So NOT Happening

So NOT Happening

A Charmed Life Novel

JENNY B. JONES

THOMAS NELSON
Since 1798

NASHVILLE   DALLAS   MEXICO CITY   RIO DE JANEIRO   BEIJING

Published in Nashville, Tennessee, by Thomas Nelson. Thomas Nelson is a registered trademark of Thomas Nelson, Inc.

Thomas Nelson books may be purchased in bulk for educational, business, fund-raising, or sales promotional use. For information, please e-mail SpecialMarkets@ThomasNelson.com.

Publisher's Note: This novel is a work of fiction. Names, characters, places, and incidents are either products of the author's imagination or used fictitiously. All characters are fictional, and any similarity to people living or dead is purely coincidental.

ISBN 978-1-59554-541-1

Printed in the United States of America

09 10 11 12 RRD 6 5 4 3 2 1

This book is dedicated to my grandmother, Mildred Jones Griffin. She was my family, but most importantly, she was my friend. She taught me so much, but mostly taught my brother and me that our tails had better be in a pew on Sundays. She is the reason I'm saved. She was Jesus in my life. She was shopping trips, long talks, sugar cookies, outrageous laughter, and chicken and dumplings. Though she had dreams of a red convertible, she helped pay for my college instead and proudly drove a green four-door Ford.

chapter one

~~~~~~~~~~~~~~~~~~~~~~~~~~~~~~~~~~~~

One year ago my mom got traded in for a newer model. And that's when my life fell apart.

"Do you, Jillian Leigh Kirkwood..."

Standing by my mother's side as she marries the man who is *so* not my dad, I suppress a sigh and try to wiggle my toes in these hideous shoes. The hideous shoes that match my hideous maid-of-honor dress. I like to look at things on the bright side, but the only positive thing about this frock is that I'll never have to wear it again.

"...take Jacob Ralph Finley..."

Ralph? My new stepdad's middle name is Ralph? Okay, do we *need* one more red flag here? My mom is marrying this guy, and I didn't even know his middle name. Did she? I check her face for signs of revulsion, signs of doubt. Signs of "Hey, what am I thinking? I don't want Jacob Ralph Finley to be my daughter's new stepdad."

I see none of these things twinkling in my mom's crystal blue eyes. Only joy. Disgusting, unstoppable joy.

"Does anyone have an objection?" The pastor smiles and scans the small crowd in the Tulsa Fellowship Church. "Let him speak now or forever hold his peace."

Oh my gosh. I totally object! I look to my right and lock eyes with Logan, the older of my two soon-to-be stepbrothers. In the six hours that I have been in Oklahoma preparing for this "blessed" event, Logan and I have not said five words to one another. Like we've mutually agreed to be enemies.

I stare him down.

His eyes laser into mine.

Do we dare?

He gives a slight nod, and my heart triples in beat.

"Then by the powers vested in me before God and the family and friends of—"

"No!"

The church gasps.

I throw my hands over my mouth, wishing the floor would swallow me.

I, Bella Kirkwood, just stopped my own mother's wedding.

And I have *no* idea where to go from here. It's not like I do this every day, okay? Can't say I've stopped a lot of weddings in my sixteen years.

My mom swivels around, her big white dress making crunchy noises. She takes a step closer to me, still flashing her pearly veneers at the small crowd.

"What," she hisses near my ear, "are you doing?"

I glance at Logan, whose red locks hang like a shade over his eyes. He nods again.

"Um...um...Mom, I haven't had a chance to talk to you at all this week..." My voice is a tiny whisper. Sweat beads on my forehead.

"Honey, now is not exactly the best time to share our feelings and catch up."

My eyes dart across the sanctuary, where one hundred and fifty people are perched on the edge of their seats. And it's not because they're anxious for the chicken platters coming their way after the ceremony.

"Mom, the dude's middle name is Ralph."

She leans in, and we're nose to nose. "You just stopped my wedding and *that's* what you wanted to tell me?"

Faint—that's what I'll do next time I need to halt a wedding.

"How well do you know Jake? You only met six months ago."

Some of the heat leaves her expression. "I've known him long enough to know that I love him, Bella. I knew it immediately."

"But what if you're wrong?" I rush on, "I mean, I've only been around him a few times, and I'm not so sure. He could be a serial killer for all we know." I can count on one hand the times I've been around Jake. My mom usually visited him when I was at my dad's.

Her voice is low and hurried. "I understand this isn't easy for you. But our lives have changed. It's going to be an adventure, Bel."

Adventure? You call meeting a man on the Internet and forcing me to move across the country to live with his family an adventure? An *adventure* is swimming with dolphins in the Caribbean. An *adventure* is touring the pyramids in Egypt. Or shopping at the Saks after-Thanksgiving sale with Dad's credit card. This, I do believe, qualifies as a *nightmare!*

"You know I've prayed about this. Jake and I both have. We know this is God's will for us. I need you to trust me, because I've never been more sure about anything in my life."

A single tear glides down Mom's cheek, and I feel my heart constrict. This time last year my life was so normal. So happy. Can I just hit the reverse button and go back?

Slowly I nod. "Okay, Mom." It's kind of hard to argue with "God says this is right." (Though I happen to think He's wrong.)

The preacher clears his throat and lifts a bushy black brow.

"You can continue," I say, knowing I've lost the battle. "She had something in her teeth." Yes, that's the best I've got.

I. Am. An. Idiot.

"And now, by the powers vested in me, I now pronounce you Mr. and Mrs. Jacob Finley. You may kiss your bride."

Nope. Can't watch.

I turn my head as the "Wedding March" starts. Logan walks to my side, and I link my arm in his. Though we're both going to be juniors, he's a head taller than me. It's like we're steptwins. He grabs his six-year-old brother, Robbie, with his other hand, and off we go in time to the music. Robbie throws rose petals all around us, giggling with glee, oblivious to the fact that we just witnessed a ceremony marking the end of life as we know it.

"Good job stopping the wedding." Logan smirks. "Very successful."

I jab my elbow into his side. "At least I tried! You did *nothing*!"

"I just wanted to see if you had it in you. And you don't."

I snarl in his direction as the camera flashes, capturing this day for all eternity.

Last week I was living in Manhattan in a two-story apartment between Sarah Jessica Parker and Katie Couric. I could hop a train to Macy's and Bloomie's. My friends and I could eat dinner at Tao and see who could count the most celebs. I had Broadway in my backyard and Daddy's MasterCard in my wallet.

Then my mom got married.

And I got a new life.

I should've paid that six-year-old to pull the fire alarm.

chapter two

There is nothing like watching your mother dance in the arms of a giant of a man who is *not* your father.

As I pick at my rubbery chicken breast and limp green beans, I stare at Jake. Wearing a goofy grin, he spins my mom to some Michael Bublé tune about how sweet love is. Sweet? I think it's nauseating. Totally hurl-worthy.

I watch my mom's aunt Shirley shimmy her girth under the limbo pole. My mother's parents died before I was born, so there wasn't a lot of family on the bride's side of the chapel.

My phone rings and I slap it open. "Hey."

"Do I hear the chicken dance?" There is absolutely no sincerity in my best friend Mia's voice. "How's the wedding of the New York socialite and the merry widower?"

The ink on my parents' divorce papers is barely dry and my mom hauls me to Oklahoma, over a thousand miles away from my friends, my dad, and my home. And for what? To live with some oaf and his two bratty sons. On a *farm* no less. If I have to slop some hogs, I am on the first plane back to Manhattan.

"Just counting the seconds until they leave for their honeymoon and I fly back to New York." I'm staying with my dad while Mom and Jake rendezvous in Jamaica. Hopefully I can talk Dad into letting me stay. Forever.

"How are the stepbrothers?"

"Mutants, just like last time I met them." I stab a piece of cake with my fork. "I don't trust these people, Mia. Especially Jake. What's that guy got up his sleeve that he would charm *my* mom into marrying him? I Googled the guy, and I found nothing. Don't you find that strange?"

"Er . . . no."

"What if Jake Finley isn't his real name? It could be his alias. He could have a prison record."

"You think he's a—"

"Psychopathic, serial-killing, online predator?" I nod. "Just one of the many possibilities I have to face here."

"I think you're overreacting."

"And I think I know trouble when I see it." I write an advice column for our school Web site, so I deal with problems daily. I know all about catastrophe.

"Oh, Bella . . ."

"My mom just married a total stranger, I will soon live at a zoo, and my new six-year-old stepbrother is dipping his Batman doll in the punch bowl." I drag my hand through my chestnut locks. "Am I the only one who sees the problem here?"

"You can do this. Where's our little optimist?"

"She's in New York. Where her life is." After we hang up, I grab a napkin and blow my nose. Right on the part that says *Jacob and Jillian Finley.*

This all happened so fast. I still don't understand it all. One minute my mom is e-mailing this guy and then six months later, they're married. And I can't call my dad. He doesn't get in from Tahiti until tomorrow morning, in time to pick me up at the airport. Yeah, he's wrapping up another vacation with his latest barely legal girlfriend, whose name I forget. Something like Kippy, Kimmie, or Magenta. I'm serious. The last girl I met—her name was Magenta. With a name like that, you *know* she has to be a stripper. It's her destiny.

So both of my parents are totally messed up right now. One thinks she's found true love. Again. And the other is currently dating through the alphabet.

"Bella!" My mother breaks through the masses, pulling What's-His-Name behind her by the hand. After a group hug, in which Jake stands uncomfortably, still linked to Mom, an awkward silence falls.

I take this opportunity to stare at Jake, taking in his gargantuan form, his outdated ponytail, and the little scar over his right brow. *Do you get that you're ruining my life? If you're an ax murderer, I want you to know I am so on to you. My dad knows tae kwon do, and if you ever raise your voice at me, he will whip out his black belt and go all Jackie Chan on you.*

"Bel, I can't wait until this week is up and we're all back together. We're going to spend some quality time with one another before school starts. Get adjusted." My mom leans into her new husband.

Gonna. Hurl.

"Plus we have to teach Bella here how to milk a cow." Jake winks and everyone laughs. Except me.

Okay, God, I don't know what You're up to, but this is not my idea of a good time. How could You do this to me? How could You rip me from my home and drop me here—in Hicksville? Because, God— Oklahoma? It's not O-K.

chapter three

I'm going to be on *Good Day, New York* this afternoon. What do
you think about this jacket? Too Justin Timberlake?"

My dad's Hugo Boss blazer hangs perfectly on his gym-enhanced
form. And he knows it.

"I'll be talking about the latest alternatives to Botox, as well as
promoting my new retreat packages in Cancún."

And that's a retreat from wrinkles and things that sag. People
don't soak up the sun and frolic at the pool when they go to Cancún
with my dad, Dr. Kevin Kirkwood. They tell their friends and cowork-
ers they're going on vacation, then come back with a brand-new face.
New York doesn't call him the Picasso of Plastic Surgery for nothing.

"Dad, I was hoping we could hang out today. I've barely seen
you this week, and in three days I'm an official Oklahoman." A
thought that incites my gag reflexes.

"I'm sorry, babe. After the TV gig, I have a coffee date. But then
I promise I'll be home."

He grabs a bottle of water out of the kitchen, one I can barely
find my way around even still. I've been here every other weekend
for the better part of the year, and it's still not home.

My dad is currently dating like he's on *Survivor* and it's an immunity challenge. If dating were an Olympic event, he'd be sporting a neck full of medals and his face would be plastered on the cover of *Sports Illustrated*.

He slides his sunglasses on his face. "Luisa will get your lunch. If you go anywhere, call me."

"Can't we just do lunch? Tavern on the Green? McDonald's?" Anything?

"Look, babe, this is a stressful week for me."

For *you*? "My mother just married a six-foot-five farmer, I have two new brothers preprogrammed to hate me, and I'm rounding out my last week as a resident of New York City." I cross my arms. "Now what were you saying about a stressful week?"

My dad stops long enough to place a hand on my shoulder. "Isabella, I know this is an upsetting time for you. But life can't stay like it was. Your mom and I are over, and she's moved on. I've moved on."

"And by default, I have to?"

"Just think of it as having the best of both worlds. You have fresh air in Oklahoma." *I see that shudder, Dad. I see it!* "And once a month you come back to Manhattan."

"You could've put your foot down. Forced Mom to stay in the state."

My dad smiles, his teeth a perfect white row. "Honey, if you feel like you'd enjoy talking with someone about these negative feelings, I can get you in to see my therapist."

"I could live here." I've only asked a hundred times.

He kisses me on the cheek and rests his hand on my shoulder. "The weeks will fly, and I'll see you next month."

I clench my teeth. "Good luck on your interview." And I leave the kitchen in search of more understanding company.

Like my cat.

I lumber up the stairs to the top floor of the brownstone where my park-view bedroom is tucked away.

"Señor Kirkwood means well, Bella." Luisa, the woman who used to be my nanny, waits for me at the last step, a laundry basket under her ample arm. She follows me into my room.

When my dad moved into this place, he got a professional designer to decorate. Was I consulted about my preferences for my room? Um, that would be a negative. Just like I wasn't consulted about whether I would like to pack up my life, leave everything I love behind, and move to farm country.

I twirl on my heel and crash onto my bed, staring at the ceiling. Where a painting of a group of cherubs glares down at me. They're supposed to look angelic, but to me they look like they're from some gang—fresh out of Compton.

"What's up with him, Luisa?" I sigh. "I just want my old dad back."

"He's a very busy man," she clucks as she places socks in one of my drawers. The drawer with the zebra stripes on it. The decorator obviously had a head injury before taking on my room. Actually the whole house is pretty hideous, but dad says it feeds his creative spirit. I'm not sure creativity is a quality people want in their plastic surgeon.

"I thought this week would be different." I spill my heart out to the woman who is basically now my *dad's* nanny. "I imagined him being grief-stricken that his daughter would be moving across the country, but between work and all his dates, he barely knows I'm here."

Moxie, my Persian, leaps onto my stomach. I pull her close and pet her silky white fur.

Luisa settles herself onto the edge of the bed and smoothes the hair from my face. "I will miss you. Does that count?"

"I'll miss you too. I wish you would come live with us."

She waves a hand. "No. I no live around pigs and cows. I was married once—I know what that's like."

I laugh, even though it saddens me to think of being so far away from the woman who pretty much raised me. But Dad got Luisa in the divorce settlement. There was no detail left unattended in my parents' divorce. Everything was split very neat and tidy.

Everything except me.

~~~~~~~~~

"So, Bella"—my friend Jasmine flips her hair—"are you and Hunter ready to do this long-distance thing?"

I sip my virgin daiquiri and look at the giant Buddha statue across the crowded restaurant. "Sure. Yeah." I nod and smile at my two friends surrounding me at the table. "Definitely."

Mia looks skeptical and Jasmine doesn't meet my eyes.

"Hunter is totally cool with the move." I force a dreamy look into my eyes and turn to Mia. "We'll just take it day by day, you know? With the phone, e-mail, text messages . . . it will be like we're not even apart."

We pay our bill and walk outside into the muggy August evening air, where Mia's driver pulls up in an Escalade. The three of us pile into the back, giggling over nothing in particular.

I smooth my miniskirt then dig through my bag for lip gloss.

"My last time for Club Viva. At least for a while." I sigh, thinking of my fond memories of our favorite teen dance spot.

Thirty minutes later, the Escalade stops at the entrance to Viva's, and we link arms and sashay to the entrance.

"Name?"

I blink at the bouncer. "Richie. It's me." I laugh. "Bella?" *I'm a regular!* I wait for comprehension to settle in.

It doesn't. "Bella?"

"Bella Kirkwood?"

"Oh yeah . . . Bella." Richie scratches his bald head. "I'm sorry, Miss Kirkwood, you're not on the list tonight."

"What? Of course I am! I'm always on the list." I gesture behind me. "We're all on the list." *Dude, we are the list.*

He taps his clipboard and frowns, his forehead wrinkling into folds. "Nope. Sorry. Your friends are here, but you're not. We have a special band performing tonight, and we can only take who's on the sheet here."

I feel the heat of my embarrassment all the way to my toes.

The bouncer runs a meaty finger under his too-tight collar. "Tell you what, I'll make an exception . . . but just this once."

I know I should say thank you, but I'm too busy holding back a good "Do you know who I am?"

"Since you didn't make the cut, I'll have to escort you in myself." Richie unhooks the cording and lets me pass, then stops me. "The back way. Only A-listers go through the front."

I stand rooted to my spot. A-listers? I *am* an A-lister! I'm an A plus! I'm A squared. A times infinity!

He travels fast on long legs, and in my four-inch heels and extra-large attitude, it's everything I can do to keep up. With a fist the size of a Hummer tire, he pounds on the door twice. The pulsing music grows louder as the door swings open.

The back entryway is dark, and I step closer to my escort. We round the corner, then Richie abruptly stops.

"This is the door to the dance floor," he yells over the music. "Knock three times, then go in. Someone will be on the other side to help you find your friends."

I lift my manicured hand and pound three times. I push on the door, but it doesn't budge. Rearing back, I tackle it with my left shoulder, sending it flying on its hinges.

I blink hard as the lights flare to full life.

"Surprise!"

My hands fly to cover my mouth as the room erupts into flashes, cheers, and shouts. The techno song is replaced with "Bye, Bye, Bye."

Banners hang from the back wall. WE'LL MISS YOU, BELLA! and WE LOVE YOU! and BELLA + NYC = FOREVER!

"Oh my gosh!" I shake my head and scan the room, reveling at the sight of a club full of friends. "You guys are the best." Tears pool and I quickly swipe them away as Hunter, my tower of studliness, ambles my way, arms open wide. I fold into him, and we stand under a strobe light, just hanging on and laughing.

I kiss his cheek. "Did you do this?"

He shrugs. "I had a lot of help." Hunter smiles and gestures to Mia, who stands two feet behind us. With a laugh, she leaps to us, moving in for a three-way bear hug.

"How am I ever going to make it without you two?"

"You're not going to." Hunter laces his fingers with mine and pulls me to his side. "Nothing's going to change just because you're moving."

"Totally." Mia's long blonde hair swings as she nods. "We'll miss you while you're away, but we'll just have to make the most of the time you spend here."

The music roars to full volume, and I can feel the bass rumble in my chest. The crowd of my friends fills the dance floor and circles around us. With a final hug to Mia, I pull Hunter along behind me, and I work the room, speaking to every person I pass.

Forty-five minutes later, I've worn out the words *thank you* and my chest hurts from excessive, jubilant hugging.

"Let's get you something to drink." I follow Hunter to the bar area, where he orders my Club Viva usual. "A Sprite with cherry syrup. Three cherries, no stems."

I smile into his beaming face. He leans down, brushes away my bangs, then kisses my forehead. Does it get any better than this boy? He's hot, he's thoughtful, and he throws a good party. What more do I need?

Hunter gets a water for himself, then we walk upstairs to find a table overlooking the dance floor. He pulls out my chair, and I smile at his ever-present politeness. Such the gentleman, that boy.

Hunter is the only guy I've dated. Well, besides Sammy Nugent in the sixth grade, but that was only so he'd share his Oreos with me during children's church. Mr. Perfect and I have been together for two years. Our meeting was like Disney-movie heaven. He was a freshman at Royce Boys Academy, and I was in the same grade at the Hilliard School for Girls. Twice a year, our administration decides to pretend there are boys in the population, so they bring the two schools together for a social. I remember I was dancing with this tall, redheaded kid who had a retainer and watered me like a sprinkler every time he used the letter s. Then with a tap at his shoulder, the boy stopped moving, turned around, and there was Hunter Penbrook.

"Sorry to butt in, but I have to leave soon, and she promised me a dance."

I giggled with relief and curiosity at this handsome ninth grader. Of course, being shut away from boys at my all-girls school, I pretty much giggled anytime someone of the male species was near.

"I don't remember you asking me to dance this evening," I had said, letting this cute stranger take my hand and lead me into a slow dance.

"You didn't. But I thought you looked like you needed saving."

He thought I looked like I needed saving. And with those words, I knew I couldn't let him go. Two years later, here we are. Hunter and Bella.

Together forever.

I hope.

chapter four

Dear Loyal Readers of Ask Miss Hilliard,

As you know, when it is time for the reigning advice queen, Miss Hilliard, to move on, she must pass the torch. It is with great sadness (believe me, you have no idea) that I type my last blog entry as your queen of advice, your royalty of reason. My successor has been chosen, and the new Miss Hilliard will begin next week. So keep those e-mails coming. The new Miss Hilliard has plenty of wisdom to share.

Thank you, my readers, for trusting me with your questions and dilemmas. As I leave our fine school, it seems I have acquired problems of my own. Who does an advice columnist go to for help? Please keep your former friend in your thoughts and prayers as I leave my beloved city and go to a place of complete and utter lack of refinement. I will be living on a farm complete with dirt roads and cows. I have been assured there are no muddy pigs, as we all know from dissection lab last year about my little swine phobia. But, ladies, my situation is dire. This town probably has no fashion. No style. No Starbucks, people! War criminals probably see better conditions.

Think of me fondly and know that your problems filled me with joy.

I shut my laptop and stare out my airplane window. Oklahoma in all its green glory stretches out beneath me.

"Thank you for flying American Airlines. We welcome you to Tulsa. If this is your final destination, you can pick up your baggage . . ."

Welcome to Tulsa. An hour away from my new home in a town called Truman. My stomach clenches at the very idea. I can't shake this feeling that I'll wake up any moment and discover this has all been a bad dream. I'll jump out of bed, find my parents drinking lattes in the living room, and be safely tucked away in our Manhattan apartment. God can do anything, right? Give sight to the blind, heal the lame, raise the dead . . . roll the stone away and resurrect my old life.

Fifteen minutes later I follow the crowd to baggage claim.

And there stands my mom.

Surrounded by my new stepfamily—Jake the Giant and his two mongrel sons.

"Bella!" She rushes to me, arms open wide, and pulls me close. "I've missed you!"

"You too." My face is pressed to her shoulder.

Mom takes a step back, her face beaming. "I can't wait to get you all settled in. We got back from the honeymoon a few days early, so I've been fixing up your room."

"Yeah, as in the room that used to be mine."

I look past my mother's shoulder to find Logan glaring at me like I'm overcooked spinach.

Robbie runs around us, a red Superman cape flying behind him. "Me and Budge are roomies now."

I stare at Logan's back as he walks away. "Remind me again why people call him Budge?"

Mom shrugs. "A nickname from his mother."

I guess it's better than Bubba.

An hour later, Jake's old Tahoe lurches to a stop in the dusty driveway.

"Home sweet home." Mom hugs me for the trillionth time. "I can't wait for you to see your room."

"Oh . . . the waiting has been just as painful for me too." I peel my legs out of the vehicle and step onto the ground.

Right into cow poop. "Ew!" Sick. "How does poop get in the yard?" I run toward a patch of grass and shuffle my feet like they're on fire.

Logan and Robbie laugh as they enter the house.

"Welcome to farm life." Jake chuckles and follows behind his sons.

Yeah, thanks a lot. Glad to be here. Stupid . . . pooping . . . cows.

The wraparound front porch looks like something from a Tim Burton movie—rickety, spooky, and ready to sprout jaws and collapse on someone at any moment.

Mom practically skips ahead of me and flings open the creaking screen door. Clutching my cat in her travel bag, I step inside.

"Isn't it cute?" Mom's smile doesn't quite reach her eyes. "It's going to be a lot of fun decorating. We can do that together."

I stare. Mute. Appalled at the décor around me. I think 1970 came for a visit, threw up, and never left. In the living room to my left is an orange couch, sagging in the middle like it gave up. Yellowed lace curtains hang crookedly over a filmy window.

Over my right shoulder is the dining room. A beaten and battered "wood" table takes up most of the space, piled high with newspapers, books, and random cereal toys. I am drawn to the mess like a moth to a bug zapper. I place Moxie's bag on the hardwood floor and slip into the room. With a ringed finger, I write my name in cursive on the dusty table.

I turn around as Mom stands behind me. "It's not too late to change your mind," I whisper, my eyes boring into hers. "We slip out the back door, we hop a plane, and—"

"Bella." Her hands clench my shoulders. "This is it. Accept it. You're not even trying."

"Trying!" I laugh. "A few months may be all you need to adjust to the idea of a new family and life in this . . . this *frat* house, but I need more time. This home isn't even civilized. I'm afraid to look in my room. Let me guess, gingham curtains and something that resembles an old doily for a comforter?"

"No. Of course not!" Mom blinks. "Maybe a Lord of the Rings bedspread, but it's gone."

"Perfect." My eyes flit across the table and take in the family's collection of junk. A newspaper from last December. Two candy bar wrappers. A stack of wrestling magazines.

Mom pushes me toward the stairs. "We need to get you unpacked."

The stairs creak with every step and lead us to a series of rooms on the second floor.

Mom points out Budge and Robbie's room, then grabs my hand and pulls me to the bedroom at the end of the hall. "This is it." Her hand rests on the knob. "Now before we go in, keep in mind I haven't had a lot of time to do much with it. We'll have to go shopping." She cracks the door, only to pull it shut again. "And another thing . . . you can't compare it to your room at your dad's. Or in our old apartment. It's a smaller space, okay?"

"Just open the door, Mom."

She turns the knob and we both step inside. "What do you think, sweetie?"

I turn a full circle. "I'm . . . I'm speechless."

My closet at my dad's could barely fit in this space. Plain white panels drape from the single window. A simple white duvet covers a twin bed, with pink pillows that used to rest on my plush queen-size bed. On the wall hang pictures of me, my family, and my friends from New York. They all smile back at me in black and white.

"Did you see my surprise?" Robbie, wearing a Superman costume, peeks into the room. He points to the center of the bed, where a homemade card sits propped on a throw pillow.

I force a smile and reach for the card. "I heart my new sister." Aw, that is really sweet. "Thanks, Robbie." I fold him in a tentative hug. "I love it."

"It's printed on post-consumer fiber."

I blink.

"Recycled paper." He rolls his eyes. "The Arctic Ocean could be ice-free by 2050. Every little bit helps."

I look to my mom as Robbie pads out of the room.

"He's a strangely brilliant child," she whispers. "He has an amazing photographic memory. But maybe watches a little too much cable."

Mom unpacks Moxie and places her on my bed. The cat sniffs her surroundings 'til I'm afraid she's going to vacuum the duvet through her nose. "Okay, so I'm going to let you unpack the rest of your stuff. And dinner's in an hour. We're all going to eat together."

I quirk a brow suspiciously. "You cooked?"

"Jake went to get pizza. I have to go clean the dining room table."

"You're going to need more than an hour." *And a forklift. And maybe the* Extreme Makeover: Home Edition *team.*

I sit between my mother and Robbie at dinner. Mom places a chipped plate in front of me, and I can't help but notice that all of the plates seem to be one of a kind. As in, none of them match.

"I'll pray." Jake bows his head and we all follow suit. "Dear Lord, we thank You for this new beginning. For our family. We ask that You bless this food and bless our time as we get to know one another. Amen."

"So, Bella . . ." Jake takes a slice of pizza and passes it to my mom. "How's the new room?"

"Oh . . . it's . . . um . . . nice." In the same way that pudding is nice. "Budge, I'm sorry you had to give it up for me."

My older stepbrother pops the top on his Coke. "It's not like I had any choice in the matter." If this boy were an animal, he'd be growling right now. "Now I get the joy of doing homework with a six-year-old jumping from bed to bed because he thinks he's a superhero and his ability to fly is going to kick in any minute."

"Budge," Jake warns.

"My new roomie goes to bed at eight, while sometimes I don't even get in from work at the Wiener Palace until eleven, and then I get to step on every Transformer in his collection as I make my way to my bed in the dark."

"That's enough, Son."

Wait—I'm still stuck on Wiener Palace.

"And tomorrow I get to take my computer in because Robbie here erased half my hard drive. Since he thought all my stuff was now his. I'm so *glad* I have a stepsister. Because before my life wasn't complete, but now"—he pushes the hair out of his eyes—"now it is. I'm so glad we're all so *happy*." He slams down his plate and leaves, his chair shrieking across the old floor.

Silence descends on the dining room.

Robbie smacks his lips. "Can I have his pizza?"

When I walk into my room for the night, I find my bed neatly turned down. I grab my favorite oversized t-shirt, a pair of shorts, and some undies and throw my hair into a ponytail. I slip out the door and listen in the hall for any signs of stepbrothers. Confident the area is secure, I tiptoe into the bathroom.

Where I scream my head off. "Get out! Get out! Get out!"

Budge, clad only in his boxers, squeals like a girl. "*You* get out!" He grabs a towel and holds it over his chest like he's hiding a set of Pamela Anderson double Ds.

I stand frozen. My limbs refuse to move, my mouth opening and closing on words that won't form. I'm not used to seeing half-naked guys in my bathroom. Especially of the rotund, 'fro-headed variety.

I regain my breath and jab a finger in his direction. "This is *my* bathroom!"

He laughs. "*Your* bathroom? *Au contraire*, my evil stepsister. This was *my* bathroom, but now it's *ours*. We'll be sharing it."

"I'm not sharing a bathroom with you. Gross."

"You are. So don't be thinking you're gonna take over with all your little girly soaps." He bumps me as he charges out the door, his hair dripping. "I'm watching you." With two fingers he points from his eyes to mine. And he disappears down the hall.

I close the door, take a seat on the dewy toilet seat, and sigh.

Hello, God? You still up there? I realize You have some big things to deal with: global warming, wars, straightening out Hollywood. But do You even remember me? I'd like to beg You to deliver me from this overflow of ick that has become my life. I would get down on my knees for this prayer, but . . . it's gross. Please help me. I don't think I can take much more of this.

Hours later I swim to the surface of a dream and open my eyes in the dark.

Where am I?

Oh yeah. Truman, Oklahoma. In the world's smallest bedroom.

The hair on my arms prickles, and I sit up. Something's not right.

I hear a noise from downstairs, and my heart leaps into over-drive. I dive for my phone, ready to call for help.

Then headlights bounce off my window, and I jump up and pull the curtains back.

Jake. Pulling out of the driveway. At 4:00 a.m.?

I sigh into the quiet room and lean into the wall. My heart slowly returns to a normal pace as I return to my bed.

Guess he has an early shift at the plant.

Or maybe he's running away.

Wish I'd thought of that.

chapter five

~~~~~~~~~~~~~~~~~~

"Bella?"

I drag one heavy eyelid open. "Mmm?"

"It's time to get up for school!"

My head throbs in protest. I flip over and burrow deeper into my blanket, sending Moxie sprawling to the floor. "Go away."

"Get up! Greet the day!" The bed gives way as my mother sits in the remaining space beside me.

"Tell the day I said to buzz off."

"Now you can't go to school with that sour face. Where's your good attitude?"

"In New York."

"I've got breakfast for you in the kitchen."

I wrinkle my nose. "No thanks."

"I didn't cook it. Just some bagels—like back home." Mom smiles and runs her hand across my forehead, pulling the hair from my face. I always wished I had been born with her blonde hair. It fixes in seconds and makes her look all California chic. Instead, I got my dad's chocolate brown hair that, without highlights, is the color equivalent of mud. At least I got her height and long legs. Also, like her, I can't roll my tongue, but so far that hasn't been much of a problem.

After a shower, I lope down the stairs and join Mom in the dining room.

Robbie sits at the table, his elbows planted next to a cereal bowl. "But I like Chocolate Puffies."

"Sorry, sweetie. I threw those out. They're all sugar. For your first day of first grade, you need something special. Like oatmeal!"

"Yuck."

"But I put a raisin happy face on it just for you."

Robbie levels his glass green eyes. "Lady, I could smell that trick before I even got out of bed."

Mom tries again. "Raisins are good for you."

"Look like rabbit turds." He rearranges the red cape around him. Except for the wedding, I've yet to see him without it.

Robbie continues to argue with his new stepmom. His own mother apparently died when he was born, so it's just been the guys here. Living it up in the shag-carpeted bachelor pad.

I slide into a seat and close my eyes. I would think about the fact that Mom just fixed breakfast for the first time in my life, but I'm too wired over school. Today is my first day at Truman High. I'm so not ready. The first day of school is nerve-wracking enough, but being the new girl on day one? Vomit inducing.

I miss Mia and my friends. And Hunter. I've been so busy disinfecting my new room and avoiding Budge and Robbie, I haven't even had time to call him since I got in yesterday. Why is everything happening so fast? It's like my world is spinning, and I'm here hanging by a fingernail. A fingernail in desperate need of a manicure.

Mom places a bagel in front of me, followed by a container of flavored cream cheese. "Just like New York." She waits expectantly. "Eat up."

I pick it up. Doesn't feel like a New York bagel. I sniff it. Doesn't smell like a New York bagel. I crunch into it.

"I don't know what that is, but it's not a bagel."

Mom stands up. "Well, I don't think you're going to pass any street vendors on your way to school, so eat now or forever hold your peace."

Budge walks into the dining room, his large feet dragging. "Hey." He warily takes in the scene before his eyes flit briefly to me. "You ready?"

I blink. "Um . . . no."

"I have a gamers club meeting before school, so hurry up. We're discussing the newest version of Halo, and I can't miss it."

I look at Mom.

"Logan is going to drive you two to school." She pulls her mouth into a smile. "You know I'd love to take you, but Jake and I have to take Robbie. It's his first day of first grade, you understand."

Robbie sticks his finger in his oatmeal. "Parental involvement is directly related to my success as a student." He levels his eyes on me. "I don't think you want to mess with my future."

Ugh. I have got to remind Dad that he was going to buy me a car. I'm one of those weird New Yorkers who actually has a driver's license. Just no car.

"Dude, I'm serious," Budge says. "I have to go. My meeting is very important. We're electing officers."

I take another bite of the cardboard bagel. "I would hate to keep you from your life's work."

"The Halo hierarchy is not something to joke about. It demands respect."

I laugh. "Get over yourself."

"Whatever. The Budge train is leaving. If you want a first-class seat, you get up now. Otherwise . . . it's coach. Something you probably know little about." He stands beside his brother and holds out his fist. Robbie hits it with his own. "Make me proud today, Robmeister. Keep your hands to yourself and remember rule number one above all things."

"Don't discuss politics."

"No, the other one."

Robbie nods. "Don't eat glue." He drops his chin. "It's my weakness."

Budge slams the back door behind him.

I jump up, leaving the rest of my breakfast.

"Have a great day, honey. I'm praying for you. I know it's tough, but you will be a stronger person for it."

I grab my purse and Dooney backpack and follow in the path of my stepbrother.

Outside, the Oklahoma sun shines on the Finleys' small farm. Somewhere in the distance, cows moo and roosters crow. I should find this all peaceful and quaint, but I don't. Gimme some smog and irate taxi drivers any day.

"Are you coming or what?" Budge steps out of an old, dilapidated garage that has seen better days. And those were probably around the World War II era.

I step inside and my breath hitches at the monstrosity before me. "No."

"Get in."

"No way." I shake my head. "There is no power on earth that's going to make me climb into that . . . that . . ."

"Hearse." Budge pats his car, his eyes clouded with love. "Ain't she a beaut?"

"A 'beaut'? *She* used to transport *dead* people, and I am not stepping foot into it. I'd rather walk."

"Driving your prissy self to school was not my idea, so I'm not going to sit here all day and wait for you." He opens the heavy gray door and scoots in. The dead-people mobile starts right up like a Formula One race car.

At the sound of another engine, I turn to see Mom, Jake, and Robbie pulling out of the front driveway. They wave happily, like this instantly complete family. Dust plumes behind the Tahoe.

The hearse cruises by me. "Wait!" I run after Budge's car, my heels punching holes in the yard.

He brakes and cranks his window down. Screamo pours out the car and pounds in my ears. Not only does he have hideous taste in cars, but his musical choices are just as bad. Clearly a sign of mental disturbance.

"You can't just leave me here."

He looks down at my heels and smirks. "Yes, I can. And will. Rich girl, there ain't room enough in my car for you, me, and your overbloated attitude. You can walk to school for all I care."

I sputter. "I don't even know where the school is!"

"Use that nose you've got so stuck in the air—and sniff it out."

And he drives away.

I stand in the driveway, torn. Do I run after him? I'd ruin my dignity. And my Marc Jacobs shoes.

Or do I just walk? Maybe skip school? Forget it all, kick back, and watch some daytime TV?

I rip my cell phone out of my purse and punch in my mom's number. In one long sentence, I fill her in.

"Bella, I can't come and get you. We're still five minutes away from the school, and we can't be late. We have a parent meeting."

A *parent meeting*! Where's *my* parent?

"Why didn't you get in the car with Logan?"

"Do you honestly need an explanation for that question?"

I hear my stepdad talking in the background. "Jake says his farm truck is in the barn. Keys are on a hook in the kitchen. But be careful. You don't have a lot of driving experience."

I sigh and consider bawling for the millionth time since arriving. "Fine. I'll take it."

Mom gives me directions to the school, and we hang up.

Barn. I think I saw one of those.

I smooth down my skirt and head behind the garage, following the sound of cows. My feet are already protesting.

At the fence opening, I maneuver a latch and drag the heavy gate until it's wide open. I teeter across some railing in the ground, losing my footing only once, and just walk.

I head to a grove of trees, and just around the corner is my mecca. A barn. Red, of course, with a paint job so fresh the house would be jealous.

I jump at the bawling of a nearby cow.

Taking three steps back, I hold out my hands. "Stay back. I'm warning you. I have . . . um . . . hair spray and Tic Tacs in this bag, and I'm not afraid to use them."

Big, blinking eyes lazily assess me, but the cow still walks closer. My heart doubles in tempo. Can cows smell fear?

"I'm not afraid of you." I'll psych it out. "I just don't want to hurt you. So for your own good, I'm asking you again to back that thing up." Nothing. "Shoo! Shoo!"

The black-and-white giant marches even closer, and I suck in my breath. New plan—I'll stand still as a statue. No eye contact. No movement. Isn't that what you're supposed to do when accosted by a wild bear?

The hairs on my arms prickle as the cow's heavy, warm breath settles over me like a blanket. Like a nasty, hideous, damp, gross blanket.

The beast smacks its lips.

It's going to eat me!

I give up on my plan to stay mute. "Oh, Jesus. Help me, Jesus. Though I walk through the valley of the shadow of death, I will fear no evil." I'm totally fearing! "Yea, though . . ." I can't think! "Something, something, something . . . uh . . . though you make me to lie down in green pastures."

The animal's expansive, wet nose sniffs me. *Excuse me, but if anyone's the offensive one here, it's you.*

"The Lord is my shepherd, I shall not want—"

Slurp!

My scream pierces the sky.

I just got licked by a giant cow tongue! I swab at my face, breaking my frozen pose. "*Ugh! Ewwww!* You know what, that is enough!" I leap back. "Now you listen to me, you . . . you . . . bovine." I roll my shoulders and straighten my spine. "You are totally violating my space here. I have had a really, really hard morning."

The old thing blinks, and I notice its full, curvy eyelashes. What a waste of a feature.

"Now I am going to just step around you, walk into that barn, and get in a truck. But I'm warning you, if you try to follow me, I will not be responsible for my actions." I lower my voice. "You should probably know . . . I eat burgers. You should *fear* me." *Oh yeah.*

I turn on my heel and sprint away.

The truck, a blue thing born about the same time as the hearse, sits beneath a covered area adjacent to the barn. I swipe at the sweat and cow slobber on my forehead and climb into the cab.

Twisting the key, I offer up a prayer of thanks when it starts. I haven't been behind the wheel since I spent last month with my grandparents in the Hamptons. With shaky hands, I maneuver the truck into the field and wave good-bye to the lone cow. By the time I hit the first paved road in town, I'm singing some classic Beyoncé.

I signal to turn at the final four-way stop. I will not be embarrassed to pull into the parking lot in this truck. I am lucky God provided it. Even though God also provided me with a *jerk* of a stepbrother, making the truck necessary in the first place.

As I lift my foot off the break, the blue truck sputters and chokes. "No, you don't. Come on. Just a few more miles. You can do it." *Break down later.*

I turn left.

And the truck gives up. No more.

With the vehicle's last few breaths, I steer it to the side of the road. Smoke pours out from underneath the hood.

I pound my head on the steering wheel. This can't be my life.

Am I on camera? A reality show, maybe, where they see how much I can take before I crack?

Barely stifling a few choice words, I call my mom again.

No answer.

Swinging the door open, I slide down to the ground, grab my bags . . .

And walk.

"You want a ride?" I jump at a voice as a truck slows down next to me. His bald head sticks out the window.

"No, thanks." Creep. Who trolls down a road and asks girls if they want to get in his truck?

"You Jake Finley's stepdaughter?"

At this I stop. "Maybe."

He looks me over, but the perv factor is pretty low. "I'm a good friend of Jake's. Recognized his truck. I'd be glad to give you a ride to school."

"I'll just walk." I pick up my pace, but he continues to drive along beside me. "I said *thank you*, sir."

"Miss?"

Exasperated, I sigh. "What?"

"You're going the wrong way."

chapter six

"You smell."

This is how the school secretary greets me.

"Thanks." *And your eau de Avon is just a total nasal delight.*

"No, I mean, seriously, hon. You smell."

I toss my backpack on the counter, drape myself over it, and launch into my sob story, emphasizing words like *hearse, attack cow, stalled truck,* and *two-mile hike in heels.*

"You probably want to wash your shoes off. I think you might've stepped in it."

And I'd like to step right back out and fly myself home to Manhattan.

"I've got some wet wipes and soap in the bathroom back here."

I scrub down as much as possible, throw my once perfectly straight hair into a frizzed-out ponytail, and walk back into the office with as much dignity as I can muster.

The thirtysomething secretary smiles and gives me a thumbs-up. "Much better."

"Thank you."

"Now your mama's already registered you and everything, so

I'll just have a student show you to your first class." She snaps her fingers and a sleeping kid in a row of chairs lifts his head. "Josh, take Miss Kirkwood to her first class. It's Mrs. Palmer's room."

With barely a glance in my direction, Josh leads me down a hall, around a corner, and to my first-period class.

He leaves me at the door, and I walk myself in. My already-queasy stomach twists itself into a pretzel knot.

The teacher stops her back-to-school spiel at the front of the room, eyes me, checks her watch, then motions me in.

I hand her my schedule and pray I washed off all the stink.

"Take a seat right over there, please."

Aware of everyone's stare, I follow the direction of her pointing finger, then stop.

Budge.

Right behind the empty seat.

"Um . . ." My voice is a croaking whisper. I check my schedule again, hoping I'm really supposed to be in another room. No such luck.

"Is there a problem?"

Lady, we don't have time to get into all my problems.

My eyes take in Budge, who regards me with nothing less than bored disgust. I limp down the aisle, every blister on my foot tempting me to scream, and settle into the desk.

"Nice walk?" Budge whispers behind me.

"Perfectly enjoyable. I was glad to catch some fresh air." I also caught some bugs in my teeth on that last two miles, but I won't give him the satisfaction of those details.

Fifteen minutes later the bell rings, and I pull the schedule from my purse to check my next destination.

"Can I help you find your class?" I look up from my seat and find a blond guy from two rows over standing near. "I'm Jared Campbell."

I smile, suddenly aware that any lip gloss I had on was probably slobbered off by cow tongue. "I'm Bella. And I would love some help."

His dark eyes glance at my schedule. "Right this way." And we walk down the crowded hall.

"Where are you from?" he asks.

"New York." I feel the ever-present pang of homesickness. "I guess you're a hometown boy?"

He laughs. "Nah, a lot of us are transplants. Many of us have parents who work in Tulsa but don't necessarily want to live there, so here we are. I'm originally from Chicago."

I sidestep a boy wearing saggy pants and a nose ring. "Do you ever get used to it? Is this ever home?"

Jared pats me on the shoulder. "Sure. It takes awhile. I've been here three years, I guess. "

We come to an abrupt halt at room 202.

"Thanks, Jared. I appreciate the help." My first kind soul at Truman High. Well, besides the secretary wielding the baby wipes.

"Why don't you eat lunch with me and my friends? We sit in the corner of the cafeteria next to the vending machines. I'll be looking for you."

A pound or two of weight dissolves from my burdened mind. I have someone to eat lunch with—a total new-kid score.

I leave my second-period art class completely high on paint fumes. Stepping into the ladies' room afterwards, I find a stall and text my mom the location of the truck.

Taking a deep breath, I open the small door and work my way

through the crowd of girls, all of us waiting to look at ourselves in the row of bathroom mirrors.

The girl beside me gasps. "Oh my gosh. Max Azria, right?"

I turn to see she's staring at me.

"Your skirt—Max Azria."

I smile in relief. She's speaking my language. "Yeah. I love his stuff." Though my outfit is now a total wrinkled, wilted mess. "I've had kind of a bad morning. I'm not exactly at my best."

"I'm Emma Daltry. I'm a junior."

"Me too!" I pull out some gloss, finding a spot at a mirror. "I'm new—Bella Kirkwood."

"You must sit with me at lunch. We can talk clothes."

"Oh, I'd love to. But I already have a lunch commitment. Maybe tomorrow?"

"Definitely. I'll see you around." Emma tosses a limp good-bye and flounces out. I guess it was wrong of me to assume everyone here would be wearing Wranglers and cowboy boots.

After chemistry, I move on to something I'm fairly decent at—math. In AP Calculus I'm given a textbook that probably weighs more than Robbie. Mr. Monotone teaches that class, forcing me to count the seconds until the blessed lunch bell finally sounds.

Following the herd, I locate the cafeteria. I wait ten minutes in line for a shriveled-up burrito, then maneuver through the crowd to Jared's table.

"Hey, Bella!"

I smile at the small gift that he remembers my name.

"This is Bella, everybody." Jared proceeds to introduce me to his friends. "And finally, this is Brittany Taylor." The girl beside him gives me the most pitiful excuse for a smile. *She* totally needs a French kiss from a cow.

"Well, hey." Emma, the girl from the bathroom, grabs a seat and sets down her tray. "Bella, right?"

"Yeah. Jared and I have AP English together, so he invited me to join you guys." I'm on the verge of babbling. There's an undercurrent here I can't quite put my finger on. My eyes drift to Brittany again. She stares at me like I still smell of barnyard. Maybe the powder-fresh scent of the baby wipes has worn off.

"So what do you think of your first day so far?" Emma pops a fry in her mouth and leans in.

Oh, how to put this tactfully? "It's fine." *Like eating nails is fine.*

"Bella's from New York." A murmur of appreciation goes round the table at Jared's announcement.

I fill them in on a brief synopsis of my life.

"You went to an all-girls school?" Brittany asks this in the same tone one would say, "You pick your nose?"

I smile. "Yes." *Sister, you do not want to knock my life as a Hilliard Girl. I will recite our pledge, yodel our fight song, and break out the secret handshake if necessary.*

"Has to be a lonely place without any guys around, eh?"

I laugh at Jared. "Not exactly. There's a nearby private school for boys." I feel a pang of guilt for not mentioning Hunter. But these people don't need to know my entire life story yet. "What do you guys do for fun around here?"

Emma sighs prettily. "Not much, I'm afraid. I'm originally from Seattle, and I have yet to adapt to the total lack of things to do in Truman. We go into Tulsa a lot. Shop, eat, hit some hot spots."

I watch the cafeteria crowd as my table enters into a conversation about kids I have yet to meet. I'm living a fashion nightmare. Jeans of every color and style. Shoes that do not match outfits. A blatant disregard for root maintenance. Is this what I'll look like in a year? *You will not suck me in, Truman!*

"So . . . Brittany . . ." Girl who is still staring me down like a rabid schnauzer. "How long have you lived in Truman? Where are you from?"

Emma giggles. "Oh, our Brit's not a transplant. She's an original."

"But we let her hang out with us anyway." Jared nudges Brittany with an elbow. Her face breaks into a reluctant smile.

"Maybe you can help me learn my way around here, then."

Brittany steals a fry off Jared's tray. "Right. Hey, Emma, are we still going shopping Wednesday night?"

"I know! Bella can go shopping with us, right, Brit?" Emma doesn't wait for her answer. "We'll show you Tulsa, then top off the evening at our favorite burger place."

My spirits lift at the magical, therapeutic mention of shopping. "I would love that." *Thank You, God, for giving me friends on day one. Especially friends who appreciate a night out with the credit cards.*

We rush through the rest of lunch, and the gang fills me in on local gossip, pointing out the troublemakers, the shady characters, and the wannabes in the room. I laugh at all their stories and file away the information.

Things learned at Truman High so far:

One, do not get on this group's bad side.

Two, avoid the burritos.

chapter seven

〜〜〜〜〜〜〜〜〜〜〜〜〜〜〜〜〜〜〜〜〜〜〜〜〜〜

*H*ow was school?" Mom closes her book, *Parenting a Teen Without Being Mean*, when I open the car door.

I shut myself in the Tahoe and dissolve into the seat, tired but grateful to be alone with my mother without the Finley men.

"I arrived a sweaty mess. The school secretary wouldn't let me into my classes until I passed a smell test, and I have English with Budge." I sigh and rest my head on the door. "I'm just a fish out of water here. A Jimmy Choo in a sea of Payless BOGOs."

"We both have to adapt. You think I'm not struggling?" She holds up her book. "I haven't had a six-year-old in the house in a long time. And when I did, I had help."

"I miss Luisa." My nanny would listen to my sad Oklahoma stories, fix me a cup of homemade hot chocolate, and tell me everything would get better. My mom used to be so busy with working out, charity events, and a collection of other random hobbies that I only saw her an hour or so a day. This new version of Mom is kinda freaking me out.

She drives us to the crumbling Victorian I am now forced to call home. The farm truck sits in the front yard, hoisted up on blocks. Two legs stick out from beneath it.

I reach for the door handle. "The day a toilet seat appears on the front porch, I am so gone."

"Give this a chance."

"Hey, guys!" Robbie tears out of the house, barefoot and wearing his usual cape. "Look what I did in school today. Guess what it is."

He holds up a finger-painted blob of red, white, and blue.

"Oh . . ." My mother frowns, clearly searching for words. "Is it a . . . ball?"

"Nope." Strike one for Mom.

"A puppy?"

"Get real, lady."

"A self-portrait?"

"It's a symbolic representation of my patriotic feelings."

I can only nod.

"I watch a lot of CNN." And Robbie pivots on his bare heel and runs back into the house.

"You probably ought to order some more of those books, Mom."

Jake slides himself out from under the rusted blue heap, wipes his sweating head with a handkerchief, and moseys our way. He wraps his trunk-sized arms around my mom and plants one right on her lips.

Ew.

"Did your day get any better, Bella?"

I give him my best plastic smile. "It was lovely. Can't wait to do it again tomorrow."

The screen door opens and smacks shut again, with Robbie squealing and running. "Oh, Daddy! Oh no, Daddy!" He tornadoes in our direction, running right into his dad. "She's gone!" His eyes are huge and serious, his breathing ragged.

"Who's gone, Son?"

"Betsy. She's run away. After all we've been through, she left me."

"Who's Betsy?" Mom asks.

"His cow."

My stomach does a strange flop. "What does Betsy look like?"

Robbie raises his head and pins his eyes on mine. "Like a cow."

"I'm sure she's there. Let's go grab her a little snack, and we'll find her."

Jake and his hysterical son disappear behind the house.

"Don't worry, Bel. This is just part of farm life." Mom wraps her arm around my shoulders and guides me inside. "Why don't you come and talk to me while I start dinner."

"You don't cook, Mom."

"I do now."

An hour later, I'm peeling carrots for Mom's secret recipe when Jake and Robbie return, followed by Budge. Jake hangs his ball cap on a peg in the kitchen, Robbie runs upstairs like his pants are on fire, and Budge lurks in the doorway, his face drawn.

"Did you find Betsy?" Mom stirs at the stove, reading from her cut-out recipe.

"No." Jake's gray eyes land on me. "Did you shut the gate when you drove the truck out this morning?"

I swallow. "No."

Budge sneers. "Didn't you see the cow?"

"Yes, Budge, I did. Not only did I see it, I was totally violated by it, in case anybody cares. I could've been seriously hurt."

My stepbrother laughs and shakes his head. "Afraid she'd lick you to death? That cow wouldn't step on an ant, let alone bother you."

I jerk the peeler over a carrot. "Like I'd know that!" I turn my attention to Jake. "I'm sorry. I was late for school and . . . stressed." *And nobody gave a crap.* "And then the cow wouldn't leave me alone. I've never even *touched* a cow before, and then he, er, she, was all up in my business, and—"

"She's Robbie's pet. He got her from his mama's parents when he was born." The room silences at Jake's statement.

I stare at the pile of orange in the bowl. "I'm sorry. I didn't know. But there was that cattle guard thingy, and—"

Budge smirks. "Cows can jump that."

"How could I know your magic cow could hurdle something *made* to keep her in? Does that make any sense? I mean, what is the purpose of having a cattle guard if it doesn't *guard* the cattle?"

"That's enough," Jake says.

"Your son leaves me stranded here this morning, and *I'm* the one in trouble?"

Jake holds up a hand the size of a tractor wheel. "Nobody said you were in trouble. I'm just trying to piece this all together. If she's been out since this morning . . . well, we'll have to widen our area of search."

Budge looks at me like I have peas for brains. "He means we might not find her. She could be caught in something and hurt by now. Good job."

My cat takes that moment to appear at my ankle and curls herself around it, purring.

Budge sneezes and wipes his eyes. "Get that cat out."

"She can't go outside. She doesn't have any claws." I pick Moxie up and pull her close.

Budge sneezes again and pinches the bridge of his nose.

"Hon, maybe you could take her out of the kitchen." Mom shoots me a warning glance. "Please."

Clutching my cat, my only piece of home, I stomp up the stairs and slam my bedroom door.

I put my iPod earbuds in, fire up my laptop, and log on to the *Ask Miss Hilliard* blog. I need to touch base with normal. Reconnect with real.

Dear Sisters of Hilliard,

    Greetings from the heartland!

    Miss Hilliard texted me today and said she has been getting lots of queries as to my situation. I am so humbled by your concern. What true friends you all are. And believe me, I could use the support.

    I will spare you most of the details, but this morning I was expected to ride to school in a hearse. I refused, of course. Then I was accosted by a wild animal in a field. This beast clearly could've used a session of Mrs. Harbinger's Manners 101.

    Next I was forced to drive an old, unreliable truck to school, but of course, it left me stranded on the side of the road, forcing me to walk for miles and practically ruin my heels. And it's not like I can just run downtown and replace them, right? In fact, if these people have a place to shop in this city, I have yet to see it. Unless you need a part for your John Deere.

    Ta-ta for now, ladies. I appreciate the thoughts and prayers passed my way. I need them. These are troubled times

we live in—the crisis in the Middle East, the decaying environ-
ment, and me stuck in cow town.

Inhale some smog for me,
Your former Ask Miss Hilliard

Forty-five minutes later, after passing on Mom's attempt at cooking, I throw on my oldest pair of jeans, a t-shirt, and a cute pair of retro rain boots. I hear the "family" in the living room watching *Wheel of Fortune*, so I ease out the back door and walk toward the field.

I make sure to shut the heavy gate behind me this time. "Bet-sy!" My voice scatters some birds. "Bet-sy! Here, cow!"

I continue walking and yelling until my feet and throat are both sore.

Sometime later, I find myself near a pond. And there's Betsy, her black-and-white fur shining as the sun starts to set behind her. She looks up, her dark eyes totally unimpressed with my presence. She continues to drink from the pond.

"Hey, girl." I smile, relieved that I have not single-handedly killed Robbie's pet after all. "Come here." The cow continues to ignore me, as if she is having a private, meditative moment with nature.

"Where've you been?" *And for that matter, where am I?* I glance around at the landscape. Nothing looks familiar.

As I close the distance, I see stickers and prickly things in the cow's tail. "Somebody's been for a walk, eh?" I get close enough to touch her face. "Well, I certainly can't blame you, but time's up. You have to come back with me. I can certainly understand wanting to leave, but if anybody's running away from this place, it's me."

I hold out my hand like I expect her to follow. "Here we go . . . This way. Be a good cow, now." Robbie's pet returns to slurping from the green water. "Bets, can I talk to you—girl to girl? I pretty much made a little boy cry today, and if I don't redeem myself, then I'm in big trouble." I move some distance away and sit down on the bank.

"But maybe today was God's way of getting my attention. The Finleys think I'm just some spoiled society brat. Well, you know what, Bets?" I stand and dust off my jeans. "I'll show them. I will just show them what Bella Kirkwood is made of. And it ain't just Macy's and Prada bags." *I totally just said "ain't."*

"Now . . . how to get us home?" I turn a full circle, eyeing the sun, the trees, some rock piles.

I am so lost.

I sit for what must be hours, hungry, tired, and mad that no one has bothered to come and find me. They probably think I want some alone time. Well, *wrong!*

The sun is almost tucked away when Betsy gets up, moos to the darkening sky, and walks herself past me.

I lift my head from my knees and watch her tail swing in a happy little rhythm. She stops some distance ahead and turns around, as if she's waiting for me.

What do I have to lose?

I stand up, pick off a few leaves . . . then follow a cow all the way home.

"I found your cow." I shuck off my boots and walk into the living room, where Robbie sits in my mom's lap.

"You did? Where was she?"

"Just hanging out." Did anyone even realize I was gone?

"I think you're really mean for letting her out."

"Robbie, Bella didn't mean to." Mother smoothes back his red hair. "She and I come from a very big city. We barely even had a yard."

Or a maze of cow dookie to step around.

Robbie glares at me all the way up the stairs as I head toward my room. I grab my cell phone and call Hunter.

"Hey, you! How's my little Oklahoman?"

I start at the beginning and fill him in on every detail. "And then this evening . . ." I sigh. "I had to launch a one-girl search party for a—" A female giggle in the background stops me cold. "Who is that?"

Hunter laughs. "Oh, that's just Mia."

"Mia?" As in my best friend, Mia?

"Yeah, she's helping me with my algebra. Here, she wants to talk to you."

When I get off the phone with Mia, all my worries evaporate like snow in California. It's the same old Mia, same old gossip, same best friend.

The only one who's different is me.

chapter eight

~~~~~~

o what do you think of Tulsa?"

I suck on my second Frappuccino, ignoring the brain freeze
and relishing the long-lost flavor. It is cruel and unusual punishment to force me to live somewhere without a Starbucks. I mean,
come on. I think there might be *three* cities in the world that don't
have Starbucks, and Truman is one of them. What are the odds?

"Not bad." In fact, I kind of like the outside shopping center. In
Pottery Barn I grab two sets of sheets, a comforter, an armload of
throw pillows, and some curtain panels for my room, all centered
around an organic Asian theme. Anything beats the garage sale
motif of my room now.

I reach for one more pillow. Then drop everything in my
arms.

"Let me get that for you." Jared Campbell steps out from an
aisle.

"Jared!" Brittany throws her arms around him as he picks up
the contents of my new bedroom.

He hands me a package with a lopsided grin. "Your Egyptian
cotton sheets, madam."

I smile. "Thank you, sir."

"So the guys and I decided to crash your shopping trip. Are you girls ready for dinner yet?"

I walk to the register with my goods, already envisioning a new paint job for the bedroom.

"Let's take Bella to Sparky's Diner downtown. What do you think, Brit?" Emma asks.

"Yeah, sure."

The cashier gives me the grand total, and I hand over my Visa.

"I'm sorry, but your card has been declined."

I flinch as if she's just insulted my mother. "Excuse me?"

"Do you have another one we could try?"

"Um . . . sure." I laugh. "I can't imagine what the problem is." And hand her the MasterCard. I smile and roll my eyes at my friends.

"Nope, I'm afraid this one is declined too."

My fragile grip on politeness slips. "That's impossible. Try them again."

"Ma'am, I'm sorry. In fact, I'm going to have to cut them up."

I turn away, unable to watch this horrific display. "Let's go. Something is really wrong. It's got to be their machines. Or maybe my identity has been stolen. Some sixty-five-year-old man in the Philippines is probably posing as me and ordering boxes of frilly underwear online to his heart's content."

"I'm sure it's nothing." Emma pats me on the shoulder.

"Let's go eat. The guys and I are starved." Jared steps in beside me. "I'll buy." He holds up a hand when I open my mouth. "I won't take no for an answer. It will be my welcome-to-Truman gift to you." Jared gives me a quick side-hug. "That's what friends are for, right?"

Sparky's Diner is nothing but a hole-in-the-wall burger joint. And aside from the fact that someone's having to pick up my tab, it's perfect. The walls are covered with black-and-white pictures of Sparky, the owner, and various celebrities who have been here through the years. Sparky and Donald Trump. Sparky and Chuck Norris. Sparky and *NSYNC before Justin left them to bring sexy back.

"Brittany, scoot down a seat so I can sit by Bella." Emma puts her purse down beside me and waits for her friend to move.

Brittany's eyes narrow as she slides across the booth. "So, Bella. Do you have a boyfriend?"

"Yes, in New York." I smile. "Hunter."

"How's the long-distance thing going?" Jared asks, swiping a fry off my plate. A plate he paid for.

"It stinks." But what about this move *doesn't* totally reck? "I left a lot back in Manhattan. I left a school I loved. A huge group of friends. A writing gig as an advice columnist."

"What? How cool," Emma says.

"Yeah, I had an advice blog. Students at Hilliard would write in with their problems, and I would answer them as Miss Hilliard. I still write in some and update my blog fans on my life. Though anymore it consists of entries like, 'Life is awful—just like last week.'"

Brittany lifts a brow. "Truman isn't the place for you?"

"Are you kidding? This is the last place on earth I want to be." I hold up my hands. "I mean, don't get me wrong, it's charming in its own way. I just need the culture and pace of New York, you know? Not to mention I have a demon-possessed stepbrother."

"Budge Finley."

"Yeah." I stare at Brittany. "How did you know?"

"Your stepdad works with mine."

"At the paper plant?"

She nearly chokes on her Coke. "If that's what you want to call it."

My eyes narrow. *Aha.* I knew Jake Finley wasn't on the up-and-up. He left at the crack of dawn *again* this morning, yet he was at the table for breakfast. Something strange is brewing. "What do you mean? They don't make paper at the Summer Fresh factory?"

"Yeah, but that's not all." She laughs. "You'll have to ask your stepdad." She picks up her purse.

"Let's head back to Truman." The group stands up at Jared's command. "Some of us have homework to do."

"Hope you get your credit card situation fixed," Brittany says as we exit. "I'd hate to see you suffer any more than you already have here."

~~~~~~~~~~

I slam the door and rush through the foyer.

"Wait a minute."

Mom and Jake sit in the darkened living room, the closing credits of *Letterman* on mute.

"Later—I have to call the credit card companies."

"In here. Now."

My foot halts on the first step. I sigh and walk in to join them. "Yes?"

Mom consults her watch. "First of all, you were supposed to be home an hour ago. It's a school night." She waits for my excuse.

I shrug and give her my sweetest smile, a face that has always worked on Mom but would never work on my nanny.

"Jake says when Budge, er, Logan is past curfew, he gets grounded." She holds up her latest parenting guide, *No Means I Love You.* "This book would agree."

Maybe you skipped the chapter where it talks about exceptions for daughters whose lives have been ruined.

Mom gestures to an empty seat and turns on the lamp. "Bella, your credit cards are no good."

"You're telling me! I tried to shop at Pottery Barn tonight and—" I sit up straighter. "Wait a minute. How did you know that?"

"I had your dad cancel them today. I forgot to tell you."

"You *forgot?*"

Mom looks to her husband then back at me. "We're a family now. And we all will live under the same roof, under the same rules. Jake and I want all of you kids to live equally—it's not fair for you to have an unlimited credit card and Logan to have to work at the Wiener Palace for extra money. So any money your father gives you for child support will now be put into a trust fund. And your credit cards are gone."

I stand up. "That's insane." It's like cutting off someone's life support.

"This is our new life, hon."

"Well, I hate *our* new life." I stomp past them and pound up the stairs. "I hate this town! I hate . . ." *Think, think. What else?* "Cows! And those *stupid* roosters that wake me up every morning!" *Stomp, stomp.* "And sheets that don't match!" The walls shake when I shut the bedroom door.

Moxie hops off my bed and greets me, wrapping her white body around my ankles. I pick her up and she purrs into my neck. Outside my window, an overgrown oak tree taps on my window.

Trying my best to ignore it, I sit down at my desk with Moxie. She paws at an imaginary bug as I turn on my Mac.

Dear Hilliard Sisters,

For those of you who pray, I need it. Your former Ask Miss Hilliard is living in the pit of the country. Nobody understands fashion here. They wouldn't know a Marc Jacobs bag if Wal-Mart put them on clearance. The school colors are a hideous green and black. The school parking lot looks like a Ford truck dealership. My stepbrothers are mutants from outer space, the oldest driving a vehicle he purchased at a funeral home's garage sale. The cheerleaders wear bows in their hair like it's 1985. And yesterday someone asked me if my Rock & Republic jeans were a new style from Wrangler!

I could go on and on, ladies. I know you feel my pain, and there is some comfort in that. So this is your former Miss Hilliard . . . asking you for advice. Short of hopping the red-eye back to my beloved NYC, what can I do?

My cat and my memories of Hilliard are all that get me through.

Oh, and my iPod.

And my Wii.

Okay, and my new Chanel bag.

But still. You understand my pain. Keep me in your thoughts during my dark hours of suffering.

That which does not kill us . . . is probably not in Truman, Oklahoma.

Your former Ask Miss Hilliard

chapter nine

"**B**ella, I have a giant favor to ask."

I put down my cereal spoon and glare at my mother. She and I haven't said two words to each other since last night.

"Oh, let me guess, you want me to go out back and get the eggs out of the henhouse?" Do we even have one of those?

Mom takes Robbie's oatmeal out of the microwave, slams it on the table, then all but jumps into the seat next to me. "I've had enough of this." She pushes her blonde bangs out of her eyes. "You think this isn't hard for me too?"

"You signed up for this! I didn't." But I would totally sign up for a stepfamily refund right now.

"All of this is just as new to me. I'm having to learn how to cook, take care of a house by myself, be a mother to two boys, and live on a factory worker's income. This is not easy." Mom's chin quivers, and I see her brave mask slip.

"We don't belong here. We're like two Paris Hiltons stuck on Planet Wal-Mart."

My mother places her hand over mine. "Yes, we do belong here. I do love Jake, and you need to accept that even though this is not a day at the Ritz, we're not going anywhere. Bella, this is all very, very difficult." Lines crinkle on her forehead. "But I need you on my side—not fighting me every step. We're in this together."

"Then why cut off my credit cards and totally humiliate me in front of my new friends? I wanted to *die*. Why leave me carless in my new hometown? I get why your life has to change—you're not connected to Dad anymore. But I am. Surely he can't be supportive of me living this second-rate life."

"Actually, he is."

"He's not! He's just too caught up in his own life to care what's going on in mine." The man has yet to call me. "You know he doesn't have time for any family discussions, so he just agrees with whatever you say. And you're using that to your advantage."

"You are my daughter, and I love you. But being here has made me realize that we led very shallow lives in New York."

"Yes. And I liked it." *I mean no!* I wasn't shallow. I was involved in my church youth group in Manhattan. I did mission work. I was a Big Sister. I took my Little Sis to Barneys every season. I dedicated my time to advising the hurting and downtrodden at Hilliard. *That's* shallow?

"Well, if you're not so wrapped up in material things, you won't mind catching a ride with Logan this morning."

I choke on a bite of Corn Pops. "No way."

"I have a job interview this morning and can't take you to school. Please?"

"I am *not* riding in that death mobile. It's ugly, it's a sign of your stepson's mental imbalance, and it's embarrassing."

Budge chooses that exact moment to raid the fridge. "Too bad you don't have a car."

I toss my hair and snarl. "I'm going to have a fabulous car very soon. Ever heard of a BMW?" If there's any perk to living here at all, it's that I get to drive.

He shuts the door and looks to the ceiling as if deep in thought. "BMW? I hear you're getting something of the used clunker variety like the rest of us *poor* Truman teens."

I suck in air. "What? That's a lie." Daddy promised I could pick out anything I wanted. I have this sporty little black one totally customized online. I turn to Mom. "Would you do something with him?"

"Logan, do mind your own business, please." Mom's eyes drop to her lap. I'm instantly suspicious.

"Mother?"

"Well . . . your dad and I have been talking. And a new car is not in the cards for you right now. It's not fair to the family for you to drive a new sports car and Logan to drive his . . . his . . ."

"Sign of my mental imbalance."

I stand up. "What's not fair is you and Dad pulling the rug out from under me! What's not fair is forcing me to move here and leave everything and everyone I love behind. What's not fair is expecting me to give everything up just because you want me to blend in here. Well, I'm not like Budge and Robbie. My dad doesn't work in a paper factory. He's a plastic surgeon to the stars, and he *promised* me a new car!" Sure, it was his guilt talking, but I'll take it.

"You will live within the same means as everyone else in this family. Anything else just wouldn't be right."

Who cares about everyone else!

I shake my head. "Is there anything more I need to know? Any other grenades you want to lob my way?"

"No, I believe that's it." Mom purses her lips as Jake enters the now-quiet kitchen.

"Something wrong?" he says, and I nearly leap out of my chair and tackle him.

Except that would be like trying to tackle a giant redwood.

I rinse my bowl out in the sink then turn around, a memory surfacing. "Jake, what is it you do at the Summer Fresh paper plant again?"

He coughs. "I'm an assembly line manager of a department."

My brown eyes lock onto his. "Really?" I lean against the counter and cross my arms. "I hear there's more that goes on at that plant than making some wide-ruled. Did you know this, Mom?"

Budge laughs as he unwraps a Pop-Tart. "Dad, didn't you tell her about the military arsenal that's stored there?"

"What do you *really* make there, Jake?" I ask. "My mom and I have a right to know."

"Bella—," my mother warns.

"Something is going on here, and I want the truth. Mom, I believe this could be something illegal. Drugs, smuggling, weapon manufacturing—"

"Dad is chief of operations on the feminine product assembly line." With a smirk, Budge grabs the keys to his hearse then walks out the door.

My world tilts and I grab the counter again.

It's worse than I thought. My stepdad is a cow-raising, truck-driving, chicken-feeding craftsman of maxi-pads.

Life could not get any worse than this.

chapter ten

~~~~~~

"Happy fourth hour, Truman Tigers! I'm Bailey O'Connell here to read your morning announcements."

Truman High's morning news show blares to life on the classroom TV.

The perky brunette spouts off the announcements like they're the juiciest Hollywood gossip.

"And that's all you need to know for today, Truman High. But before we sign off, we here at Tiger TV would like to personally welcome our newest students." A PowerPoint follows of the new kids, using their school ID photos. Great. Mine looks like a mug shot. Maybe God will grant me a favor and they'll skip me.

"...And welcome to junior Isabella Kirkwood, who comes from the prestigious Hilliard School for Girls in New York City. Did you know Callie French, lead singer of the Killer Petticoats, is a famous Hilliard alumna?"

People in the class murmur and turn to stare in my direction. I smile bravely.

"And according to a reliable source, Bella is known for her advice-giving skills and has a super-fun blog you'll want to check out on the Hilliard Web site. I can't wait to look at it myself! Get to know this new Truman Tiger. Next we have senior Lance Denton . . ."

The breath lodges in my throat.

The voice on the TV becomes a buzz in my head.

No.

They can't go to the *Ask Miss Hilliard* blog! They'll read all the horrible things I wrote! I was mad. I was sad. I was hurt. I didn't *exactly* mean all that stuff.

Okay, calm down. What are the odds someone will actually Google Hilliard and locate the blog? Hardly anyone even knows me here. Just Emma, Jared, Brittany, and that group—and they'll probably just agree with it. *Don't freak out. This is not a big deal.*

I take the hall pass and escape to the girls' bathroom. Shutting myself in a stall, I pull up the blog. It won't accept my password! I call Mia, knowing this is lunchtime at Hilliard. She answers on the second ring.

"I'm locked out of the blog. You have *got* to delete my last post to *Ask Miss Hilliard*!"

"No way. That was good stuff. The Pulitzer people ought to be calling you any day now. It was better than anything J. K. Rowling's ever written."

"This is not funny," I hiss. "By some freak twist of fate, everyone at Truman High could be pulling it up after school today. Mia, you have to remove the post. It's easy to do, you just—"

"I know how to do it. I'm just not." She snaps her gum. "Transitioning to a new Miss Hilliard has been hard. My readership took a total dive when you left. But everybody's been reading your entries."

"Oh, really?" *That is so great. I have such loyal friends, and—* "No, wait! Seriously, if these people here read what I said about them— about their town—I am dead. Don't hurt their feelings just for the sake of your blog. I'll send in another post. I'll write something else."

"I came up with this totally cool idea to have the readers write in with their advice to you. You should check it out. There's some really good—"

"Delete it!" I've created a blogging monster! "You have to get rid of it. Mia, how can you do this to me? I have to live here. These people will run me out of town if they read it."

"Oh, will they be wearing their cowboy boots when they run? If so, send me a picture to go with the blog."

"Why won't the blog let me on?"

"Because I have full administrative privileges now. There's no need for you to have full access. So from now on, please post your letters where reader comments are."

I close my eyes and lean on the less-than-clean metal divider. "You're not hearing me."

I recap the morning and explain the situation detail by detail.

Mia laughs. "Bella, you're overreacting. Do you really think those people you go to school with are going to read the blog?"

"Yes. No." I groan. "I don't know. Probably not. But just in case—"

"Fine."

My heart returns to beating. "Really? You'll do this for me?"

"Yes. I guess. I'd hate for my best friend to be hog-tied, or what- ever it is they'd do to you. I'll do it next hour in the computer lab."

"Great. Thanks. You're the best, Mia."

"That's what friends are for. Oops, there's the bell. Ta-ta. Call me later."

God, please don't let anyone at Truman get to the blog before Mia does. I'll do anything—I'll feed Jake's stupid roosters. I'll teach Mom how to make toast without burning it. I'll play baseball with Robbie. I'll let Betsy lick me in the face. Anything.

I exit the stall.

And come face-to-face with Emma and Brittany.

"Hey, girls." I slip my phone into my purse. "Thanks again for taking me shopping last night. I—"

"We wouldn't know a Marc Jacobs bag if Wal-Mart put them on clearance?" Emma plants herself right in front of me.

"I . . . um . . ." How? Why me?

Brittany scrolls through her iPhone. "Nobody understands fashion here?"

"I didn't mean you guys. Come on, I would never make fun of you all."

"Living in the *pit* of the country?" Emma shakes her head and looks at me like I'm dog vomit. "You know, it's kind of like family. When you're part of the family, you can talk about them. But nobody else can."

"I'm really sorry. I'd had this horrible night—oh, not the shopping. Well, the credit card thing was awful, but that's all because—"

"And I *do* happen to know what a Marc Jacobs bag looks like." Emma holds hers up, a lovely butterscotch number.

"You have to believe me. I wasn't including you in that blog." I push my hand through my hair and force myself to inhale. "Look, I was mad and upset when I wrote all that. My life is totally in the crapper right now. I was lashing out at anything I could. Had I known there was any way someone from Truman would find that blog, I wouldn't have written it. I still don't know how that girl from Tiger TV found out about the Web site."

"It doesn't matter." Brittany's lip curls. "Maybe you should go back to your fancy private school in New York where people know how to dress and talk and act civilized. Sorry we're not good enough for you."

With matching eye rolls, the two swivel on their heels and storm out the bathroom door.

The fluorescent lights hum overhead. I look at myself in the mirror. My face is flushed like I've run a marathon, my eyes wide and panicked. My heart pounds beneath my funky Betsey Johnson t-shirt.

Oh, God. What have I done?

I punch a button to redial Mia. I need a status report. Now.

No answer.

Redial.

Straight to voice mail.

Rounding my shoulders and straightening my spine, I fling open the door and walk down the hall back to class. So two girls know. They have nothing to gain by telling anyone. And the blog should be down by now. *Please, God. Please, God. Please, God.*

When lunch comes, I'm praying for the rapture. A lightning bolt to take me out. A plague of locusts to carry me off.

But the only catastrophic occurrence is that all the school knows.

"I wear Wranglers." The cafeteria lady hands me my fruit plate. "You got a problem with that?"

I swallow. "No, ma'am." I throw out some money and leave the kitchen.

Half the room stares at me. Old conversations stop. New ones begin. The cafeteria is engulfed with talk of my *Ask Miss Hilliard* blog. Groups are gathered around printed-out copies. They pass it around and fan the flames that are destroying my reputation—my life—by the millisecond.

I clutch my fruit and all but run out of the building. I fly by tables and hear my name, taunts, threats, my own words twisted and thrown back at me.

Outside, I keep going until I reach the parking lot. I yank out my phone and call my mom.

"You have to pick me up."

"What's wrong?"

"My life." I sit down between two cars, out of sight. "My life is wrong."

———————

"What are you doing here?"

My stepdad reaches across the truck and throws open the door. "Climb in. Your mom's got another job interview."

I hesitate, but really, what choice do I have? Go back into the building where the student body is waiting to attack me and use my body for a bonfire, or get a ride home with my non-dad.

I step into the cab and buckle up. My mom working . . . what is this world coming to?

"Are you okay?"

"Oh, fine." *Great. Wonderful. Could not be better if the parking lot swallowed us whole.*

He guides the truck, now running like a new model, onto the road. "Your mom said there was some trouble at school."

I stare out the window at pieces of the town. "Yeah, the fact that I'm enrolled there is trouble."

"You want to talk about it?" Jake doesn't take his eyes off the road.

"Nope."

"I know you're having a hard time adjusting here."

Really? What was your first clue? I thought I was hiding it so well.

"It's like everything I do here is wrong." I can't believe I'm talking to this guy. "You know that story of Midas and everything he touched turned to gold?"

"Yeah."

"Well, I'm the opposite. Everything I touch turns to poop."

Jake laughs, then sobers at my expression. "*Ahem.* I guess I can see what you mean. It will get easier though."

"Your sons hate me."

"They don't hate you. They're just not used to girls in the house. It's a huge change for them too." Jake turns the wheel with one hand, and we're at McDonald's. "You got one of these in New York City?" He gestures toward the golden arches.

"Um, yes."

"Well, they don't serve Häagen-Dazs, but it's not a bad place to get a hot fudge sundae. Do you want yours with or without nuts?"

"Without." I'm maxed out on all things nuts.

He holds the door open for me, and I step inside. The place is nearly empty except for a group of old men in the corner having coffee and reading their papers.

We wait at the front while a pregnant girl who looks younger than me throws fries in the basket.

"You know," Jake says, "the boys haven't seen a female in the house since their mom died six years ago." He shakes his head, and his blond ponytail swipes his shoulders. "And now there are two. They need time to adjust too."

We lock eyes, and my stepdad waits for me to say something. Something profound. Something meaningful in return. Something that reeks of understanding.

"I gotta pee." I disappear into the bathroom, leaving Jake to order.

When I come back out, Jake is filling a large cup with Coke, his phone at his ear.

"Hey . . . um . . . no, I won't be coming in this afternoon. I know, I know. Something's come up." His deep voice drops. "I'll see you when I can see you."

I step in closer, my senses on high alert.

"I know I said I'd be in, but I just . . . can't. I'll explain it later. I need to be with the family right now." He punches his straw in the lid. "Tomorrow. I promise I'll get away. I *will* be there. You're not the only one who has a lot riding on this."

His back is to me and I wait a few seconds before I sidle up next to him, as if I hadn't been there the whole time. "That looks good." I take a hot fudge sundae off his hands. I smile like the world doesn't hate me and I didn't overhear any of that suspicious conversation.

He studies me for a bit before handing me a drink. "Your mom said you like Sprite."

I force another smile. "Very thoughtful of you."

A few minutes later we're back on the road, and I'm inhaling my ice cream like I need it to breathe.

My life just went public for all the town to see.

But now it's time to do a little digging and uncover all of Jake's secrets.

Because something smells rotten in the town of Truman. And it *ain't* the cow pasture.

chapter eleven

~~~~~~

*B*ella, wake up. Your alarm has been going off for forty-five minutes."

I cover my head and whimper. "Go away, Mom."

"Logan's leaving in twenty minutes."

"Tell him to have a swell day at school."

"I can't take you today, so he's your ride." Mom swats my rear and plops down beside me. "Are you ready to talk about this?"

"Two words," I say beneath a blanket. "Life. Over."

"We got a few random calls last night. People shouting horrible things into the phone then hanging up."

"And those are the ones who still like me."

"What exactly did you do?"

"See?" I throw off the covers. "Why is it always my fault? From the moment we've stepped foot onto Truman soil, I'm to blame for everything."

She frowns. "So you didn't do anything?"

"Of course I did. But must we assign blame here?" Sitting up, I stare at my mom with serious eyes. "I'm never going back there. I think I should move back to Manhattan. This isn't working out for me." Or the school-load of people I insulted.

Mother rolls her blue eyes. "Right. I'll give that some thought." She doesn't even try to sound believable. "In the meantime, you're here, so off to school with you."

"But you don't understand. Those people want to—"

"See you downstairs."

If my mother has any small traces of sympathy left, she takes them with her as she leaves. I pull Moxie closer to me and find comfort in her warm fur and rumbling purr.

"All right. Let's do this day." Moxie hops down only to run herself into a chair. I plant my feet on the floor, a total achievement considering everything.

I slip into some faded jeans, a vintage Chanel tuxedo shirt, and black flats. I leave my contacts in their case and reach for my small wire-rimmed glasses, a total package that says, "Though I am semicute, I am hung over with misery."

Downstairs, I find Jake has already left for the day, and Budge and Robbie sit at the kitchen table with my mom. The three of them laugh over some shared joke, and the sound jars my already-pounding head.

I clear my throat. "Hey."

The laughter stops and Budge slashes me with his narrowed gaze. "I gotta go."

"Wait." I fall in behind him. "You have to give me a ride."

He looks me up and down. "I'm a mutant from outer space, remember? I don't *have* to do anything." And he stomps out the back door.

Grabbing my bags, I chase him outside. "Budge, hold up."

For a big boy, he can move quickly. I don't catch up with him until he's in the garage.

I move to the passenger side and fling open the door. "Please stop." He starts the car, but I talk over the loud roar. "Look, I'm sorry. I know you've read the blog." Though Mia assured me last night my posts were deleted, it had been too late. They had already been copied into e-mails and Facebook and permanently branded into people's brains.

"I don't care about your opinion of me. You're nobody to me."

My heart pings a little at that. "You don't know what my life has been like."

"Thank God for that."

"I mean my life now . . . it's hard."

Budge cranks up his radio but yells over it. "I guess we mutants from outer space have it easy." He looks up, his curly hair covering his eyes. "Get out of my car—you know, the car I got at a funeral home's garage sale."

"Budge, I hurt your feelings, and I'm sorry. I was mad when I wrote all that."

"Whatever, Bella. I'm out of here."

He revs the engine, and I dive into the seat, barely shutting the door before he clears the garage.

Budge growls. "This is the last day I take you to school. I don't care about you—couldn't care less if your spoiled butt had to walk every day."

"Thank you." I lay a hand on my racing heart, grateful all my limbs made it into the car with me. "I really appreciate that—"

"Shut up. Just don't even talk." He turns the music up even louder and the bass vibrates the windows.

Ten minutes later Budge pulls over on the side of the road. The radio goes dead. "Get out."

I blink. "What?"

"You're two blocks from school. It's not a long walk."

"Are you kidding me?"

He reaches across me and opens my door. "I don't want anyone to see me with you. Just because you've ruined your reputation doesn't mean you're going to jack up mine."

I open my mouth. Then close it. "But these are two hundred-dollar shoes."

"Then watch where you step." He points to the road. "Out."

With as much dignity as I can muster, I heave my purse and backpack over my shoulder, slam the hearse door, and get to stepping. "I said I was sorry!" I yell. These people around here do *not* understand the word *forgiveness*.

Two blocks later and I'm standing in the school parking lot.

I stare at the building, unable to move any farther. *God, please help me. I don't even know how to pray in this situation, but I need some holy intervention.*

With the weight of the planet and every other galaxy on my shoulders, I enter the building and head toward the English hall. I keep my gaze on the linoleum floor as I squeeze through the masses of students.

"Hey, rich girl!"

And the verbal game of darts begins.

"Can I get the numbers of your friends at your old school?"

"I got a one-way ticket back to New York for you right here."

I duck into room 104 and take my seat in AP English.

Nobody says anything to me, but there's really no time. As soon as the bell rings, Mrs. Palmer passes out *The Scarlet Letter* and goes into lecture mode.

She gives us a little background on the time period, then the characters. "Hester Prynne was a marked woman. She had committed a huge sin."

The blonde in front of me turns around and glares.

"Hester was an outsider . . ."

Three more students look my way. I feel my cheeks burn.

"She had offended the entire community and was a constant reminder of shame."

So basically Hester and I could be twins. Could the teacher not have chosen something like *Death of a Salesman*? *Huck Finn*?

"She wore a scarlet A on her clothes at all times—*A* for adulterer."

I turn to the gawking boy on my left. "I don't know what you're staring at, but my similarities with Hester just ended."

When the bell rings, I all but run to art class.

My head snaps up when a shoulder connects with mine.

Brittany Taylor.

"Hey," I say weakly.

Though her mouth doesn't move, the rest of her face says, *Drop dead.*

This is going well. Can't wait to come back next week and do it all again.

When I get to my assigned seat in art, a big glob of wet clay is waiting for me. A girl beside me snickers, but without so much as a flinch, I scoop up the wet mess, throw it away, and clean up the seat.

Mrs. Lee flutters into the room, stands in the center, then spends the next fifteen minutes discussing the joy of drawing an apple. She then places an apple on a table at the front of the room, claps her hands, and says, "Draw what you see!"

There are four of us at my table, and every single student surrounding me knows who I am.

"Hey, you—rich girl."

I keep my eyes on my sketch pad.

"I drive a Ford F-150. You got a problem with that?"

No, in fact, I'd give my entire purse collection for one of those myself.

"She thinks she's something, doesn't she?" Ford boy nudges a tablemate, who joins in the conversation.

"I got a pig farm I'd like to show you, Miss Hoity-Toity." He laughs. "You don't mind a little mud, do you?" He and Ford boy proceed to see who can *oink* the loudest.

"Leave her alone." This from a tall girl with a Lady Tigers t-shirt.

"Students, I need to see you working!" Mrs. Lee circulates through the room, checking for progress. "And cease the barnyard noises." The teacher *tsks* as she nears our group. "Bella, you've drawn a poodle with gigantic teeth. I need to see the fruit. Be the fruit, my dear. Be the fruit."

"Maybe if she had a pair of Wranglers on, it would help." The whole class dissolves into giggles at this random comment.

"Students!" The teacher claps her hands, but the room doesn't quiet. "We need silence for the inspiration to flow! Concentrate!"

"I personally get inspiration from my *big bow.*" A student two tables over smirks. "You know, 'cause I'm a cheerleader from the eighties." More laughter. More comments.

I want to curl up beneath the table and cover my ears. I can't take much more of this.

Just as I contemplate the safety issues involved in jumping out the window and making a run for it, Mrs. Lee puts two fingers to her mouth and sends up a whistle that could break glass.

"Stop it!"

The talking comes to a halt.

The dirty looks do not.

The petite teacher surveys the room, taking in every single student. Then she focuses on me. "Come with me. Yes, you."

I pick up my stuff and follow her down the hall.

"Don't take this personally, dear, but the students cannot work with you in the room. You're disturbing the flow of creativity."

She smiles and pats my shoulder, then escorts me into the counselor's office. "Mrs. Kelso, I believe we need a schedule change here."

The counselor, a blonde woman with a mile-high stack of files on her desk, looks up. "Your name?"

"I'm Mrs. Lee."

She sighs. "The student's name, Mrs. Lee."

"I'm Bella Kirkwood."

"Funny you stopped by." The counselor leans back in her chair. "I've had a lot of students in my office since yesterday—very worked up and upset. Seems they all claim the same malady—Bella Kirkwood."

*

chapter twelve

unday morning finds me squished between Budge and Robbie in the backseat of the Tahoe. This is my first taste of the Finley family's church and, irony being what it is lately, of course the church is in the Truman High cafeteria. I'll be so busy reliving last Friday that I won't catch a word of the message.

Or I'll be mesmerized by Robbie's Sunday attire. Surely he will be the only six-year-old wearing spandex pants and a Superman cape complete with inflatable chest.

As soon as Jake stops the vehicle, Budge jumps out and disappears. He probably needs to discuss secret Halo strategies found in the book of Revelation.

While Jake escorts his youngest to children's church, I keep my focus on the floor as Mom and I make our way to a row of seats. Smoothing my skirt, I sit down and open my program.

Then I feel the stare.

My eyes jerk to a man two rows in front of us. Chill bumps skitter across my skin.

The bald man. The one who tried to give me a ride to school.

He turns back around, suddenly immersed in his own program.

"Mom." I nudge her. "I, um . . ." How do you tell your mom that you think her husband is up to something shady? He could be dealing crack. Working for the mafia. Selling half-price panty liners in back alleys. "I think something's going on with Jake."

"He has been a little stressed. But he's been working a lot of overtime lately."

Overtime? You have no idea.

"Something's not right with him," I whisper, glancing at the back of the bald man's head. "I saw him—"

"Didn't think Robbie was going to turn loose of me." Jake steps over me and sinks into the seat by my mom. "He changed his mind when the teacher broke out the Oreos." He smiles at both of us.

I see through you! I know you're hiding something, Mr. Tall and Sneaky.

My stepdad introduces us to a few people nearby. I shake hands like I'm thrilled to be in a church. In a school. In a town that hates me.

We sing a few contemporary choruses, then a middle-aged man in khakis and a plaid shirt walks to the podium.

"Welcome to Truman Bible Church. I'm Pastor Wilkerson, and I'm glad you're here."

Oh, I'm thrilled too.

"Today we're going to finish our series. We've been talking about something really important. Deception."

I hope Jake Finley is paying close attention.

~~~~~~~~~~

I spend the rest of Sunday talking to Hunter and Mia on the phone. Before I go to bed, my cell rings one more time.

"Hey, kid!"

I lean into my pillows. "Dad?" That voice . . . sounds so familiar. Could it be?

"Who else? How's it going?"

"Terrible."

"Now it can't be that bad. You want to talk *bad*, I had to remove twenty pounds of excess skin from a woman yesterday. Try living with that."

"Yeah, right. My minor issues will never compare to those who undergo the almighty knife. Who valiantly fight the battle of the bulge or wage war on wrinkles."

He sighs. "I hear your sarcasm. You're frowning right now, aren't you? What did I tell you about that?"

If he gives me the whole frowning-uses-more-muscles statistic again, I think I will projectile vomit through the digital sound waves.

"Tell your dad all about Truman."

I give him the abbreviated rundown, tidying up the blog-leakage story but still giving him the important details.

"People here want to run me out of town." I twirl Moxie's stuffed mouse in front of her face. She only blinks and goes back to growling at her tail. "I was thinking I could move in with you for a while. Maybe try this again next year." Or *never*.

Silence crackles in my ear. "Bella . . . I love you. You know that."

Here we go.

"But my therapist says I'm in a selfish phase, and that's just not a good environment for you—not full-time anyway."

It's good enough for his bimbo-of-the-month club.

"This is a learning experience for you. Your mom called me

Friday, and we both agree that you need to walk through the consequences of your actions."

Walk through the . . . ?

"No, I don't! Yes, I get that posting my rant about Truman for the
whole world to see was stupid. I won't do it again. Lesson learned.
Send me a plane ticket."

"I'm sorry, Bel. I really am. But I'll see you in a few weeks."

"Yeah. Whatever." And I disconnect from my dad.

Just like he's disconnected from my life.

chapter thirteen

~~~~~~

When I enter the kitchen Monday morning, Budge is sneezing all over the table.

"Gross. Cover your mouth." Neanderthal.

He lasers me with a glare, then sneezes again, sending Moxie scampering for safer, quieter territory.

"Bless you." Robbie smiles at his brother. "Did you know that saying probably comes from the days of the bubonic plague?"

I glare at Budge. He *is* the plague.

Mom sits down, a nervous look on her face, and rubs my back. At last! I finally get some sympathy around here. "Honey, I have some bad news for you."

I grab the bowl of oatmeal she slides my way and inhale its mapley goodness. "You mean something worse than today I'm going to go to school and be pelted with insults, spit wads, and stray pieces of gravel? I won't have anyone to sit with at lunch, and everyone in class will shun me and egg my car? Oh, wait. I don't have a car."

"Um, yes, there's more."

I drop my spoon.

"Sweetie, Budge is allergic to Moxie."

He sneezes on cue.

"So? He can get some shots or something."

He stands up and takes his bowl to the sink. "Or you get rid of your cat."

I grab my mom's arm. "What? No!"

"I'm really sorry, but he's tolerated the cat for as long as he could. He didn't want to upset you."

Budge stands behind Mom and smiles. He's evil! Evil, I tell you!

"He lives to upset me. You can't make me get rid of Moxie. She's all I have."

"I wouldn't go *that* far," Mom says.

"Well, I would. She and I have been together through thick and thin. And she's special—not just anyone would know that you have to moisten her food. Not just anyone would dig out her toys when she loses them. Not just anyone would know that she needs extra pets when she walks into walls or falls off of staircases. Moxie needs me!"

"Bella, we are part of this family now, and we have to make decisions that benefit everyone."

"Besides," Budge adds, "it's gross to have a cat in the house."

"Oh yeah, because you Finley guys are *really* into hygiene and tidiness. Moxie could get lost in the dust in your room alone."

Budge rears back and blasts another sneeze.

"That's so fake! Look at him—how can you buy into this?"

"Jake will find Moxie a good home, Bel."

I stand up, my chair squawking across the linoleum floor. "Tell him to find me one too." And I race upstairs.

~~~~~~~~~~

Knowing I'd rather dance in the front yard topless than ride to school with Budge, Mom drives me herself.

"Have a good day, Bella."

For seconds I stare at her. It's like telling someone on death row to keep her chin up. Closing the door, I walk away.

God, please get me through this day. I'm like Job in the Bible—losing everything. Okay, so, like, everyone he knew died. And I haven't lost any cattle or anything. But still—I got it bad.

I crank up my iPod, bypass my locker, and head straight for English class.

I can do this. I can do this. I can do this.

With room 104 in sight, I pick up my pace.

Mrs. Kelso jumps out of nowhere, stands in the middle of the hall, and blocks my way. "Miss Kirkwood, come with me, please."

"But I need to get to—"

"Now."

The blonde woman leads me to her office and motions to a less-than-plush seat, and I sit. She props a hip on a corner of the desk and looks into my eyes.

"I'd like to pick up where we left off Friday afternoon."

Oh yes please. I'd love to relive every moment of Friday!

"I don't really care that Mrs. Lee thinks you bring bad vibes to her art classroom. But we did schedule too many students in there that hour, so somebody has to go." She raises her brows. "And it's you."

Like I care. Right now dropping out and joining the circus sounds more my thing anyway.

"The question is where to put you." She moves to take her seat behind the massive oak desk. "I got online and read your blog postings—oh yes, they're still out there. Captured for all eternity in numerous places." She taps her acrylic nails together. "It occurred to me that since you like to write, you might do well on the newspaper staff."

"Or I might not." I pick a string from my Betsey Johnson skirt. "I'm not interested, but thanks."

"I really wasn't giving you an option." She returns to her seat and clicks away on her computer. And before I can say, "Homeschooling sounds fun," I'm clutching my newly revised schedule. "I'll meet you after English class to escort you to your new destiny as a journalist."

"I know nothing about writing for a newspaper."

Her passive face breaks into its first smile. "Oh, but you're a smart girl. Let's just hope they don't ask to see any of your previous work."

I suffer through English class, showered with only a handful of slurs. When I wasn't writing my hand to the bone on an essay, I was praying for an Old Testament curse upon Budge's frizzy head.

When the bell rings, I find Mrs. Kelso waiting for me in the hall. "Right this way, please." She stops a few doors down, and we're in an officelike space, with old framed newspapers hanging from the walls, as well as row upon row of awards and certificates. "This is Mr. Holman. He is the paper advisor."

I smile at the white-haired man who shakes my hand. "New student, eh? Can she write?"

"Oh, she's got all sorts of experience. She has a revealing . . . honest approach to her work." Mrs. Kelso sends me a wink. "Now Mr. Holman just oversees the paper. You'll learn the ropes from his editor."

"And that would be me."

I turn around, my eyes widening at the vision in front of me. A vision with hostility flaming in his blue eyes. Mr. Holman might not be familiar with my attack on Truman, but this guy sure is.

"Isabella Kirkwood, I'd like you to meet my editor, Luke Sullivan."

I hold out my hand for Luke to shake, but he ignores it, staring at me like I'm contagious.

"*This* is our new staff member?" He runs a hand through his black hair. "We have a waiting list two pages deep to get on the paper, and *this* is who we get?" Luke shakes his head and huffs. "Unreal. I can't work with this."

"You can, Mr. Sullivan," the counselor says evenly. "And you will. Like all staff members, you will teach Bella the ropes of writing for a newspaper. Are we clear?"

Luke Sullivan walks away as the ten other people in the class openly stare in my direction.

"He cares a lot about this paper." Mr. Holman looks toward his protégé. "It's very important to him. We are an award-winning publication, Miss Kirkwood. I hope you're ready to do everything you can to maintain our standard of excellence."

I smile weakly. The me from last week would say something about Truman's standard of excellence. "You can count on me, sir."

Satisfied that no one is going to tar and feather me today, the counselor leaves. Mr. Holman shows me around the room and introduces me to the other staff members. None of them embraces me in jubilant greeting. Nobody cries tears of joy at my presence.

"Luke here will get you started. Our first edition comes out next week, and the back-to-school issue is an important one." Mr.

Holman pats me on the back, shoots a warning glance at his editor, then leaves us alone.

I stand next to Luke's desk and wait for him to turn around and look me in the eye.

Two minutes pass. I clear my throat.

Sixty more seconds. "Look, Luke—"

"You think you can just waltz in here and play the prima donna?"

I check behind me. Is he seriously talking to me? "Um . . . no."

"I know who you are, and I know about your little gossip column."

"It was an advice column, and I'll thank you not to use the word 'little' like it was nothing. I mean, granted, the last few postings weren't my best work, and I'm sorry about those, but it's time we all get past it and—"

"If you bring even a hint of trash to this paper, I will go to the school board to get rid of you."

"Calm down." I drop my own volume. "What is your deal? You know, you really ought to get some help for your anger issues."

Luke stands to his feet and towers over me. I inhale a light, musky cologne. "The only thing that makes me angry is having to work with some debutante just because the counselor has nowhere else to put you. I have Ivy League schools watching my work, Bella. And when I graduate next year, I don't want to have to go to the community college just because the princess here brought our paper down and I lost all my scholarship opportunities." He takes a step closer until I can smell his Dentyne. "See, my daddy isn't on E! on a regular basis and he isn't going to write me a check for college. Do you think you can wrap your little brain around that?"

My cheeks are hotter than a flatiron. "Gee, I don't know. You use such big words." I pout my glossy lips. "They make my head hurt."

"I'm warning you, Kirkwood. One misstep, and I'll see that you're transferred to advanced competitive weightlifting."

I grind my teeth together to keep from totally unleashing on this pompous pig.

"Do you know what the inverted pyramid is?"

I snap my gum. "Um . . . something in Egypt?"

Luke glowers behind his glasses and tosses me a binder. "Read this. It's my tutorial on the basics of journalism. I'll quiz you tomorrow."

"I can do this, you know."

"Whatever. Just stay out of my way." He points to a desk. "Go study, rich girl. Writing is more than just cheap shots and a cutely turned phrase or two. You can't buy your status in here. You gotta earn it."

Straightening my spine, I pivot on my heel and walk away. Will I ever live down the Great Humiliation? Everyone thinks I'm some sort of celebutante with nothing in my head but hundred-dollar bills.

"He's intense." A dark-complected girl sits down beside me. "But he's good."

Yeah, good at being perfectly horrible.

"I'm Cheyenne, by the way."

I force a smile. "Bella Kirkwood."

"I know. Good luck—with everything." She glances at Luke's back. "You're gonna need it."

Twenty minutes later, Luke's shadow falls over my binder. I take my sweet time looking up. "Yes?"

He hands me a sheet of paper. "Here's your first assignment."

"Already?" My heart flutters with excitement. "I knew you'd come around. I really am responsible and a hard worker, and I—" My eyes focus on the description on the page. "The cafeteria Dumpster?" I read it again. "A story on the excessive waste at Truman High? You want me to investigate the school trash heap?"

He lifts a coal black brow. "What's the matter, princess? I thought you could handle it."

I'd like to handle *my fist up your nose.* "It will be my pleasure to observe the activity surrounding the Dumpster."

He laughs and it lights up his eyes. "Surrounding the Dumpster? Oh no, Bella. You'll be observing *in* it."

My.

Life.

Stinks.

chapter fourteen

Is there anything lonelier than eating lunch by yourself?
I might as well be the only girl on the planet for all the attention I'm getting. The embers of anger have died down, and now
instead of battering me with insults, everyone is just flat-out ignoring me. Looking through me.

I take my yogurt and apple outside and sit under a distant tree,
where the occasional ant scurries by.

My favorite song plays in my pocket, and I reach in and grab my
phone. "Hunter!" I instantly feel better.

"How's my favorite Oklahoman?" His familiar voice has my
lips curving into a smile. I fill him in on the latest. "Can you believe
I have to give Moxie away?" Pain shoots through my heart.

"So you're basically friendless, carless, and catless?"

"And those are the bright spots in my life." I lean back into the
big elm and sigh. "I miss you. I'll be home in a few weeks though.
Not that Dad cares. I think somebody used the cellulite sucker on
his brain."

"Things definitely haven't been the same since you left."

"I know—it's like I took all the cool out of New York, right?" I laugh. "Hunter, tell me what to do. Give me some advice. How do I win these people over?"

"Why would you want to?"

I frown and pick a weed. "Because I live in their town. Go to their school."

"They're obviously beneath you. Get over it. Find some people to hang out with that are more like you. Have some class."

"Hunter, you haven't even met them."

"I read about them on your blog."

Yeah, you and the rest of the northern hemisphere. "I was mad when I wrote that. Angry."

"So they're none of those things you said?"

"Well . . ."

"Exactly. You can do better than that."

"I don't think you understand. Are you hearing yourself? You can't just discount these people because they dress differently or don't know the significance of Forty-second Street."

"All I know is the Truman folks are making you miserable. And I don't like to see my girl unhappy. It makes me unhappy."

Aw. Hunter's mad on my behalf. Isn't that cute? Like a knight in shining armor, he wants to defend me. Slay my dragons.

"Your girl's unhappy because every person in this town wants to torture me—like pluck out my nose hairs or force-feed me pig snouts. I'm not used to *not* having friends." I hear the whine in my voice. "People usually like me, Hunter."

"I know they do."

"But I need *these* people to like me."

"There's my bell. I'll talk to you later, okay? Hang in there. I'll tell Mia you said hi."

"Oh, are you going to be seeing her?"

"Yeah, there's a back-to-school party at Viva's."

My bottom lip pooches out like I'm two. "Have a good time."

"You know it won't be any fun without you."

Right.

We hang up. After I scoop the last bite of yogurt, I rest my head on my knees and send up another S-O-S to God.

All right, Lord—me again.

I need a miracle. Anything—I'll do anything to get back in good graces with everyone I've offended. I can't stand this—being hated. I want to be popular again. And I want to show them who I really am. Please . . . just one miracle?

"You Bella?"

I lift my head so fast it hits tree bark. "Ow." A girl with the body of an Olympic hopeful stands before me, looking none too pleased to be there. "Um . . . yeah." I look around and survey the area. "Are you here to beat me up?"

"Depends. Are you gonna say something stupid?"

"I will sincerely go out of my way not to." And then I see a flash from last Friday. "You're the girl in art class—the one who took up for me. That was really nice of you. I know you didn't—"

"I'm Lindy Miller. Do you mind?" She points to a giant root sticking out next to me and sits down.

"If you're here to tell me off, you probably need to take a number. You might get a turn about mid-December."

She shakes her head and her ponytail bounces with hair the color of an Oklahoma wheat field. "I . . . um . . ." Lindy traces a pattern in the dirt with her Nike running shoe. "I need your help."

I drop my apple. "I'm sorry . . . I didn't hear you right."

Her brow furrows and she stares at me. Hard. "I said I need your help."

I lean in. "Look, if you need money, there's not much I can do for you. I've been cut off like Lindsay Lohan and the booze, you know what I'm saying?"

Her voice booms. "I don't need your money." She glances behind her, like she's afraid our conversation is being bugged. "I need you to make me more girly."

"Whoa—" I hold up a hand. "Just because my dad is a plastic surgeon—"

She rolls her eyes and huffs. "Forget it. I knew you were a waste of my time." And she jumps up and stomps away.

That girl may be weird, but she also could be my only ray of hope here. I mean, she did actually speak to me.

"Wait!" I run after her. "Stop! Lindy!" At this point I would totally hit my dad up for a boob job for her. Anything. "Please—" I catch up to her and tug on her shirt.

She spins around, her eyes burning hotter than a campfire. "I said forget it."

"No, come on." I brave a smile. "Look, I'm going to be honest with you. I've got no one here. My home life is a disaster, the bathroom walls are filling up with my name and number, and not because I'm a good time. And I can't get a soul to so much as look at me—well, not without flipping me off. The only people left on the planet for me to talk to are in a totally different time zone. Do you understand what I'm telling you?"

"That you're a pathetic loser?"

I bite my lip. "Okay, do you understand what *else* I'm telling you?"

She draws in a deep breath and contemplates the sky. "My problem's name is Matt Sparks."

"Is he harassing you?"

"No." Lindy almost smiles. "I wish. Matt Sparks is the running back for the Truman Tigers. And . . . he's my best friend."

"And you're afraid all his head injuries are affecting your friendship?"

"No." Her hazel eyes drop to the ground. "I . . . Look, it's obvious that you know a thing or two about fashion and crap like that."

"It's true. I know both fashion *and* crap."

"I want you to teach me how to be all girly so Matt will notice me—really notice me."

I study this girl in front of me—her cheeks colored a pink shade of embarrassed, her baggy athletic shorts revealing toned leg muscles, and her school t shirt hiding who knows what beneath it.

"I don't know . . ." I twist my hair around my finger. "Have you tried just being yourself?"

She snorts. "All my life. It's time for drastic action. Whatever it takes."

"Anything?"

"Except that waxing business."

"And what do I get in return?"

"The satisfaction of helping a sister in trouble?"

I shake my head. "Nah."

"You get friends. I'll need you to hang around me so you can get to know Matt and me better. We're not exactly on the bottom of the social food chain around here, so I think you'll see some benefit to associating with us." She looks across the courtyard at all the students *not* paying attention to me. "Your scandal will blow over eventually. People will forgive you."

"Not likely."

"You just need to . . . I don't know, do something to get back on their good side. Maybe show them you're serious about getting to know them and Truman a bit better."

And if I'm not?

"It's not as if you *really* meant all that stuff you said on the Internet, right?"

"Right." Well, maybe .01 percent right.

"Think about it. But whatever you decide, keep this to yourself. I'm trusting you with this information—I don't know why, but I am. But if you tell anyone about our conversation, I will sic the entire Truman cheerleading squad on you."

I draw a cross over my heart. "I won't say anything."

"If you're up for the challenge, call me." She hands me a piece of paper with her number on it. "See ya, New York." Lindy walks away, her steps quick and efficient. And not an ounce of grace to be found.

The three o'clock bell rings, and I jump out of my seat and am the first in the hall. Still leery of the full-size lockers and my nightmares of being shoved into one, I adjust the weight of my four-hundred-pound backpack and—

"*Oomph!*" Plow right into an argyle sweater. "Sorry."

Luke Sullivan glares down at me, his hands clutching my shoulders. "Going somewhere?"

His eyes cloud, and I notice they're a strange, deep blue. Like spilled ink. "I . . ." *Focus, Bella.* "I'm going home."

"You have an assignment to do. That's an ongoing investigation, and it starts today."

"I think the stinky Dumpster can wait a day. I'm not wearing my 'sit in trash' outfit, but I'll be sure and pack it tomorrow. And get your hands off me."

"Only if you remove yours."

I startle as I realize my palms are splayed across his chest. His surprisingly hard chest. I tuck my hands behind my back, and Luke releases my shoulders, his eyes never leaving mine.

"Luke, seriously, I need a little notice. My mother is waiting in the parking lot, and I have things to do at home." Like lie on the floor and scream until Mom says I can keep Moxie.

"I knew you couldn't do this. You don't have it in you."

"No! I totally have it in me." I have no idea what we're talking about here. "Tomorrow. Really, I'll investigate your Dumpster tomorrow. I think one day won't hurt our foray into the many things I'm sure the cafeteria is covering up." I wince when I hear the mockery seep into my tone.

"Forget it. I'd hate for you to miss a nail appointment or something."

"I don't have a nail appointment!" *You jerk.* "Um, but if I did . . . where would that appointment be?"

He growls low and pivots on his heels. "Consider your assignment revoked."

I'm so sick of everyone's low opinion of me. If it's going to change, I'm going to have to *make* it change. Whatever it takes. *You can do it, Bella. You can do it.* "Fine!"

Luke stops and walks back my way. "What's that?"

I swallow. "I said fine. I'll do it."

"Today. Now."

I force a smile. "Can't wait to get out there. My journalistic fingers are just itching to . . . to . . ." My forced enthusiasm falters. "Look, I'll go sit in trash. That's all I can give you right now."

"I want a full report. Dig around in that Dumpster for at least two hours. Got it?"

"And you promise this isn't some way to make me disappear? Some big truck isn't going to show up and scoop me up, right?"

For a millisecond I think I see a flicker of humor in his eyes. But if it was there, it's gone now. Just his cold, assessing stare. "Any trouble you get into will be of your own making."

Oh, I would love to rake that prim and proper smirk off his face. "Yes, sir, Mr. Editor. And maybe if you're nice to me, I'll bring you back a souvenir. Like a petrified burrito or a decomposed hot dog." Because that's all I'm going to find on this pointless errand.

His eyes flicker over me again before he turns around and walks away. *That pompous, arrogant little—*

Outside I find my mom in the parking lot. I slide into the passenger seat but leave the door open.

"I've got news," I say.

"Me too. I got a job!" She pulls me into a fierce hug. I close my eyes and drag in her comforting smell. I remember when I was little I would count her hugs like prizes. They were few and far between, unlike Luisa's open arms. Mom was rarely home. And when she was, her ear would be connected to her phone or she'd be taking care of someone else in one of her charity organizations. I always wanted to start a charity for myself. The Where in the World Is My Mom Foundation.

"I'm going to be working at Sugar's Diner downtown."

"*What?*"

"Yeah, I start tomorrow. I'm going to wait tables."

"Mom, you don't even know your way around a kitchen." I stop myself from rolling my eyes. I don't want to hurt her feelings, but this is a disaster in the making. "Wouldn't you like to find something more suited to your skills?"

And then her lower lip trembles. She drops her head to the steering wheel. "I don't have any skills." She sniffs and wipes away a falling tear. "It's so hard."

"Tell me about it."

"Okay." She blows her nose and holds me with a watery gaze. "I married your dad when I was so young. I was in love." She shakes her blonde head. "I dropped out of college to marry him and support him through med school."

"See, you've got work experience. What did you do back then?"

"I mean I supported him emotionally. I kept the apartment pretty—myself pretty. Then your dad's career took off and you came along." She smiles and pats my knee. "And I just forgot about my own dreams. Your dad became this giant personality . . . and I seemed to have lost mine. Bella, I don't even know who I am anymore."

Aha! "Mom, it's okay. We can go back to New York and figure it out. You were confused when you married Jake. I understand."

"Oh no." She closes her eyes, further smearing her mascara. "Marrying Jake was a turning point for me. He encourages me to be . . . me. And now I've got to figure out who that is."

Yes, please hurry. Because I think the real you will want your Manhattan address back.

"I need to figure out what I'm good at. What my interests are." Mom smiles slowly. "I need to get to know my daughter. I've missed out on a lot. But no more, Bella." She swipes at her smudged under-eye area. "You want to know what I decided today?"

"Mom, I don't know if I can take any more of your life changes."

"I'm going back to school!" She giggles. "Isn't it great? Just a few classes next semester, but I'm on the right track. I know it."

I glance at my watch and feel the dread coat my stomach. "I'm really glad for you." Aren't I? "But I've got to go. You're looking at the newest staff member of the *Truman High Tribune*, and my first assignment starts right now. I couldn't get out of it." Or avoid getting *in* it.

My mother straightens and turns the key. "Oh. Well, I was hoping you could help me with dinner tonight. It's my turn to cook, and"—she shrugs—"you know what a disaster that is. Plus I thought it would give us a chance to talk more. But I'm glad to see you making connections already! I told you all that would blow right over."

Yeah, like a dead tree.

I stick a leg out the door and force the rest of my body to follow. "I'll call you when I'm done. Shouldn't be but a few hours." And then a couple *more* hours of showering. My hand hesitates as I shut the door. "Mom . . . I really am proud of you. But promise me you'll keep your eyes and ears open. I really think Jake might be—"

Her cell phone erupts in an obnoxious chime. "Oops, got to take this. Call me when you're done, sweetie."

And my mom drives away. Still oblivious to Jake's deception.

And the fact that her daughter is about to get totally violated by a Dumpster.

chapter fifteen

Assignment Rules: Garbage Exposé

1. *Investigation is confidential and will not be discussed with anyone not on Tribune staff.*
2. *Reporter is to secure the area and make sure no one sees entry into Dumpster.*
3. *Reporter is to stay concealed within Dumpster for a minimum of two hours.*
4. *Reporter is not to do anything but observe and take pictures during this time.*
5. *Anything confiscated during the investigation is the sole property of Truman High School; should anything be kept by reporter, it will be considered stolen property.*

I refold my assignment description from Luke and grab a few necessary items from my backpack. Can you believe those rules? I'm so sure—like I'd *want* to keep anything from the trash. That boy needs to get over himself. Mr. Power Trip.

"Okay, here goes nothing." Throwing my bag on the ground, I

"secure the area" and find the coast is clear. Unfortunately. I walk to the back of the rusted brown Dumpster. And stop. If I get hepatitis or some sort of rash out of this, I will have Luke Sullivan's head on a platter.

Closing my eyes, I take a deep breath. *Ew!* Too deep. Breathe through the mouth.

I grab a milk crate from a nearby stack and set it beside the Dumpster. Right now I think I would rather pluck out my own fingernails than do this.

I plant one foot on the crate.

This is so unfair. The nerve of that guy. You *know* he created this assignment just to smoke me out of the class.

Both feet on the crate.

I'm through being a disappointment to Truman High. If Luke tells me to swim across the Mississippi River in my winter coat with my arms tied behind my back and weighted fins, I will do it.

My hands clutch the top of the metal wall and I peer in.

Truman High is going to see that no matter what they throw at me, I can handle it. I can do anything. I am Bella Kirkwood. I am made of tough stuff—strong resolve, tons of courage, heaps of strength—*sick!* Is that a dead mouse?

With a final look behind me, I stick my heel into a foothold, heave myself up, and hurl my body over the side.

"Yuck!"

And face-plant into a puddle of old spaghetti. My breath coming in gasps, my hands fly to my face and swipe the red stuff off. I think I'm going to be sick. I lift the tail of my top and bury my head in it. There's one shirt ruined. Along with my dignity.

God, I don't know why I've got a front-row seat on this little jour-

ney *into humiliation, but whatever You're trying to teach me, I'm here.*

And if we could hurry the lesson along, that would be great too.

My feet find the floor, and I find a spot and sit on a trash bag. Time to start opening some of these bags, I guess, because I sure don't see anything suspicious here. Five giant trash bags. A batch of old spaghetti that was stronger than the bag and worked its way to freedom. A few plastic bottles that should've been recycled. And a paint can.

I grab my notebook and jot the items down. Oh yes, I can see the story already. *Cafeteria has perfectly normal, smelly garbage.* Front-page news. Can't wait to have my name attached to that.

Reaching for a bag, I breathe through my mouth and untie it. On second thought, I am *not* digging through that. I don't have gloves. I don't know if my tetanus shot is up to date. And I could get cut on something like glass or metal. Or the cafeteria's rock-hard cookies.

I pry the bag open further and take a few pictures. Maybe I'll get the photos blown up into eight-by-tens and frame them for Luke. Since he's so into trash.

After snapping a few more pics with the digital camera and nothing else to do, I settle onto a bag.

And wait.

Only one hour and forty-seven more minutes.

I pull out my phone and text Mia in New York.

Hunter sez ur going to party 2nite. Make sure he's not slow dancing w/some hot girl. Ha!:) Sorry I haven't called. Fallout from blog has been nuts. U would not believe where I—

"We've got trouble."

My head snaps up at the voice.

Who is that?

Male. Young.

What if he finds me? How will I explain this? Um, just hungry for a little spaghetti and look where I found some!

Another guy answers. "I know who you mean. I'm on it."

"He's on the verge of talking."

"I said I'll take care of it."

"He could blow the cover on ten years of the Brotherhood. We can't risk that. Do you still want to go ahead with the new recruit? Are you sure he's ready?"

Recruit? Ready for what?

"We'll talk to Sparks at the Thursday night party, then decide. Hopefully he'll show. I see no reason to stop now."

Sparks? As in Matt Sparks? That's Lindy's friend.

"Anything to make the coach happy, right?" Silence stretches, and I risk a shallow, quiet breath. "Are you sure you don't want me to handle Reggie?"

A breeze blows and I flinch as something flies up my nose.

I rub my eyes and check out the box next to me. Pepper!

My sinuses constrict. *Oh no.*

I pinch the bridge of my nose. Must. Not. Sneeze.

"No. He's all mine. He needs to learn that we come first. None of us will be talking about last year's mishaps."

I bury my face in my armpit. My eyes water.

Here it comes! Can't. Hold. On. Any. Longer.

"Later, dude."

"Achooo!"

My hands fly to my mouth and I freeze. Who throws away an industrial-sized box of pepper? That is *so* going in my report.

"Did you hear that?"

Silence.

Then feet shuffling. Getting closer to the Dumpster.

My nose burns again. I pinch it and hold my breath. A sneeze is seconds away.

"Hey, somebody's coming. Let's get out of here."

Great idea! Go!

"I'll talk to you tomorrow—with a plan."

Their feet pound the pavement in a hard run.

"Achoo! Achoo!"

"Bella?"

"Achoo!"

"Is that you, Bella?"

I know that voice. The Evil Editor.

I step on my trash bag and hang over the edge of the Dumpster. "Who else would be neck-deep in day-old marinara and used forks?" I glare down at the boy who sets my blood to boiling.

"Are you okay?"

"Yes." *Like you care.* "Why?"

"You seem to have a little . . . uh, something here." He steps forward and brushes my cheek with his knuckles. A featherlight touch. Our eyes lock.

And I fall backward, my trash bag imploding beneath me. "Ugh! I hear you laughing out there, Luke Sullivan!" I brush clinging tea grinds and banana peels off my skirt.

"I'm not laughing."

I peek over again. "Did you get a good look at those two guys?"

He looks behind him. "Who?"

I roll my eyes. *Boys! So unobservant!* "They were just here. You had to have run into them."

"Nope. Didn't see anyone. But I was jotting down some notes on my BlackBerry too."

"Great. So I sit in a giant box of trash and see nothing but an improperly disposed of paint can, yet when a *real* story shows up, you totally miss it."

Luke frowns. "What do you mean?" He holds up a hand for me to grab. "Jump out."

I barely resist a second eye roll. "I'm in a skirt." I motion for him to face the other direction, then with very unladylike grunts and probably a flash of my undies, I crawl out of the dump and back onto terra firma. "Okay, you can turn around now."

His nose wrinkles. "You smell."

"And you're obnoxious. But, Luke, I have a real story. At least a piece of one. These two guys were here and—"

"Save it, Kirkwood."

"What?"

"You are assigned to *this* investigation." He points to the trash. "That's all I want you to cover." He wrinkles his nose. "Maybe not so literally next time."

"But I overheard this conversation and—"

"What was it about?" He grabs the camera out of my hand and slips it in his front pocket.

"Well . . . I don't know. But they were being all secretive. Somebody's got a plan for this hush-hush meeting, and something about the first football game." *Wow. I really do smell.*

"Bella—"

"And they would've talked more but then I snorted a bunch of pepper, which I definitely don't recommend."

"Bella—"

"And I couldn't sneeze, so I was holding it in, and I thought my eyeballs were going to pop out of their sockets, and—"

"Would you be quiet?"

"Oh." I blink. "Were you saying something?"

"You have been assigned a story—"

"An exposé on *trash*?" How can you even call that a story?

"—and you will focus only on your assigned story. So I don't care if someone comes up to you with details of an Orlando Bloom sighting—you will ignore it. You have a long way to go to prove yourself. And this is not a good start."

I open my mouth in helpless outrage. My brain whirs with insults, blistering words, and slurs against his mama. "I am telling you, something is going on at this school. Something related to the game and Matt Sparks—and maybe he's ready, maybe he's not—and they want to stop Reggie from talking about last year." I catch a breath. "What happened last year? Anything? Any sports fiascos?"

"What you probably heard were a few football players discussing game strategy."

"Behind a Dumpster? Luke, this could be big. I smell scandal."

"I smell old cafeteria burritos. Go home, Kirkwood. Don't give this situation another thought. Sort through your notes from this afternoon, and we'll discuss the progress on your research first thing tomorrow in class." And he turns on his perfectly polished leather shoe and walks away. Dismissing me. And my juicy news. As if we're both nothing. Totally insignificant in his little world.

I reach for a crumpled piece of paper in my purse. Checking it, I punch in the numbers on my phone. Voice mail.

"Lindy, this is Bella Kirkwood . . . I'd like to take you up on the offer we discussed today. I'll see you tomorrow at lunch. Can't wait to hang out . . . and meet Matt Sparks."

~~~~~~~~~~

Mom picks me up, and we're both quiet on the way home. She doesn't even ask about my appearance. When she turns on the dirt road, the dry dust swirls around us like a fog.

"Bella, I'm really sorry about Moxie. I know she means a lot to you."

Just everything.

"I want you to know that I placed an ad in the paper. It will start running tomorrow."

I turn my head and look out my passenger window.

"Did you hear me?"

"What do you want me to say, Mom?"

She pauses. "Anything. Tell me what you're thinking."

"I don't think it would change anything."

We pull into the driveway and I jump out, slamming the door behind me. Seems all I do anymore is slam doors.

"Grab a plate!" Jake calls when I enter the house. "Spaghetti's on."

My stomach rolls. "I'll pass." I've seen enough spaghetti for today.

Mom's voice stops me on the stairs. "The whole family is sitting down for dinner together. Wash your hands and take your seat at the table." I turn around, and the set of her jaw tells me she won't be taking no for an answer.

With a long, overdone sigh, I walk past her on the staircase and plop myself into *my* seat at the table. I feel two eyeballs on me. Slowly I face my younger stepbrother.

"What are you staring at?"

His brown eyes narrow. "You look like you've been wrestling in pig slop."

"And you look like you've been eating paste again." I brush a white fleck off his cheek.

"Guilty." He shakes his head. "I try to be strong and resist, but it calls out to me."

"At least you're admitting to your addiction, Robbie."

"People don't understand the burden I carry." He passes me a bowl of salad.

Budge shuffles into the kitchen, glares in my general direction, then sits beside his brother. "You stink."

"Beans for lunch." Robbie rubs his stomach. "Sorry."

"Not you." He punches his thumb toward me. "Her."

"Shut up, Budge."

"You shut up."

"Cat hater."

"Prissy Paris Hilton wannabe."

"Computer techie gamer dork."

"Spoiled brat of a—"

"Enough!" Jake's hand comes down and the whole table shakes. "Now whether you two like it or not, we are a family. And we *will* get along. But I will *not* have you yelling at the dinner table."

Burp!

All heads turn to Robbie.

"Sorry. But this disharmony is affecting my digestive system." He shrugs. "It's very delicate."

"Bella," my mom says. "Would you like to pray for our food?"

"No."

Her lips thin. "Fine. I will."

My mom is going to pray? Until we got to Truman, my mother hadn't even been in a church in nearly three years. I usually went with friends. Sunday became just another day for my parents to work. Well, that's what Dad said he was doing. Work probably went by the name of KiKi or Barbi.

At her amen, food is passed again.

Robbie slathers butter all over his roll. "So how was work today, Dad?"

Jake smiles at his son. "It was fine. We had a machine break down for a few hours, but I fixed it. We had a quota to meet, so it was a sticky situation."

I would think it's always a sticky situation in the maxi-pad business.

After dinner I go upstairs to shower, do my homework, and spend some quality time with my cat. We sit together in the window seat until darkness spills over the sky like black ink.

A breeze blows my hair and shakes the oak limbs outside. Moxie jumps off my lap at the scraping noise.

I study the window screen that looks like it's made of metal floss and has seen better days. With light fingers and a heavy heart, I grab the edge of the screen. It pops out easily, and I place it on the floor. Then, grabbing the Bible on my bedside table and my phone for a light, I climb out onto the roof.

Caution in every step, I work my way to the edge and grab hold of a big thick branch. And I nestle into its crook and sit.

An hour passes before I'm through telling God all the things I'd like Him to fix and come back inside. I set my alarm and nestle into the cool sheets with Moxie purring at my ear.

At 3:55, the buzzing clock blasts me from a dream. I drag myself back to the window seat, my eyes struggling to stay open.

Five minutes later, I watch my stepdad get into his truck. And with the headlights off long enough to get out of the driveway, he steers his truck toward the road.

Jake Finley is up to something.

And I, Bella Kirkwood, intend to find out what it is.

chapter sixteen

～～～～～～～～～～～～～～～～～～～～～

Good morning." My mom kisses me on my cheek as I reach in to
get a bagel.

"Hey." It's the best I can do. She's *choosing* to separate me and
Moxie, so excuse me if I don't exactly feel like blessing her with
some kindness. How come the Bible doesn't address this issue?
Where's the chapter that deals with parents who throw your pet
onto the street? Or daughters who see their stepdads sneak off in
the wee hours of the morning?

"Good morning, new sister." Robbie pours more syrup on his
Eggo. "Did you know today is National Towel Day?"

"Um . . . no." The collection of facts in this kid's head scares
me.

"Well, it is. I thought we could all go around the table and tell
why we're thankful for the bath towel."

"Actually, Robbie, I thought we could discuss something else." I
wait until Robbie, Budge, and my mother are all looking at me.
"Like why Jake snuck out of the house at four this morning."

Mom's eyes widen.

"I'm sorry, Mom. I couldn't keep it to myself any longer. But I watched him sneak out of the house. Your husband is up to something, and we deserve to know what that is."

Her face falls. "Oh, honey . . . I had wanted—"

"Things to be perfect? I know. I'm sorry. But they're not." *Far from it.*

"I had wanted to surprise you." She looks over my shoulder as Jake enters the kitchen through the back door. "Jake, it seems that Bella—"

"I know." I shake my head in disgust. "I saw you leave this morning." *The jig is up, dude.* "I think you owe my mom an explanation." And then we'll be packing our bags and getting out of your way.

And then my stepdad . . . laughs. He laughs! "There's just no getting anything by you, is there?"

"No." Okay, confused here. Now Mom is laughing.

"Come with me." Jake gestures toward the back door. He sees my hesitation. "We'll all go."

The whole family, minus Budge, walks outside.

And there in the driveway, the same dusty path that I watched Jake travel only hours before, sits a lime green VW Bug. With a giant red bow on top.

"Surprise!" My mom squeals and pulls me into her arms. "Isn't it great? Jake found it!"

"Yeah . . . great." I watch him through narrowed eyes. "So this is what you've been working on?"

"I've been a busy guy. We got it last week, but it needed a few repairs." He pats my car. "And a killer stereo system."

Mom pulls me close, her mouth at my ear. "Don't you feel silly now—all that suspicious talk?" She giggles. "You always did have a big imagination."

"These are *all* the notes you have?"

Luke paces in front of me, running a tanned hand through his black hair. The other newspaper staff members are busy writing, but me? I'm getting my daily dose of Luke harassment.

"Um, yes. Frankly, for two hours of swimming through trash bags, rotten food, and old boxes, I thought I did good to come up with *that* much." *Jerk.* "What did you think I was going to find—the secret recipe for the cafeteria meat loaf? The formula for world peace? The whereabouts of Michael Jackson's old nose?"

He stops, lifting his eyes from my notes. "Very funny." He leans in, his arms braced on each side of my chair. "Bella, if you can't take it here, you know where the counselor's office is. She would be glad to change your schedule again."

I blink into his ocean blue eyes. "I sat in trash for you. I think I passed your stupid test, so let's get on with the real stories."

"You've got one." He rises up, crossing his arms over his chest. "Stick to it."

"What are you working on? Maybe I could help?"

He coughs to cover a laugh. "My story is a piece I've been working on for two years. Our advisor is entering it into a national contest. I don't think I need *your* help, but thank you."

Maybe he ought to do a piece on humility, the arrogant little—

"Luke, are we going to talk about the conversation I overheard at the Dumpster yesterday? *That's* the real story here. Not the shameful way the school doesn't recycle."

"If I catch you pursuing anything but the trash article, you're off the paper. And within a few days, the only electives open will be Professional Weightlifting and Parenting 101."

"But something *is* going on, and I—"

"No." He thrusts my notes back in my hand. "This conversation is over."

Your oxford shirt is so over. Ohhh, he makes me *so* mad!

A few hours later, I slip into the cafeteria, my lunch bag under my arm. I think I saw a little too much in the Dumpster to risk school food.

I weave through the tables. I catch a few glares, stares, and some stray insults.

"Hey, Bella."

I sigh with relief when Lindy Miller calls out to me. Part of me thought she'd stand me up. That I would spend yet another day here at Truman High without friends. A total loser and loner.

"Bella, this is Matt Sparks." I shake hands with her sandy-headed BFF, then introduce myself to a few more people at the table.

"You're the girl who wrote the bad blog about Truman?" Matt asks.

"Yeah." I continue to stand, not sure I'm welcome here. "It was a mistake. It was a really bad time for me, and I . . . messed up."

He considers this. "It's going to take awhile for them to warm up to you." His eyes pan the whole cafeteria. "Not everybody's as forgiving as Lindy here." He bites into a French fry. "Or me." Then he smiles.

And I sit down. "So you play football?"

"Yeah, and Lindy here is a beast on the basketball court."

She blushes pink. "I wouldn't say that."

"Oh, I would. She could totally be WNBA material. Hey, Jared."

I turn around, and behind me stands Jared Campbell, the first person who spoke to me at Truman. Before the Great Disaster.

"Hey." His gaze drops to me before focusing on Matt. "Just wanted to remind you to bring your physics notes to practice."

I scrutinize his every word, trying to see if he sounds like either of the two voices I heard yesterday. It's so hard to tell.

"Jared, do you know Bella?" Lindy asks.

"Yeah." His face is a neutral mask. "We've met."

His words contain no heat, and I'm encouraged. "How are . . . things?"

"Fine."

I decide to push my luck and keep talking. "How about that pop quiz in English, huh? I did not see that coming."

"Jared, come on." Brittany Taylor arrives and links her arm into his. If looks could kill, I would be splattered on the wall. "I have a seat for you over here."

He throws up a weak wave, then allows Brittany to escort him away.

I break the awkward silence. "I'd love to see the team practice sometime. I kind of missed out on the whole football thing going to an all-girls school. Maybe Lindy and I could watch you guys today?"

"What?" She chokes on her water. "Why?"

I kick her under the table. "Because we want to support the team." *And your cause, Lindy.* Not to mention, it will give me a chance to watch the football players and see if I can learn anything more about the conversation I overheard. See if I recognize any voices.

"Um, yeah. Watching practice would be ... fun."

"You girls—anything to watch some sweaty guys, eh?" Matt laughs.

"Well, maybe for me." *Forgive me, Hunter.* "But I think Lindy here has already got her eye set on somebody." I nudge her with my elbow.

"You do?" Matt frowns. "You like somebody and didn't tell me?"

"Uh ... uh ..."

"A girl has to keep some of her secrets, right?" My fake smile is bigger than the Oklahoma panhandle. Lindy only stares and nods.

"So Lindy and I thought we saw you at church last Sunday."

My mind reviews last Sunday. I didn't really notice anyone. Well, except the creepy bald guy in front of us. "Really? So you guys go to the Church of the Holy High School?" As soon as it's out of my mouth, I want to stuff it back in.

But Matt only laughs. "Yeah, nothing like coming to school *six* days a week. We should be in our new building sometime next year."

"Is that where your family is going to go to church?" Lindy offers me a fry, and I take it.

"Actually, my stepdad and his kids are from here. Just my mom and I are from New York. Do you know Budge Finley? He's my stepbrother."

"Oh." Matt and Lindy bob their heads. "He's like a computer genius, isn't he?"

Um, he's like a social moron.

"Yeah," Lindy says. "He's on the student team of techies. It's pretty elite—students are trained to fix the school computers and stuff."

"Bella—"

I'm mid-bite as Luke approaches our table. I swipe my hand across my mouth and come back with a mustard-coated finger. Great. Mouth full. Yellow mustache. "Hmmm?" Chew, chew. Swallow.

"I forgot to mention that I'll need you to resume your research today."

"What?" Pieces of sandwich shoot out of my mouth. He motions me over to a nearby wall, out of earshot.

"I am not climbing in that Dumpster again."

"Of course you're not."

That's what I'm talking about. He needs to recognize I have my limits.

"You'll be in the one on the opposite end of campus. Near the gym."

"No! I'm busy. And I think I can still smell myself from yesterday." Even though I spent half the night in the shower to degunkify.

"How are you going to write an article on the contents of school trash if you don't *look* at the school trash?"

Jesus, I'd like to ask for a little restraint. Because I'm about to tell him I think I might be looking at school trash right now.

"Look, I said I would do the article, and I will. But your hounding me at my every step isn't helping."

"I have college recruiters watching our paper. Ivy League."

"Yeah, I think you've mentioned that."

"So get serious about the paper or get lost." He does a perfect heel spin and walks away.

"Wait—" I catch up as he exits the cafeteria. "I need more notice, okay? Believe it or not, there's more to my life than garbage watching. I have to be somewhere after school. I'll do it tomorrow." He looks skeptical. "Seriously."

He exhales loudly and I smell his cinnamon gum. "Is there anything you take seriously, Bella?"

I inch closer to him, closing the distance. "Your lack of faith in me is so encouraging. Tell me, Luke, is this how you treat the rest of the newspaper staff? Is this how you boost morale—by constantly letting them know how little you think of their abilities?" I am *so* channeling Oprah right now.

His eyes darken. "I won't let my paper go down the toilet just because some prissy socialite got stuck in the class. I care too much about my staff and the integrity of the paper."

Have I ever noticed he's like a cross between a preppy Jake Gyllenhaal and that Superman guy from TV? *Wait, did he just say "prissy socialite"?*

"Even though I think this assignment is a total scam to get me to bail, I will dive into every Dumpster in the county if I have to. You're not getting rid of me, so get used to it." Plus I don't want to take that class where you have to take home a computerized baby. I need my beauty sleep, thank you very much.

"You want my faith, Kirkwood, you gotta earn it." And Mr. Dismissive marches down the hall, out of sight. Hunter could so give him some lessons in manners.

~~~~~~~~~

After school, I walk across the street with Lindy to the football field. The boys are already in their practice uniforms and in motion. I have no idea how this game of football works, but apparently it involves lots of sweating, grunting, and drinking water like thirsty dogs.

It's kind of hot.

"Lindy, you have to show interest in what Matt does—like his sports." We take a seat midway up on the metal bleachers. "When's the last time you watched him practice?"

"Never. In a few weeks I'll be at practice myself, so that's not really an option."

"Do you go to the games?"

"I'm the water girl."

"Oh." I guess she couldn't get any closer to him on the field if she were a cheerleader. The hot Oklahoma sun beats down on my head, and I swat my limp bangs away. "Hey, I was thinking . . . I'm getting away this weekend to Manhattan . . . Would you want to go?" Nerves spike my stomach. "You don't have to. I totally understand if you'd rather not. You don't know me *that* well and all, and I haven't really—"

"Are you serious?"

I see nothing but excitement in her face. "Yeah, totally. We could get our hair done. Shop. I could show you the sights."

Lindy is speechless for a few seconds. "I would love to. It might take some work talking my dad into it."

"Perfect." I smile. Maybe I'm really making a friend here. "So . . . I was wondering what you could tell me about Truman High. You know, any gossip? Any stories? Any scandals I should know about?" Like something to do with the football team last year?

Lindy swats a bug off her Nike t-shirt. "Can't think of anything."

This is getting me nowhere.

"How did the football team do last year?" I watch Matt throw the football to Jared Campbell.

"We went to the state play-offs. That hadn't happened in a long time. Truman used to be known throughout Oklahoma for our football team. So last year we finally made it to state. We played our archrival, River Bend. The game went into double overtime, but we lost in the last minute."

"What happened?"

"Reggie Lee, our kicker, missed."

As in *the* Reggie? The one the guys at the Dumpster were talking about?

"Between that and some other stuff that happened last year, he's never quite been the same." She points across the field to one of the padded players. "He's a senior this year. He's got recruiters watching him."

Apparently everyone does.

"What do you mean he never got over it? It's just a game."

The head coach blows his whistle and calls for a water break. "That's Coach Lambourn. His son, Coach Dallas, is an assistant." Lindy then does her best to explain the basics of football. The girl is a walking Wikipedia of the sport. About ten seconds into it, my eyes are glazing over and my attention goes elsewhere.

I spy a lone football player heading toward the field house. Reggie Lee.

I interrupt Lindy. "Where's he going?"

"I don't know. Probably to use the bathroom in the locker room." A couple other football players head in his direction.

"I need to grab something out of my car. I'll be right back."

And I make my way down the bleachers, my flats proving to be a good choice today.

I walk toward my Bug, then keep going, following Reggie and the other players at a distance. I have no idea why. I'm kind of new to this investigative reporting stuff, so it's not like I know what I'm doing.

They pass by the field house entry and keep going, walking around to the back of the building.

I stop at the corner and dare a quick peek around.

The tree-sized guy on the left punches Reggie in the shoulder. "Your allegiance is with the team. Are you in or not?"

Reggie bows up. "Back off, man."

"Don't make this hard for us," the other player says.

"Hard for—" Reggie spits on the ground. "You have no idea what it's like to be me—to live with this."

"Can I help you?"

I jerk my head back and flatten myself to the wall. "Um . . ." It's one of the coaches. I read his shirt. Dallas Lambourn. Guy looks young enough to be in high school himself.

Coach Dallas lifts a brow and waits.

"I was just trying to find a bathroom." That's somewhat true. A girl can always use a bathroom.

"Really? Because it looks like you were following my boys here." He gestures behind me, and slowly I turn around.

There stands Reggie Lee and his two teammates. They don't look happy. In fact, I think they have their tackle faces on.

"I'm new here." I smile prettily. "I'm a friend of Lindy Miller's. We're just watching practice. I come from an all-girls school, see, and Lindy was teaching me all about football." *Am I still talking? Why can't I shut up? Stop talking!*

"I don't like anything to distract the team from their practice. Do you understand, Miss—?"

"Yes, I understand completely," I blather, not bothering to fill in the blank with my last name for the good coach. "I'm sorry, I just got a little lost. But hey, Coach, your team looks great." My eyes widen. "Er, not necessarily these three. I didn't mean they're hot and I'm stalking them or anything." One behind me growls. "Not that you're not hot. No, totally fine and all that. Well, the pants might be a little too tight, but I meant the whole team"—I make a swooping gesture toward the field—"looks very professional . . . and, um . . ." I back up slowly. "I'm just going to take my seat with Lindy now. We should actually be going, now that I think about it." I continue retreating. "Good-bye." I wiggle my fingers at Reggie Lee. "Good work." I toss a wave to boy number two. "Go team!" to guy three.

And I speed-walk back to the bleachers. I barely contain a sigh as I resume my seat beside Lindy, who keeps an eye on Matt below.

She tears her focus away from him. "Did you get what you needed?"

I glance back to the field house where Coach Dallas still stands with his players, all eyes on me.

"I'm not sure."

chapter seventeen

~~~~~~

I peel Lindy's fingers from my arm as the plane starts its descent. It took Mom and I going over to Lindy's to meet her dad to convince him to allow her to go to New York with me. It's just Lindy and her dad, so he's pretty protective.

"This is only my second flight in my life. Can you believe it?"

I pat her shoulder. "You're doing fine." Oh my gosh. Her fingernails are embedded in my arm. "Not much longer now." My heart does a little somersault at the thought that I will be on home turf in less than thirty minutes. Unless Lindy leaks all the blood from my veins.

"I can't wait to meet your dad," Lindy says, her eyes clutched tightly shut. She's had her eyes closed the entire flight. Even when she went to the bathroom—she just felt her way there. Ran into one drink cart and an old lady. "I think I've seen him on *E!*, right?"

"Yeah, he's a guest commentator on *E! News*. Whenever they think a star has had plastic surgery, they call him for his opinion." Though Dad never really rats anyone out.

"Are you excited to see your boyfriend?"

I lean my head into the seat. "Yeah. It's hard to do this long-distance thing." So hard we haven't talked since Monday. "We're both so busy." Hunter with school and sports. And me with . . . um, sitting in Dumpsters and spying on football players.

When the plane touches down, the weight on my shoulders lightens. I'm home. Hello, New York City!

We weave through LaGuardia Airport—as well as you can weave when you have to pull a transfixed Lindy behind you the whole way.

"This airport is so big they have two Chili's!"

"Come on." I pull her around the corner.

And there among the crowd stands my dad. Like I'm seeing him with new eyes, I take a moment to compare him to Jake. Dad is a good six inches shorter—not quite six foot. He wears clothes tailored for his body, unlike my stepdad, who wears whatever flannel shirt he pulls out of the closet. Dad's jeans look worn and faded, yet I know they were hand-picked by a stylist. And Jake's are also worn and faded. From the barn. And hanging out with cows. And feminine products.

"Bella!" Dad throws his arms out wide, and I run into his waiting embrace. He twirls me around in the middle of the airport. "I've missed my girl."

"Missed you too." I inhale his scent, a mix of cologne and shampoo, and smile. Why do things ever have to change?

"Who've we got here?" He sets me down and I introduce Lindy.

"I'm honored to meet you. I've seen you on TV." She stands in awe, like Dad is Brad Pitt or something.

"Why don't we get your bags and go get something to eat?" He throws an arm around both of us.

"At Chili's?" Lindy asks, her eyes wide.

"No. How about some pizza?" And he takes us to Tony's, my favorite pizza place in all of Manhattan.

We three scoot into a booth and give the waiter our drink orders. "So, Bella—" Dad interlocks his fingers. "I, uh, had plans for tonight that I couldn't exactly get out of."

I lower my menu and stare at my dad. "I'm here for two nights, and you're going out?" I feel *so* wanted. "Who is she?"

"Bells, you know I'm glad you're here, honey." He reaches for my hand. "This is not just a date though. It's more like a business appointment. It's important."

Right. Important. Glad you have your priorities straight.

"I'll be out tonight, and then I'm all yours. I thought tomorrow you could take Lindy shopping." He waggles his eyebrows, a sure sign that (a), he feels guilty; and (b), he'll be loaning me his credit card to make up for it. "And then maybe you girls can go to your favorite salon—you've been complaining about a manicure lately. And after you get all beautiful, we'll go out to dinner and catch a show." His eyes twinkle.

"*Wicked*?" I clap my hands in glee as he nods. "Oh, thank you, Daddy!" And I plant a sloppy kiss on his cheek. *Wicked* is just *the* best musical in the history of theater. I've only seen this retelling of *The Wizard of* Oz like ten times. But I love it. I have all the songs memorized.

After dinner, we take a cab to Dad's.

"So everyone in New York City lives like this?" Lindy points to the rows and rows of apartments as we climb out of the cab. "I mean, where are your yards?"

Dad and I laugh, then help our native Oklahoman inside.

"Bella!" Luisa barrels through the living room and wraps me in her strong hug. "Country life suits you." She pinches my cheeks. "Your face has color."

It's probably a rash from the gym Dumpster I was in a few days ago.

I introduce Lindy to my former nanny. Lindy sticks out her hand, but Luisa pulls her into a bear hug too. "I like this one." Luisa clasps Lindy's chin. "This one is nice; I can tell already."

Yeah, Luisa has never quite warmed up to my friends. I don't know why.

"Your friend Mia left a message." Luisa follows Lindy and me upstairs. "She said to meet everyone at the club at nine thirty. That's awful late for my Isabella to go out, yes?"

"No, it's not. I'll be fine." And I cannot *wait* to see everyone. And dance my butt off.

"I changed the sheets on your bed, so it's all ready!" Luisa scurries ahead of us and flings open my bedroom door.

"Augh!" Lindy clasps her heart and freezes in her tracks. "What is *that*?" She points to the mural over the bed. The evil cherubs.

"Don't worry. They won't come down and get you." I don't think.

"And that?" She points to the matching red chairs in the corner.

"Um, they're supposed to be lips." I shrug. "The theme of the room is love. At least that's what my dad's designer said." I say the theme is Designer Smoked Too Much Crack.

"Do my girls need anything?" Luisa turns on the lamp beside the queen-size bed. The lamp in the shape of Shakespeare's head.

"We're just going to get ready and head out for Viva's." I open my suitcase and start pulling out my party clothes. "Dad's got a date." Luisa and I share an eye roll. She mumbles in Spanish all the way out the door. "Get changed, Lindy. It's time to see some New York nightlife."

Her eyes glow with excitement. She wheels her small suitcase into the bathroom. Seriously, she has such restraint. All she came with was this carry-on. Me? I brought my whole Louis Vuitton luggage collection. A girl never knows when she's going to need something!

While Lindy's in the bathroom, I quickly slip into a funky chic dress and some heels and plug in my flatiron for a touch-up. When my phone pings with a text, I giggle at the name of the sender. Hunter.

Can't wait 2 C U. I've got a Sprite w/ur name on it.

He's so sweet. Why can't all guys be as gentlemanly as Hunter? Like Luke the spastic editor.

"Okay." Lindy opens the door. "I guess I'm ready." And steps out, wearing Abercrombie cargos and a plain red t-shirt.

"Um . . . are these your party clothes?" I can hear Mia and the girls already.

"Yeah." Her spine straightens. "What about it?"

I plaster on a smile. "Because we want people like Matt to notice you're a girl."

"Are you saying I don't look like one?"

Tread carefully. "Lindy, you came to me because *you* said you wanted help looking more feminine. If that's going to happen, you can't get offended every time I try to make a suggestion. Tomorrow we'll go shopping"—on Daddy's money, thank You, Lord—"and I'll show you exactly what you need."

"I don't know, Bella."

"It will be fun." I toss my lip gloss back in my purse. "Let's touch

up your makeup"—as in put more on your face besides Chapstick—
"and hit the club."

~~~~~~~

I pay the cabdriver and all but drag Lindy to the door of Viva's.
"Come on, you can do this."

"My face looks like a clown."

"You look amazing." And she does. Turns out Lindy has some
enviable hair wrapped up in that ponytail. And lips that would
make Scarlett Johansson jealous.

"Have I mentioned I'm not much of a dancer?"

Clearing the bouncer, I pay our cover and walk in. "Is Matt?"

"Yeah, he's totally got skills."

"Then tonight you'll learn how to dance."

"Bella!" Mia and two friends rush me, squealing my name. We
clutch each other in a group hug and jump up and down.

I cling to Mia like a fabric softener sheet on a sock. "Oh my
gosh. I have missed you guys!" We pull apart, and I introduce them
to Lindy.

"Hi." Mia smiles prettily. "I like your lip gloss. Is it MAC?"

Lindy blinks. "No. It's pink."

The girls dissolve into giggles.

"Come on, Lindy. Let's get something to drink." And I lead her
to the bar area. "Aren't they great?" I ask, pointing to my friends.

"Oh yeah, they're . . . something."

"Bella! What's up?"

"Colton!" I bump knuckles with Hunter's friend. "Just the guy
I was hoping to see. This is my friend Lindy." He holds out his fist
for her. "And this guy right here is the best dancer in the city."

"Oh, go on, girl. Get out of here."

"No, seriously." I pay for our drinks and hand Lindy her Coke. "My friend would like to learn some basic moves. Can you handle that, Colton?"

"Anything for you, Bella. Come on, Lindy. Let's get started."

Her eyes widen like he's offering to push her in front of a moving train.

"If you want Matt, you gotta do the work." I jerk my head toward Colton. "He's the best. Take advantage of the opportunity."

"I'll go easy on you." Colton pulls a hesitant Lindy onto the floor.

And I walk upstairs, sipping my Sprite, the bass of the song sending my head to bobbing. I stand on an open balcony and overlook the dance floor. Colton is laughing at something Lindy said. Her body is stiff and uncomfortable. And so far the girl has no rhythm.

Hands cover my eyes, and a deep laugh rumbles near my ear. "Don't tell my girlfriend, but I was wondering if you'd like to dance."

I giggle and turn around. "Hunter!" I throw my arms around him and just hold on. His hands find my face and he leans down, his lips on mine.

Seconds later we pull apart, but I rest my forehead on his. "Tell me I never have to leave here."

He runs a hand over my hair. "Sorry, Bel. Can't do that. But I wish I could."

I take a step back, keeping his hands in mine. "Why haven't you called me this week?"

"I talked to you Monday." He plays with the hoop in my ear.

I swat his hand away. "That was four days ago, Hunter." I try to keep the hurt out of my voice, but it comes through anyway.

"You know how crazy the first few weeks of school are."

My eyes narrow. "Yeah, I'm sure it's been a very stressful time *for you.*" Are you kidding me?

He pulls my chin up with his hand. "We knew this would be hard."

"But we also knew we'd have to try."

"Are you saying I'm not trying?"

I look away and stare at the dance floor. "I don't know what I'm saying."

"Don't tell me you've found yourself a cowboy in Oklahoma."

My lip curls and I return my attention to Hunter. "Don't be small-minded. That's a stupid stereotype."

He steps back and holds his hands up. "Whoa, what is this? I'm just kidding. Somebody sounds a little possessive. Maybe you *do* have another guy."

"Oh yeah, Hunter, I've found someone else. After I sat in a few trash heaps for the paper, then did my new list of chores at the house, and my hours of AP homework, plus the time I've put in helping Lindy, I managed to find a moment or two to cheat on you." My anger could incinerate this whole club. "Do you *want* me to see someone else?"

Hunter just stops. Says nothing.

His eyes fuse with mine. "What's going on with us?" He braves a smile. "Bella and Hunter do not fight."

"I don't know." I shake my head and run a hand through my hair. "This wasn't how I pictured our little reunion."

He tucks a stray lock behind my ear, his hand sliding down my jaw. "I'm sorry I haven't been good about calling. I know you've had a tough few weeks, and I haven't been there for you."

"And I'm sorry I snapped at you."

"Why don't we start over?" The dance floor lights flash in his brown eyes.

He spins me around and his hands cover my eyes.

"Don't tell my girlfriend, but I was wondering if you'd like to dance."

I swivel on my heel and wrap my arms around his neck. "I'd love to dance with you."

chapter eighteen

~~~~~~

I'll see you ladies at dinner, okay?" Dad kisses my cheek and hands me his credit card.

I swear I hear angels singing the "Hallelujah" chorus. Oh, credit card! How I've missed you. Your plasticky goodness. The zipping sound you make when the clerk runs you through a machine. The rattle of a long receipt being spit out by a boutique register.

"Go easy on me today, okay?" He points to his card.

"But, Dad, I haven't shopped in *forever*." Ever since Mom married Jake and somehow *I* got financially cut off. So unfair.

"You've only been in Oklahoma two weeks."

"But in my heart . . . it's an eternity." I push Lindy out the door before my dad goes back to his idea of curtailing my spending and teaching me a lesson. *Hmph*. Whatever. It's teaching me misery, is all. And causing me to lust in my heart—over other people's clothing.

I step outside onto the front stoop and breathe in the familiar Manhattan air. *Ew*. Maybe I shouldn't breathe too deeply. We are a little smoggy at times.

A yellow cab speeds us away, like a chariot taking me to heaven.

Shopping—oh, I could just burst into song. The closest I've come to shopping lately is squeezing the melons at Wal-Mart with Mom. And that's just indecent, if you ask me.

"Okay, Lindy. Our first stop is Marco Ricci's salon. While Marco's working his magic on your hair, I'll be getting a manicure and a pedi. Then we'll switch." Dad totally called in a favor to have my stylist work us in on such short notice. Marco's usually booked, like, a year in advance. Maybe Dad's giving him a discount on a new nose or something.

"I don't know." Lindy fingers her ponytail. "I kind of like my hair."

"But it's not about what you like. It's about what *Matt* might like." I thought we established this last night when we stayed up 'til 2:00 a.m. talking. I felt like Dr. Phil, coaching Lindy toward a new vision of herself.

The taxi pulls up beside Marco's, and I have to force Lindy out of the car and into the salon.

Lindy plants her feet in the lobby and just takes it all in. The pink walls. The techno music. The ladies in the chairs sipping champagne.

"Um . . . isn't there a Supercuts or a Regis somewhere?"

A squeal has me clutching my ears.

"Profanity! Profanity!" Marco, head to toe in black, scurries from behind the front counter, his beret bobbing on his head. "Who is zees you bring to Marco?"

I swallow. "This is my friend Lindy." I elbow her. She doesn't move. "Greet Marco," I say through gritted teeth.

She tries to shake his hand, but he clutches his hands to his chest.

"Do you know who I am, leetle girl?"

Lindy shakes her head. "N-n-no."

"I am Marco Ricci"—his hand sweeps the room—"hair arteest." He leans forward, his pinched face inches from hers. "Dream maker." He draws himself up, his spine as straight as a hair pick. "Now would you like to greet Marco again?"

With rounded eyes, Lindy looks to me. And back to Marco.

Then she drops herself into an awkward curtsy.

Laughter fills the entry as Marco doubles over and howls. "Zees girl you bring me—she is priceless." He grabs a shaking Lindy by the shoulders. "Kees, kees." And smooches the air beside both cheeks. Then his face sobers. "Oh, we have work to do, no?"

"Yes," I say. "Now you're the expert." I know this man so well. "But I was thinking maybe some blonde highlights. Four or five inches off. Some bangs."

"What?" Lindy squeaks. "Five inches off my hair? Are you crazy?"

"Marco eez crazy about art. And your head eez a canvas vaiting to be painted, no?"

"No." Lindy steps away from Marco. "Nobody's gonna paint my head."

Marco crosses his arms and huffs. "I cannot work with zees."

"You'll have to excuse her. She's very upset." I put my hand over my mouth and lower my voice like Lindy can't hear me. "She desperately wants to impress a boy. They met as young children and have been best friends ever since. But now . . ." I look away with a dreamy gaze. "Her heart has changed, Marco. She loves him, but does he even know the real Lindy exists?"

He shakes his head and clucks his tongue. "Oh no. No, no, zees vill not do." He nods his head once. "I vill do zees for you." Marco pulls Lindy to him. "I vill do zees . . . for love."

"Give her the amoré special on those brows too," I whisper to Marco. And I go in search of a foot bath.

Two hours later, Carmina, the shampoo girl, signals for me to follow her. I clutch my toweled head and join her at Marco's station.

I would let my jaw hit the floor, but there's hair on it. "Lindy . . . you look—"

"Ah, ah, ah." Marco shushes me. "Marco vill now show her vhat she look like. Are you ready?"

Lindy rubs the spot between her eyes. "He tried to rip my flesh off."

He rolls his eyes. "You had caterpillars taking over your face." He looks at me. "Zees one ees tough cookie, no?"

I laugh. "Yeah, she is." I smile down at Lindy, who sits with her back to the mirror. Her face is a mask of calm and nonchalance. But her hands beat a punchy rhythm on her knees.

"Marco geev to you . . ." He whirls her chair around. "My neweest creation!"

Lindy gasps, and her hands fly to her mouth. "Oh." She touches a piece of hair. "My."

"You're hot, Lindy!"

"It doesn't even look like me."

"Of course it does—only better."

"Marco make your true love crazy in ze head. He vill not stop looking at you, no?"

"Matt's going to flip." I hug my new friend. "You look great. The blonde and caramel highlights really make your eyes pop."

Lindy sighs, sending her new bangs flying. "Let's just hope Matt's eyes pop."

We spend the rest of the afternoon shopping. I take Lindy all over Manhattan, from the ritziest boutiques to my favorite discount stores, like H&M on Thirty-fourth Street.

At five o'clock, we wait outside of Bergdorf's for my Dad to pick us up.

"Bella, I just want to thank you." Lindy sets her packages down on the sidewalk. "When I said I wanted help . . . I didn't expect all this."

I take in the revamped Lindy, who now looks nothing like a basketball star. More like a buff runway queen. "I had fun." And I really did. "Well, except for when I had to chase you through the salon during the eyebrow wax." We laugh at the new memory. "But you look amazing."

"I do feel . . . different."

"And that's a good thing, right?"

Her answer is interrupted by the arrival of my dad's Mercedes. We climb into the backseat and smother him with girl talk.

He parks his jet black car then escorts us into Tao, a New York City hot spot sometimes frequented by the Hollywood elite. We sit on the main level by the giant statue of Buddha, which actually is not a very appetizing place to eat some spring rolls. But the whole restaurant is filled with soft shadows, candlelight, and the buzz that is only found in New York. I just want to freeze it and never let it go.

"Luisa tells me you got in late last night," Dad says later, spearing a piece of his sea bass.

I shrug and watch Lindy navigate her way to the bathroom in her new heels. "I guess."

"Your curfew was eleven thirty, was it not?"

"Yes." I feel my cheeks redden. "Can we talk about this later?" I force the corners of my mouth to lift. "It was only forty-five minutes late."

"You were past curfew."

"So were you." I instantly regret my words. Well, regret that I *said* them.

"I'm the parent here."

"Really?" Oh my gosh. This salmon I'm eating . . . It's . . . it's like truth serum! I can't stop myself.

"You and your friend have been shopping all day on my credit card. I think the least I deserve is some respect."

I peep over my shoulder to the table next to us then back to Dad. "I am grateful. But what I wanted this weekend was to spend some time with my father. You've been *occupied* all weekend. I haven't seen you in weeks, and we've barely had a chance to talk. I thought you'd *want* to spend time with me. Instead you booked your schedule and handed me your Visa."

"You know I work long hours."

I nudge the vegetables on my plate with my fork. "You get me once a month. Couldn't you adjust your schedule?"

"Bella, I work very hard at what I do. I have goals. And right now I'm pursuing some opportunities that I've been waiting a very long time for." He rests his hand on mine, and I watch our shadows overlap in the candlelight. "Don't you want a dad who succeeds, a dad who becomes something?"

I slide my plate away, my appetite gone. "I just want a dad, period."

chapter nineteen

Three-forty-five in the morning.

I sit straight up in bed and slam off the alarm.

Exhaustion drags my eyelids down, but I shake it off. I have work to do. Two and a half hours before I have to be up for school . . . but if my hunch is right, ten more minutes before I have to be out the door—hot on Jake's tail.

I jump out of bed, knocking the cat to the floor. She meows and slinks away. With my phone as a flashlight, I find a pair of black sweats, throw my hair in a ponytail, and lace my feet into some running shoes.

I crouch on the floor and peek over the windowsill.

Seconds later, Jake's giant form appears. He looks back toward the house then climbs into his truck.

In a flash, I grab my car keys and sneak down the stairs like I'm a world-class spy.

In the kitchen, I watch Jake's truck pull out of the driveway, and when it's a distance from the house, I run outside and jump into the Bug. Taking his cue, I leave my headlights off and navigate the car using only the moonlight. Which isn't easy.

I see the outline of his truck ahead as I pull onto the dirt road. I keep a safe distance behind him and hope he doesn't even think to look in his rearview for someone tailing him at four in the morning.

When we hit the first paved road, I hold the brake down, letting him get even farther ahead. Though his lights are on, I leave mine off and pray the illuminated streets will be enough to see by. And keep me hidden.

He turns onto Central Street.

Fifteen seconds later, I do the same.

Three more turns, and we're heading the opposite direction out of town.

He hangs a left at Mohawk Avenue and wheels into an alley, and that's when I stop.

I frown at the landscape around me. I'm not familiar with this area. Kind of industrial looking. Lots of metal buildings. This is definitely *not* the maxi-pad factory.

I park the car a street away and grab my cell phone, my keys, and the best pepper spray New York sells.

I crouch low—why, I don't know—and tiptoe toward the alley Jake disappeared into. Casting a nervous glance behind me, I stop at the corner of the alley and listen. Two buildings line the small street, and music blasts from the door closest to me.

And yelling.

A shiver dances up my spine. I clutch my phone in a shaking hand. Should I punch in 9-1-1 and have it ready just in case? Am I stupid for doing this? What if I open that door . . . and I'm never heard from again? *Lord, please help me. Protect me from anything scary. And if something scary does happen, help me to be strong . . . and not pee my pants.*

I stand there for a few minutes and just listen. And think. And sweat.

I ease my hand out and touch the knob. Inhaling deeply, I twist it, and the door opens easily. The shouts continue from the far recesses of the building. Somewhere in another room.

I step into a garagelike entryway.

No one in sight.

Sticking close to the wall, I follow the voices down a hall.

"This is the last time you cross me!"

I stop. My breath hitches. Jake—that's Jake.

"You can't stop me! No one can!" Evil, menacing laughter echoes through the building, making the hair on my neck rise.

I take three more steps but freeze at the sound of punches thrown, grunts of pain. What if Jake's in trouble? What if Jake *is* the trouble?

My feet have carried me to a set of double doors. He's in there.

His voice booms again. "I can stop you! I don't think you know who you're dealing with."

I sure don't know who I'm dealing with.

I've got to go in.

Somebody falls to the floor. A scuffle. And then a loud, piercing roar.

And I bust through the doors. "Stop!" My camera phone flashes. Crap! I meant to hit SEND. "I'm calling 9-1-1!" *Or taking your picture.* Whatever.

Two men lie tangled in a heap on the floor. Jake has a man pinned to the ground with his legs. Sweat drips from his face.

Jake's eyes are crazed, wild. "What?"

I stomp forward, my legs trembling. "Let him go." My voice squeaks. "I said let him go, Jake."

He stares at the man beneath him. Then back at me.

"I don't know what this man has done to you, but strangling him with your thighs is probably not the answer." I brave a glance at his victim and notice he's naked from the waist up. "I'm onto you, Jake. I've known about your sneaking out for a long time. Secret rendezvous are one thing, but killing someone is *so* not going to go over with my mom." Unless he offs me before I tell her.

Jake releases the guy then jumps to a standing position.

And that's when I notice that he's just wearing pants too. Black spandex. And his foe is in hot pink.

I take a giant step back. "What kind of place is this?" Two guys wearing spandex rolling around on the floor is *not* a healthy sight.

"Bella, I—" He moves toward me.

"No!" I hold out a hand and jump back. "Keep your distance, you—you—spandexy perv! I'm calling Mom. And the police. And . . ." Jerry Springer?

"It's not what you think." Jake swipes a hand through his dripping hair.

"Oh yeah?" I plant a hand on my hip. "So I *didn't* see you entangled with another man, decked out in shiny Lycra, and your legs in places that scream *highly* inappropriate?"

He blinks. "Um . . . okay. That part is right. But let me explain."

"Save it." I spin around, showing him my back, and head for the doors. I can't wait to pack my bags and get out of this town.

"Bella, wait! You have to listen to me."

I glance back. "Why?"

His Adam's apple bobs. "Because . . . because I'm—"

"Captain Iron Jack." A cape appears over Jake's shoulders.

Out from behind him steps that man—the bald guy from church. The one who stopped when the truck broke down.

I wrinkle my nose at Jake. "Are you an exotic dancer?" *Ew!*

"Of course not."

The bald man speaks. "He's a wrestler, that's what he is. And soon to be a professional. I've never trained anyone so talented— even if he is a little late coming into the game."

My head hurts. Can't process it all. "Mom doesn't know." It's not a question.

Jake's eyes briefly flit away. "No. But she knows I get up early and leave."

"And what does she think you're doing, warming up the maxi-pad maker?"

"She thinks I'm working out. And I am. I'm training."

"But she doesn't know why." She is so going to flip when she hears this. She doesn't know she's married to Hulk Hogan.

"I was going to tell her."

"When? When you were on Pay-Per-View?"

"No. But that would be kinda cool." He shakes his head. "No, I mean of course I was going to tell her. Soon. Bella, this is really hard to explain."

"Well, the visuals have been *quite* lovely so far."

The other two men leave us and retreat to another part of the room.

"I know it's crazy . . . but have you ever wanted something so bad you could taste it?"

Like a one-way ticket out of the heartland?

"Ever since I was a kid, I would watch wrestling on TV and I would think, I want to do that. It's been my dream for as long as I can remember. I wrestled in high school. Then a little bit after that, and things were going really well. But then my family came along, and one day I woke up and I was raising two boys by myself and I didn't have time for silly little dreams."

Silly little *spandex* dreams.

"You've betrayed my mom's trust. There's this huge part of your life that she doesn't even know about."

"I couldn't tell her at first. I had enough trouble with all that online dating business. I sure couldn't say, 'Hey, my name is Jake and when I grow up I want to wrestle.' I just wanted to wait until I had gained some ground with this before I talked to your mother about it. It's just been the last six months that things have taken off."

I run a hand over my face and wonder why I got out of bed this morning. I so need a latte or two right now.

"It's not just a pipe dream, Bella. This is going to work. I have a manager now." Jake gestures to the back where the bald guy re-arranges some weights. "Mickey's training me. I've had a few matches, and . . . I think I might actually be good at this."

"You have to tell my mom." *And the sooner you do, the sooner I can get back to Manhattan.* "Like today. This morning." I pull on the door handle and swing it open.

"I'm sorry I've disappointed you."

I just stare at my stepdad. There's just something about looking at a grown man in tights that robs a girl of any words. "I gotta go."

"Don't tell your mom before I get home."

Right.

The drive to the house takes forever, but it's much easier with the rising sun and headlights.

"Mom!" I tear through the kitchen and down the hall. "Mom!"

She sticks her head out of the downstairs bathroom. "What's wrong?" The towel on her head falls to the floor.

"Your husband . . ." My brain is on warp speed, words and thoughts spinning like there's a tornado in my head. "He . . . he's a . . ." I close my eyes at the image. "A pirate."

"What?"

"Jillian?" Mom and I turn toward the sound of Jake bursting through the kitchen. "Jillian?"

"In here!" She picks up her towel and bestows her "disgruntled mom" look on me. "Bella, I am trying to get ready for work—my first day. I don't know what you're trying to pull, but if I'm late, I *will* ground you."

"I am telling you, Mom, the man you married is not who you think he is. You think you know everything about him, but you don't."

Heavy breathing and pounding steps precede Jake's appearance in the hall. "Jillian." He studies her face, then goes to her, his arms manacled to her shoulders. "I have to talk to you."

My mom looks between the two of us—her out-of-breath husband and her ticked-off daughter. "What in the world is going on here?"

"He plays dress-up!"

"I'm a wrestler!"

Our voices overlap and cancel each other out.

Mom shakes her wet head. "What did you say?" I open my mouth, but she stops me. "Jake first."

Um, putting Jake *first* is what got us onto this tragic detour of life.

"Jillian . . ." Sir Spandex takes a slow inhale. "You have to know I would never do anything to hurt you. You believe that, right?"

Her smile is hesitant. "Yes. Of course."

Lemme talk! Me! Me!

"When we met online six months ago, my life changed. Within weeks of our first phone conversation, I *knew* I wanted to spend the rest of my life with you."

And that's fine—if you're on an MTV reality show!

"And I was afraid to do anything that might scare you off."

Like show you his collection of Hulk Hogan pants.

My mom's smile fades and worry tightens her brow. "What are you talking about, Jake?"

"You and I progressed so fast . . ."

Maybe not in dog years.

"And I thought I'd have plenty of time to tell you, but before I knew it, we were making plans, and I just didn't want to do anything to mess it all up. I tried so many times"—Jake looks toward the ceiling like he's trying to will down some holy help—"but I never could find the words to tell you."

My mom steps closer to her husband. "Are you sick?"

"No, no, nothing like that." His laugh contains no humor. "I'm botching this up."

But on the bright side, if you were trying to tell my mom you're dying of brain rot, this would be going really well.

"Jillian, when a man puts off a dream, something he's wanted his whole life—it doesn't just go away. It haunts him, follows him for the rest of his life."

Should I start humming a Josh Groban song here?

"And . . . see, my dream . . . it's like a tree. And then you came along . . . and that tree grew these new branches—"

"Oh, for crying out loud! This morning I caught your husband with his legs wrapped around another man!"

chapter twenty

~~~~~~

J walk out into the Monday morning sunshine and shut the door on an explosive argument between the newlyweds.

And find a couple waiting on the front porch, ready to knock.

"Um . . . can I help you?" *If you're selling Avon, now is so not a good time.*

"We're the Petersons."

"Uh-huh." My attention strays to Budge, who pulls his hearse out of the driveway with his brother slumped in the passenger seat.

"We're here to get the cat."

I snap back to focus. "What?"

The wife speaks up. "The Persian cat—we talked to Mrs. Finley about it. We're here to pick the cat up."

"It's for our son," her husband says. "He wants to call him Tigger."

Tigger? They want to take my precious cat, give it to a snotty-nosed kid, and rename it after some ADD character from *Winnie-the-Pooh*?

"I'm sorry, but *she's* spoken for." I'm not totally lying here. I'm speaking for her. And Moxie wouldn't want to go home with these people.

"But Mrs. Finley said—"

"Mrs. Finley is busy right now." Hopefully calling the airport to get two one-way tickets. "But the cat is not available. I'm sorry."

The woman lifts a dark brow. "We'll come back this evening, then."

And I'll be waiting.

I skirt past the pair and escape to my sherbet-colored Bug, for the first time somewhat relieved to be going to school.

I barrel down the dirt road and punch in Hunter's number. Voice mail.

I try again.

"Hunter, it's me." *You know, your girlfriend.* "Where are you? I tried to call you last night when I got in." I dodge a crater-sized pothole. "Anyway, I miss you already . . . and I'm sorry I was so moody this weekend. Some stuff's hit the fan here, so call me."

In English class, I reach into my backpack and dig for *The Scarlet Letter*. When I come back up for air, novel in hand, Budge has parked himself in the seat beside me. "Hey," I mutter.

"I don't know what you're up to, but whatever you pulled this morning has my little brother very upset."

I feel a rubber band snap on my heart. "I'm sorry that Robbie's—"

"Crying," he bites. "My brother was crying all the way to school. He wanted to know why his dad and new *mommy* were yelling. And when I looked in their bedroom, there you were. Right in the middle of it."

I swivel in the seat and face him with my whole body. "What are you getting at? That their argument was somehow *my* fault? That makes a lot of sense, Budge. For your information," I hiss, "*your* dad is the problem here. Why don't you ask him what he did?"

"Why don't you and your mom go back to New York?"

"Why don't you jump off a cliff?"

He draws himself up. "I know why that couple was at the house this morning."

My face sobers.

"They came to get your cat." Now Budge grins. "And let me guess—you didn't let them?"

"So? They can't have my cat."

"We'll see about that."

"Hey, I know! Maybe you can talk to your dad about it in between his shift at Summer Fresh and slamming somebody to the ground in his pirate suit."

Budge's face turns one shade darker than his hair.

"That's right, *step*brother, I know. So apparently this was a cute secret between the Finley men, but I found myself in the neighborhood of a certain gym this morning. It's amazing what people are up to at four in the morning."

"And I bet you couldn't wait to tell your mom."

I roll my eyes. "Her husband plays dress-up. She needed to know."

"You think you're so much better than everyone else." He faces the front as Mrs. Palmer enters the room. "I'm proud of my dad. He was on his way to making it in the big-time until you and your mom showed up."

I snap open my binder. "Anything else you want to blame me for? Global warming? World hunger? Lindsay Lohan's last movie?" I gather my things and move to an empty seat two rows away—but still not far enough from Budge Finley.

In journalism class, I sneak a peak at my phone to see if I have a message from Hunter. Nothing.

"Bella, I need you to outline your article ideas you've been working on. Have that for me in fifteen minutes." Luke paces near my desk. "Looking at your preliminary notes and some of your pictures, I think you have a strong lead for a few articles on the need for recycling."

I push my phone back into my purse and try to look interested.

Luke jots something down in his pocket notebook. Yes, seriously, the boy keeps a fifty-cent notepad in his shirt. If it weren't for the fact that he has the face of that Clark Kent guy from *Smallville*, he would be a full-fledged dork.

His pen stops. "We've been trying to get recycling bins for years, but the board won't go for it—too expensive. Your story could change all that. I want you to go to the library and do some research. And hit the last campus Dumpster after school."

"Can't."

"What?" He rolls up his sleeves, exposing tanned forearms. "I didn't really mean you had an option."

"I told you about giving me notice."

"I tried. I called your phone three times this weekend. I left a message for you to contact me."

Oh. That.

Sounds vaguely familiar. I think I was in a Barneys dressing room when the calls came. Who could blame me for forgetting about it?

"Sorry, Luke, but I have to go straight home after school." I have a cat to save and a room to pack up. And I want to say good-bye to Robbie. "But I was wondering if you know anything about a party Thursday night?"

He blinks at the topic change. "No."

Of course you don't. I'm sure he's too busy reading the *Wall Street Journal* or watching PBS to get party invites. Especially from athletes.

"Bella, I don't really care about your need to get your dance on."

I turn my head before he sees my face split into a wide grin. Somebody's been watching too many *Fresh Prince* reruns.

"But we have a story to do. Trash does not wait on us."

Can't contain my laugh this time.

Luke swings a chair around and straddles it. His face is inches from mine. "The trash will be picked up tomorrow. This is your last chance before your deadline." His smile is far from friendly. "And your last chance before you're out of here. I hear the small engine repair class now has a few openings."

"Are you threatening me?"

"As your editor in chief, I'm saying that if you don't follow through, you're gone."

I stare at the center of his chiseled chin, willing myself not to spill out my whole morning's story and beg him for mercy. But I refuse to grovel. "You . . . are a piece of work, *Chief.*"

By lunchtime I have the whole high school percussion section pounding in my head. Neither my mother nor Hunter has returned my calls. I have to find a way to intercept that cat-stealing couple this afternoon, and I have *another* date with a Dumpster.

"Whoa, you look like somebody just kicked your dog." Lindy slides her tray next to mine. "Bad day?"

I pick through the lettuce in my salad and go straight for the croutons. "One bad day, I could take. It's my entire life that's totally jacked up."

Lindy runs a hand through her highlighted hair. "You should come to Wednesday morning FCA—Fellowship of Christian Athletes. We meet once a week in the library before school."

Duh. "I'm not an athlete." But if being a loser were a competitive sport, there would be a trophy with my name on it.

"You don't have to be an athlete. Matt and I go. Lots of people go. Come on." She opens her Gatorade bottle and tips it back.

"No!" I snatch it back. "Remember what I told you?"

She huffs. "I won't burp when I'm done. I told you I wouldn't share that talent anymore."

"A straw, Lindy. You don't want to mess up your lip liner."

Muttering under her breath, she gets up and walks back to the kitchen area.

Seconds later, Matt Sparks sits down. "Hey, heard you girls had a great time in the Big Apple."

I manage a weak smile. "Yeah, we had lots of fun." And I really did. Lindy might not know a pencil skirt from an A-line, but she didn't bore me for a second. And even though I don't get her sports world, we do have some things in common. We're both closet *High School Musical* fans, neither one of us can stand the smell of green peas, and if sad movies have us reaching for the Kleenex box, it's only because we're laughing so hard.

I bite down on a carrot. "So you haven't seen Lindy yet?"

"Not since Friday. I talked to her a few times, but—" The nugget in Matt's hand plops to the floor. His eyes go round.

I follow the path of his hypnotized gaze, and there stands Lindy.

She looks from me to Matt, chewing her lip. "What's wrong?" Her hands fly to her hair. "Do you hate it? It's too blonde, isn't it? I knew it."

"Um . . ." He clears his throat. "Your hair looks . . . great." His voice is completely without enthusiasm. What's that about?

"It's the skirt, then?" She plops into the seat across from me. "I knew it. I look stupid, don't I?"

Matt says nothing.

I fill in the silence. "I think the skirt really accents her legs. I mean the girl has a sprint runner's calves. You shouldn't hide that."

"No. Er, yeah." Matt's look of shock melts into a frown. "I was just surprised, that's all. You look . . . different."

Lindy's newly shaped brows snap together. "Different?"

"I mean you look . . . nice."

Ouch. "You look nice" is not what a girl who just underwent a major makeover wants to hear. Especially when she's crammed her feet into some fashionable yet pinching flats just for the sake of looking stunning.

"Well, I like my new look. And it's totally me. So get used to it. In fact, I might not have as much time to hang out with you anymore because I'll be, like"—she throws her hand about—"shopping. All the time."

"You?" He finally smiles. "Shopping?"

"Yes." Her nose lifts. "Now that Bella has introduced me to it, I simply can't get enough. I'm going to New York with her next month, too, and I'm counting the days 'til I can return to Marcy's."

"Macy's," I mouth.

"Macy's," she corrects. "Macy's and Blarney's—I love them."

"Are you mad, Lindy?" Matt asks in boy-ignorance.

"Of course not. Why would *I* be mad?" She jabs her straw into the Gatorade and sucks it down like her throat's on fire.

A few tense minutes pass, and finally I can't take the weird quiet any longer. "So, Matt, I heard a rumor about a party Thursday night." My voice is sheer nonchalance. "Are you going?"

Lindy looks up from her tray. "What kind of party?"

I shrug. "I don't know. Maybe it's for the football players?"

"I didn't know anything about that."

"Lindy," Matt says. "It's not a big deal. Some of the guys asked me to one of their get-togethers. It's nothing."

"Are you going?" Her tone is as sharp as a switchblade.

"No . . . Well, maybe."

"Are you crazy?" she bleats. "There's probably alcohol there."

"It's not like that. I'm just going to hang out. Lots of people don't drink. I'm not."

"Yeah, you say that now. But if you've caved in to their pressure to go to their party, then who's to say you won't cave in to their pressure to drink a six-pack or two?"

Matt points a fry at Lindy. "You know me better than that."

"Could we come?"

The two twist their heads and stare at me like I just said I want to be Tom Cruise's next bride.

"I mean, if you're just going for the fun of it, then Lindy and I want to tag along."

"No way," Lindy says.

"Seriously, it would be a great place for me to meet people. And it's time everyone got to know me and see I'm not the spoiled brat they think I am." I nudge my friend's foot with my toe. "And I bet there will be someone of interest there *you* could keep an eye on."

"The guy you like is on the team?"

Lindy's face is a neutral mask. "You never know."

"Come on, Matt." If I find out what the football players are up to, I can totally stuff it in Luke's trash-loving face. "If it's just a casual party and everyone won't be drinking, then it will be fun." If I'm even still here. It will probably take Mom and me a few days to pack, now that I think about it.

"Yeah, if it's no big deal like you said, then what's the problem?"

Matt considers Lindy's words. "Okay. You guys can go. But if things *do* get crazy, we're all three leaving. Deal?"

"Deal. Bella, you might see more than you bargained for."

I smile. "That's exactly what I'm hoping for."

chapter twenty-one

After school, I climb into the cafeteria Dumpster. This would be the fourth one I've sat in, so by now I don't even bother dusting the rust and taco sauce off my pants. I squeeze my hands into a pair of elbow-length rubber gloves and get out the rest of the equipment for my head. I fit Robbie's diving mask over my face and add the final touch of a snorkel.

Before I begin the ridiculous snooping process, I check my phone for any messages. Nothing from Hunter, but a text from Mom.

Meet me at diner after school. Sorry about this morning.

Maybe she packed our stuff and we're leaving straight from her work. Or we're going to eat first, then leave.

A miniscule wave of sadness comes over me. I will miss Lindy. And Matt Sparks. And I'll always wonder what the big secret with the football team was. And if I could've been a good enough writer to break the story. And Robbie. I'll miss that little genius.

Time to start opening bags.

I search through trash, making notes and taking a few pictures, but mostly finding nothing new. Same garbage, different day.

"You sound like an asthmatic Darth Vader."

I jump and find Luke leaning over the edge.

"*Ewwstaymee.*" I spit out my mouthpiece and try again. "You scared me."

"I was about to tell you the same thing." His black hair ruffles in the afternoon wind.

I rip off my headgear. "I find it more bearable if I can't smell the contents of the Dumpster."

And then the weirdest thing happens.

Luke Sullivan actually smiles. "Every reporter has her secrets."

Reporter! He called me a reporter!

"Well, this one is about to climb out. I've been here forty-five minutes and nothing's new. Same expired generic bologna. Same excessive use of Styrofoam. I think my work is done here."

He holds up a hand, and this time, I reach for it.

"Um, Bella, do you want to take off those gloves before you touch me?"

"Are we afraid to get our hands dirty, Chief?"

He pulls me up, and with his hands still wrapped around mine, I jump out. And leap away from him like he's radioactive.

"So did you want anything?" I shield my eyes from the sun and squint in Luke's direction. "Or were you hoping you wouldn't find me here so you could fire me?"

"I check on all my staff. Just wanted to see how your progress was."

And I'm Britney Spears. When will the boy learn to trust me? "See you tomorrow, then. I gotta go." As Luke and I part ways, I feel the day catch up with me. I've been up forever. A hot bath and a nap would be fabulous.

I drive the Bug as fast as the Truman streets will let me. And unlike New York, this town isn't about speed. Creeping along at thirty-five gives me a chance to really look at the city. There are mom-and-pop restaurants I've yet to eat at. A few video stores. A movie theater flashing the titles of two almost-new releases. A tiny library. A water tower with a roaring tiger on it. So different from back home. And I can see so much of the sky here. Nobody's honking. No crazy cabdrivers. People taking their time—not rushing like their life depends on how fast they walk.

The door jangles as I walk into Sugar's Diner.

Everyone turns around as if on cue and yells, "Hey, sugah!"

I hold up a hand in awkward greeting. My eyes search for Mom, but my focus gets lost on Sugar's décor. It's like 1950. Metal and Formica tables. Shiny red bar stools. A jukebox blasting "Hound Dog" in the corner.

And then my mom appears, beelining to a table, doing her best to balance three plates of burgers and a large order of fries. Her pink poodle skirt swishes as she stretches to settle the plates in front of her customer. She spots me and her tired face brightens. Mom says something to her table, then flounces my way.

I watch her customers switch plates and claim their correct orders.

My mom settles onto a bar stool and pats the empty one beside her. "Want a shake? I learned how to make one."

"No, I just want to know what's going on. What time are we leaving?"

She straightens the salt and pepper shakers on the counter. "Leaving?"

"Yeah, as in first class back to Manhattan."

"Bella . . ."

Great. Here we go.

"This isn't how we deal with things—just running away the first chance we get. I packed you a bag, and you and I are spending the night at Dolly's."

"Who?" I follow the direction of Mom's pointing finger, where a woman who could be Pamela Anderson's older sister stands holding seven plates and one tea pitcher. "We don't even know her, Mom."

"I know her."

"I realize you're into quick relationships, but you've only worked with her one day."

"She's offered us a place to stay for the night. I need some time to clear my head."

"What's there to think about? Jake lied to you. I warned you from the beginning that he could be hiding something, that there could be terrible things in his closet." Granted, I didn't think there would be a collection of spandex Onesies in this closet.

Mom takes off her apron and folds it in her lap. "It's complicated. I need time. Jake and I still need to talk—but when we're both calm and levelheaded." She taps my nose and smiles. "Stay here. I have to go wash a few dishes, then I'll clock out."

I twirl myself on the stool a couple of times. Then a couple more.

"You're gonna fly off of there."

I stop. And my world continues to spin. When I'm no longer seeing three of everything, my eyes zone in on Dolly. She leans over the counter and slides a piece of chocolate pie my way.

"You must be Bella. I hear we're going to have ourselves a slumber party tonight."

I take her outstretched fork. "That's what I was just informed."

She throws her platinum blonde head back and laughs. "You *are* an uppity thing."

I gasp, my mouth open and full of pie. "Am not!" *Why does everyone think that?*

"Your mama needs a friend, and that's what she got today. I'm not going to go through your purses and steal the family jewels when you're asleep."

"I didn't think anything of the sort."

And though she doesn't make a sound, her face says she's laughing at me again.

"Kid, not everyone is out to get you in this world."

I smile politely. "Thanks for the pie."

Fifteen minutes later, Mom walks me to my car. "Bella, Dolly's been a waitress all her life. While I'm grateful she's opened up her home to me, I'm sure her house is of modest proportions. If you so much as snarl your nose one time—"

"Mom!" Seriously, am I really *that* much of a brat? "I know how to behave." But would it have been so bad to go to a hotel? Not to mention Mom left my cat back with the Finleys. Alone. Budge will probably give her to the next person who steps on the porch.

"Okay, y'all, let's go!" Dolly pats her big eighties hair as she ducks into her Jeep. "Follow me."

"Your best behavior, Bella." Mom swats my tush then lets herself into Jake's Tahoe.

We caravan through town, weaving through streets, finally winding up on a dirt road. Why are these people so stingy with the asphalt around here? It's not 1880!

Six miles of dust later, we climb a hill. On my left the shoulder gives way to trees. And beyond that a lake. There's a lake in this town and nobody told me? It sparkles bright blue with what's left of the sunlight. In the distance two boats cross paths.

The hill forks, and we veer right.

A sprawling two-story cabin waits for us at the end of the drive.

A tall gate swings open and Dolly's Jeep leads us in.

I shut off the car, grab my backpack, and get out. Tall trees stand guard over a house that could be the centerfold in *Southern Living*. A kidney-shaped pool is tucked into the side yard, surrounded by tall topiaries and shrubs. Flowers cascade out of pots every few paces, and wild blooms line the path to the front door.

They sure pay their waitresses well here in Truman.

After Dolly shows Mom and me to our separate rooms, I force my gawking self to return to the kitchen, where our hostess stands at the island alone, dicing vegetables.

"I hope you like stir-fry."

"Sounds good." Anything would be good actually. It's been a long time since lunch. I run my hand along her granite countertop, checking out some of the pictures she has there on display. Two identical blonde girls look back at me from a black-and-white photo. From their retro garb, I can tell it's not a recent shot. "Are these your girls?"

The knife slices one final time. "The one on the right is Mary Grace." Dolly barely glances up from her cutting board. "She was my quiet one. The one on the left is Cristy. To her, talking was like air—she couldn't get enough of it."

My unspoken question hangs in the air.

"Car wreck. Twenty years ago."

The faint hum of the air conditioner mixes with the call of some distant birds. "I'm sorry."

For lack of anything better to do with the heavy silence, I continue looking at her arrangement of pictures. When my eyes land on the next one, I can't help but grab it, finding a younger version of a familiar face. "You know him?"

She grabs another carrot and studies the image. "Mickey Patrick." *Slice. Slice.* "We were married once."

"How long have you been divorced?"

"Nineteen years, six months, and eight days." She shrugs a shoulder. "But who's counting?"

"I saw him in the gym. Jake said he's working with him."

"So he is."

"Did you tell my mom about the connection? That your ex-husband is training her soon-to-be ex-husband to become a professional wrestler?"

"It's not my place." She points to a cabinet over my head. "Grab some plates. And it's not *your* place to decide whether she stays or goes."

I sniff. "It kind of affects me."

Dolly turns the chicken over, then adds the vegetables. She says nothing more as I watch her work magic on the skillet until the smell all but calls my name. "Fill your plate, Bella, then let's go eat down by the pool."

"Um . . . shouldn't we wait for Mom?"

The doorbell rings, a great chiming number that reverberates through the rafters. Dolly steps out into the living room and calls toward the stairs. "Jillian, you have company!"

The doorbell rings again as Dolly fills her plate and retrieves two forks.

"Aren't you going to get that?"

She pulls open the back door and props it open with a rounded hip. "It's not my place."

"You called Jake, didn't you?"

She winks and steps out into the sun. "Bella, sometimes staying in one's place is just really boring."

Two hours later, I'm drinking Dolly's powerful sweet tea, swirling my toes in the pool, and watching my mother and her husband come out the front door. Hand in hand. Jake leans down and stops her with a kiss.

I don't know what happened in there. I don't know what got settled.

But one thing's for certain—the honeymoon's back on.

~~~~~~~~~~~~~~~

"So you see, Jake just loved me so much that he was afraid of doing anything to push me away."

My eyes burn with exhaustion as I sit on the horrendously vintage couch along with Robbie, who is garbed in a Spiderman costume and petting Moxie. Budge, fresh from his shift at the Wiener Palace, stares out the window and sneezes at perfectly timed intervals. I can't take my eyes off his silky sheikh pants. They're puffier than an eighties prom dress.

"We want you kids to know that we are absolutely committed

to each other and to this family. It's just that when you find some-one like Jillian, you wonder . . . what does she see in me?"

I've been asking myself that on a daily basis.

"But not trusting her with that part of my life was dishonest, and it was wrong of me to keep something so important from Jillian and Bella."

Mom smiles at her husband and wraps her arm around his Goliath waist.

Great. Now Jake is officially out of the spandex closet, and where did that get me? Nowhere. They can't take their eyes off each other. It's disgusting, is what it is.

"*Achoo!*"

"Bella, take your cat to your bedroom. You know the rules." Mom pulls Moxie off Robbie's lap and hands her to me. "And Logan mentioned that Mr. and Mrs. Peterson stopped by this morning to see the cat."

I shoot death-rays at my stepbrother, called Logan only by my mother. "Um . . . yeah, I didn't like them. You can't just give my cat away to anyone." Maybe we should've asked them if they'd have taken Budge instead. "They said they had a little kid. Moxie doesn't like little kids."

As if on cue, she jumps out of my arms and back into Robbie's lap, rubbing her face against his hand.

"Moxie wouldn't have liked *their* kid." My mother just stares at me. "Seriously—they were all wrong. The woman had on mom-jeans and Keds. And the dad . . . Don't even get me started on his tie-and-shirt combo."

"*Achoo!*"

I'm seriously about to let loose on Budge.

Mom sighs. "It's not like Logan is doing it on purpose. You know we have to do this."

"No, we *don't* have to do this." With another evil eye to my stepbrother, I grab Moxie and retreat to my room.

After a quick e-mail to Mia, I walk to my window and struggle until it lifts. Breathing in the fresh air, I smell the promise of rain. Wish it could wash away all my troubles here.

Stepping across the roof, I take a seat on my favorite branch and let myself lean into its strength. With the sticky air around me and a giant half-moon above, I flip through the pages of my Bible, going straight to the topical index.

And for some reason "hideous stepbrother" is nowhere to be found.

chapter twenty-two

J don't know about this, Lindy. I'm so not in the mood for it." She
totally knows I have woes that are straight from a soap opera.

"Come on. You'll have fun. Seriously. And maybe some bonding
time with God is exactly what you need."

I halt outside the school library door and watch other Truman
students file into the Wednesday FCA meeting. They talk, they
laugh, they high-five and hug. They know each other.

And I only know three people on this campus. And one of them
is Budge the cat-hater and doesn't even count. I miss walking the
halls of my school and knowing everyone. I miss Mia and my gang
of girls. I miss seeing Hunter anytime I wanted. And God and I
haven't been so close lately either. It's like when I moved, I left Him
behind too.

"Okay." I pull open the wooden door. "Let's do this."

Lindy leads me toward Matt, who's surrounded by a group of
friends. They laugh over some shared joke.

"Hey, guys. I want to introduce you to my new *friend*." Lindy's
voice issues a challenge, and I feel my cheeks tingle with pink.
"This is Bella Kirkwood."

A tall African-American girl pins me with her dark eyes. "Former author of *Ask Miss Hilliard*? That was some interesting reading."

Jesus may wipe the sin slate clean, but these people sure don't.

"I'm Anna," the girl continues, her face still impassive. "And I bet you're really uncomfortable right now."

Why lie? "Praying for a distraction so I can slip out the door."

And then she laughs, revealing a mouthful of pink-banded braces. "It takes some guts to be here, Bella." She slaps me on the back. "You're in the right place. If you don't find yourself treated right, you let me know. I'll take care of them."

Like an idiot, I smile wordlessly at this Amazon of a girl. She must be close to six feet. "You must be one of Lindy's friends from the basketball team."

She tosses her wavy hair and laughs. "I couldn't hit a basket if it was the size of a pool. I'm the captain of the cheerleading squad."

If we were keeping points based on my ability to impress the good people of Truman, I would be at a negative five hundred.

Lindy jabs Anna with her elbow, her voice hushed. "There's Kelsey." In a blaze of whispers, the group around me watches a blonde girl across the room. She sits in a chair, staring in a zombie-like fashion as her friends chatter on. This Kelsey seriously needs a cheeseburger. She makes Keira Knightley look like a sumo wrestler.

Lindy quietly fills me in. "Kelsey Anderson hasn't been back to school since the end of last year. Her boyfriend, Zach Epps, was a star football player, had a full ride to OU . . . Then he wrapped his car around a tree. He's been on life-support ever since."

"Kelsey fell apart," Matt adds. "They say she goes and sees him at the nursing home in town every day." He shakes his brown head. "It was a really bad year for the team."

"Must've been hard for all the players." I twirl all this information around in my head.

Matt shakes his head. "Zach wasn't our only loss. Last October we also had a teammate commit suicide."

Anna looks over our heads toward Kelsey. "It's like the Tigers are cursed."

"Okay, guys. I'm glad to see everyone." My English teacher, Mrs. Palmer, stands at the front of the room as we all quiet down.

"She's our advisor," Lindy whispers in my ear as we take a seat on the carpeted floor beneath a display of Manga novels.

"Today we have Grant Dawson from Truman Bible Church."

Matt leans in. "He's our youth pastor."

Oh yes. At the Church of the Holy Cafeteria.

Grant takes Mrs. Palmer's place in the center. "Good morning, Truman Tigers!" The crowd cheers in reply, Anna being the loudest. "You know, it's not even close to Christmas, but today I want to talk about Mary—the mother of Jesus. She led such a cool life, she's worth talking about anytime of the year." He opens up his Bible and reads a few passages.

Beside me Lindy picks at her fingernail polish. I slap at her hand. "Stop that," I whisper. "You'll ruin your manicure."

"It's driving me nuts. And so is this t-shirt. It's too tight."

"It's perfect. Shows off all your curves, and it screams 'style.'"

"It screams, 'My chest is trapped and can't get out.'"

I roll my eyes and tune back in to the pastor.

"Did you know Mary was just a teenager when she had Jesus? Can you imagine being handpicked to be the mother of God at your age?" Pastor Grant asks the room.

I can't even remember to floss at my age.

"But see, guys, God uses teenagers—does it all the time. After an angel told Mary about her new future, what did she do?"

Hyperventilate?

He pauses and scans the crowd. "She rejoiced. She got excited. And then she not only obeyed God, but she went and praised God to others. Mary *knew* God was leading her on a totally different path. He was really taking her out of her comfort zone."

I can totally relate. Mary got a manger, and I got Truman.

"But she knew God's plans for her were huge and that it was totally possible the Lord wanted to use her." Pastor Grant runs his fingers through his spiky, highlighted hair. His large eyes are intense, like he's trying to send us a message with mind power alone. "What about you? Has God asked *you* to step out of your comfort zone? To be somewhere you don't want to be for a bigger purpose?"

Does a Dumpster count?

"As you go about this semester, I want you to be praying about God's purpose for you. Guys and girls alike—He might be calling you to a Mary moment. The question is . . . will you be like her—and tell Him yes?" Pastor Grant closes his NIV. "Let's pray."

As I lower my head, I catch a glimpse of familiar black hair a few rows over.

Luke Sullivan.

He's here? Like, he's a Christian? Surely not. I would've sworn he was a minion of Beelzebub. Anybody who makes a girl climb into trash bags cannot be walking in a path of righteousness—can I get an amen? Maybe he's just here for the paper.

I ask him during second hour.

His eyes darken, "What do you mean what was I doing there?"

I spin a pencil in my hand. "Well, you're not an athlete, and I have my doubts that you're a believer."

"That's funny"—he lifts a dark brow—"I would've said the same about you."

Oh, now I'm just offended. "Of course I'm a Christian." How rude.

He shrugs. "Couldn't tell."

I make a strangled noise as my mouth drops. "Right back at you, *Chief.*"

"And for your information, Miss Kirkwood, I *am* an athlete."

"Sudoku is not a contact sport."

He huffs and walks away, his azure eyes piercing. *Oh, he'll have me investigating toilets for that one.*

At lunch I can't seem to quit watching Kelsey Anderson. I know I shouldn't. From the look on her face, she's obviously struggling just to be at school, so I'm sure a cafeteria of people staring at her doesn't help.

"Here are your tickets for the party tomorrow night." Matt passes out a purple piece of paper to me and Lindy.

"We have to have tickets?" Lindy fidgets with the waistband of her skirt until she catches my frown.

"It's a private party. Very exclusive. This is the first year I've gotten an invite. And you can't tell anyone you're going." Matt stuffs his own ticket in his pocket. "We're to meet at the old graveyard on Knotts Hill. From there we're picked up."

"Sounds kind of creepy to me."

"It's going to be fun, Lindy. We'll just go for a little bit, see what it's about, then come home. No worries." But even I'm wondering about meeting in a graveyard. Ick.

"Let's ride together. I'll pick you girls up. Seven?"

The bell rings for fifth hour. I grab my backpack. "Why don't you pick me up last." I send Lindy a secret smile. "I'll need a little extra time to get ready."

I wave a final good-bye, turn around to find a trash can, and find myself nose to chest with Luke.

"You are always in the most inconvenient places," I say to his Abercrombie polo.

"Have a little date tomorrow evening?"

"No." How long has he been standing there?

Then he dismisses the topic like it's already left his oversized brain. "One of our reporters is sick and is going to miss her deadline."

He honestly didn't know I was a Christian. How sad is that? I mean, I don't care what this guy thinks or anything, but I at least don't want to be discounted as a potential believer. I mean, what is it about me that says, "*Soooo* not a Christian"?

"So I'll have it later, right?" Luke pats my shoulder and snaps me back to the present conversation. "Thanks for being a team player."

"Wait—what?"

"Your article on recycling. I want it in my in-box by Thursday at 8:00 p.m."

"I—I can't."

He parks his khaki-covered hip on a table as other students file past us. "Can't or won't?"

"Cant. I'll work on it tonight, but I'm going to need at least the weekend. I'm busy Thursday."

"Busy meeting in the graveyard? Are you really so hard up for entertainment here that you're going to go traipsing over people's final resting places?"

"Yes." *Duh.* "And you were eavesdropping."

"I was merely waiting to get your attention and didn't want to interrupt. We have to have the story, Bella."

"You can't just give me a day's notice."

He steps closer, and I instantly compare his slight stubble to Hunter's always-smooth face. "This is a real working paper we run here. And it's not just a class, but a job. So like a real paper, some-times we have to pitch in at the last minute to make sure it gets done. If you can't handle that—"

"There's a class called Tire Changing 101 with my name on it?" I poke his chest. Oddly enough, there's muscle there. "Save your threats, Luke. I have gone above and beyond to be a *team player.*" And I totally pull out the quotey fingers here. In his face. "I've done everything—*everything*—you've asked. I've sat in moldy food. I ruined a pair of suede flats. I sunburned my face while digging around in decomposing refuse." My voice rises, though we're inches apart. My breath comes in ragged heaves, and I'm so focused on this one boy that the rest of the cafeteria has faded away. "I will stay up late Friday night and try to fin-ish the piece, and that can either be good enough *or* you can send me to whatever class you want. In fact, I'd be glad to be rid of you."

"Would you, now?" His voice is as quiet as mine is loud.

His eyes hold mine for seconds. Minutes.

But I finally step away. "I have to go text my *boyfriend* before class starts."

"Don't you think I hate the fact that our deadline depends on *you*, Bella?" His tone is like a low saxophone and tingles my skin. There's no spite in his words, but I feel their prick all the same. "But irony of all ironies, you *are* our salvation here."

"You do whatever you have to do, Chief. But I'm done with threats and I'm done giving up all I've got for somebody else's sake." My mom, my dad, now this stupid paper.

And I adjust my backpack and push past him. I rush to the bathroom and hole myself in a stall, punching in a text to Hunter.

Why didn't U return my call last nite? Need 2 talk.

I shove the phone back into the pocket of my jeans, open the door, and give myself a final check in the mirror. My face is flushed like I've run the Boston Marathon.

Another stall door opens as I'm blotting my cheeks with powder.

"I think you dropped this."

I lower my compact and watch the person in the mirror.

Kelsey Anderson.

She holds up a purple ticket. "You're going to need it for the Thursday party, right?"

I take it from her pale hands. "Yeah, you must be going too?" I try to coax her with a smile.

She shakes her head, her face as solemn as death. "No."

"Then how did you know about the ticket?"

"My boyfriend had one." Empty eyes meet mine. "The night he hit the tree."

chapter twenty-three

~~~~~~~~~~~~~~~~~~~~~~~~~~~~~~

J'm sorry, the cat's not available."

This is the tenth person I've talked to this week and it's only Thursday evening.

"What do you mean not available?"

"I'm going to be honest with you, sir." I clench the phone to my ear. "You don't want the cat. It has a massive shedding problem."

"That's okay. I have other cats. I'm used to it."

"Oh, she can't stand other cats. Last time Moxie was around another cat . . . she ate it." Okay, she bit it. But one could interpret it as a sign of borderline cannibalism.

"Well, I don't know about that. Muffy and Mr. Whisker Britches are gentle souls. They won't take kindly to someone coming in and taking over the herd."

"And take over Moxie will, sir. With her teeth, if you know what I mean. Your Muffy and Mr. Whiskery Bottoms—"

"Whisker Britches—"

"—will not fare well at all. If you value their lives, I would find yourself a different cat, I'm afraid."

"Bella?"

I jump, dropping the phone. Jake.

Hanging up, I square my shoulders and compose my most innocent expression. "Yes?"

"Was that someone calling about the cat?"

"Who, that?" I point to the phone. "Um . . . yes, but they called to say they're no longer interested."

"We've had a lot of people back out on taking Moxie this week."

"Indeed we have." This guy still makes me uncomfortable. I mean he pounds people into the ground for sport. And I want to be around him because . . . ?

He pours a glass of orange juice then hands it to me. "Take a seat."

"Oh, thanks, but I really have to go. Don't want to be late for the get-together tonight."

"Do you want to tell your mom about intercepting the phone calls for Moxie, or should I?"

I toss back the juice and pull out a chair.

"Bella, I'm really sorry the cat has to go. But I know you don't want Budge sick."

"Budge isn't sick. He's totally faking it."

Jake's look is patronizing at best. "He wouldn't do that." If he pats me on the head and calls me a silly little girl, I am so out of here.

"I'm telling you, I seriously doubt your son is allergic to my cat. He just hates me, that's all."

"Budge doesn't hate you." Jake steeples his fingers and inhales deeply. "This has been a tough transition for him too. But nobody wants to see you hurt over your cat. I am sorry. I know she means a lot to you."

Tears cloud my vision. "She's totally my BFF." Yes, that's right, Bella Kirkwood is on the verge of crying here. I don't think I've teared up since I was in diapers. No, I *will* hold it together. "I would do anything to keep her. Anything."

"It's just not going to be possible." His hand settles over mine. Actually, it covers it like a giant's manacle. "I'm sorry. I want you to be happy here, and I know you're not. I've really been praying about this, and—"

"Then pray for me to keep Moxie." I jerk my hand away and explode from the seat. "She's all I have left." And I storm out the kitchen and up to my room, wiping my eyes, my fingers black with melted mascara.

At six forty-five, I check my reflection in the mirror, satisfied with my wavy hair, Fred Segal sundress, and trendy retro sandals. I search under the bed for Moxie to tell her good-bye, but she's not there. Grabbing my purse, I head to the living room to wait for Matt and Lindy.

Halfway down the stairs, I stop.

"So I would make a great home for her. I love animals. The cat I just lost was with me almost twenty years."

I all but fall the rest of the way down. "What's going on here?"

A white-haired woman sits on the couch—Moxie in her queen-sized arms.

Mom stands up. "Bella, this is Marjorie Bisby. She's here to take Moxie."

My throat burns. Words slam-dance on my tongue, desperate for release. "No" is all I can manage.

My mother's arm slips around me. "We've found the best possible home, honey."

"But she's mine." There goes the mascara. Again. "You can't take her away from me. You've taken *everything* else away from me."

Marjorie Bisby's mouth forms an O. She scoots from the middle of the couch to the end—away from me.

"I need her!" I run a hand across my dripping nose. "Does anybody ever stop and care what I need anymore? Nobody cares that I left my home. My boyfriend. My friends. My dad."

"Bella, I do care." Mom tries to hug me to her, but I throw off her embrace. "I love you, but we have the whole family to consider now. I tried to include you in picking where Moxie would go, but you wouldn't have it. It simply came to this." Mom glances at our guest. "And I would never turn her over to someone I thought wouldn't take the best care of her." She stares at the floor. "I'm sorry, but this is it. Moxie will go home with Ms. Bisby. Say good-bye to her, sweetie."

If looks could wound, I wouldn't be the only one moaning in agony here.

With trembling hands, I reach for my cat. I hold her close and listen to her rhythmic purr one more time. Through it all, she's been my constant. Not my boyfriend, not my parents, but a stinkin' cat.

I whisper words to her—mumblings of good-bye, fragments of apologies.

"It's time to give her up." Mom holds out her arms. "Let me have her."

My throat tightens and burns. "You can't change her name. She knows it."

"I won't, dear," the old woman says, her own eyes pooling.

"And she runs into walls. She'll need extra pets when that happens."

"I'll do it."

"And she has a toy mouse that she likes. She likes you to throw it, but"—I sniff loudly—"she won't bring it back to you. And she falls off the bed on a regular basis, so maybe pad the floor with pillows. She's hit her head a lot."

"I promise to take good care of her." The woman stands up from the couch. "I tend to run into walls myself."

That does not comfort me.

"Let her go, Bella." Mom pulls the cat out of my arms just as a car pulls into the drive. Matt and Lindy. I fully release Moxie. Look at her one last time.

Then run out the door.

chapter twenty-four

~~~~~~

S not and parties do *not* go together.

I blow my nose one last time as Matt shifts his truck into park.

"Are you sure you're okay?" Lindy asks for the fifth time.

I just nod my head. Every time I open my mouth, pitiful squeaking sounds are all I can manage.

"We don't have to go tonight." Matt watches the dirt road as headlights approach.

"No." I daub at my eyes. "Let's do this." And then I'll go back home and look for my beating heart somewhere in the yard, where I'm sure I dropped it.

I jump at the knock on Matt's window. He rolls it down.

"Tickets, please." A football player I recognize from the field house sticks his hand into the truck and takes our purple passes. "We need you to get out of the vehicle, and my boy Adam here is going to blindfold you."

Um, excuse me? I know my makeup looks pretty bad right now, but no need to cover up my face.

"We'll help you to our cars then drive you to the secret party location."

Lindy leans over Matt. "I'm not wearing a blindfold, Dante."

"Then this meeting is over. That's the rules." He slaps the hood. "Have a nice night."

"No! Wait! We'll do it." I unbuckle my seat belt and open the door. "Come on, Lindy. Be brave."

She scoots across the seat. "I don't know about this, Bella. We'll be stuck out there with no car, no way home until they bring us back."

"You both know all these guys. I'm sure we can get a ride if we need one. Let's just go and have some fun." I think I deserve fun right now. And a cat.

"Fine," Lindy huffs, then swings her pointing finger between me and Matt. "But if there's any funny business, we are out of there. We walk if we have to. No kegs, no drugs, no streaking."

"No streaking? You could've mentioned that *before* I took the time to shave my legs." I pull her toward Dante and Adam. "Kidding. I'm kidding."

I feel a moment's panic as a black handkerchief falls over my eyes and is tied behind my head.

Dante gently guides me toward a car. "The two girls will ride with me. And Matt will ride with Adam."

Second frisson of panic. *We're being separated?*

When the football player opens his car door, I hear the voices of other girls but don't really recognize them. But I breathe easier that they're giggling and apparently not concerned with their safety. Lindy goes in first. Then me.

Fifteen minutes later my stomach is in my throat as we've weaved through winding roads and whiplash curves. The girl on the other side of Lindy has made choking noises the last five minutes, and if she blows chunks on me tonight, I am going to rip off this blindfold and hurt somebody.

I hear the music before we even stop.

"Here we are, ladies. Party central."

A warm breeze hits me as the door is opened. Dante pulls me out by the hand and uncovers my eyes.

I struggle to focus before finally making out an old cabin. "Are we at the lake?"

Dante reaches for Lindy. "I can't tell you anything." He lowers his voice, his dark eyes intense on mine. "If you want to stay, you can't ask any questions."

The car carrying Matt pulls up behind us, and a minute later he joins Lindy and me in the yard.

We follow the pulsing music inside to a large but outdated living room. Outdated as in early nineties. Not as in total antique like the Finleys' taste in décor.

"Hey, Matt! Lindy!" Jared Campbell pushes his way through to us, holding a cup in one hand and a bag of chips in the other. His face dims when he spots me. "Oh . . . hi."

I smile anyway.

He returns his attention to Lindy and Matt. "Grab some food. There're some Cokes and stuff in the kitchen in a cooler. Some harder stuff on the back porch."

"We'll just be sticking with the easy stuff tonight."

Jared pounds his knuckles to Matt's. "I know, dude. Just thought I'd offer."

After grazing in the kitchen for a while, the three of us walk single file back into the living room. The music rattles the windows and shakes the rustic wood paneling.

"You girls want to dance?"

Lindy pales, but I nod. "Yeah. Lead the way."

As Matt clears us a path through our fellow students, I grab Lindy. "This is your chance to show him you can dance."

"I can't dance!"

"Yes, you can. Just remember what Colton taught you in New York." Not that one lesson is enough, but it's a start. Couldn't get any worse than her old way of sliding from foot to foot and snapping her fingers. "Come on, I'll help you. Just follow my lead."

Though I receive a few rude stares from some Truman Tigers who have yet to forgive and forget, most people are too caught up in the music and dancing to care about my past transgressions.

My arms go over my head, and I let the music take over.

Lindy starts out with some basic moves, her arms stiff as broomsticks. But by the end of the second song, she's got it. Well, minus a few obnoxious head bobs.

An hour and a half later, the speakers pour out a slow song. The floor clears a little.

"Do you want to dance?" Matt asks me, nothing but friendship reflecting in those eyes.

"Um..." I can nearly taste Lindy's disappointment. "I think I'm going to get another Sprite. But, Lindy, this is your favorite song, isn't it?" I lightly push Matt toward her. "You two should totally dance." I sidestep them and make my way through the swaying masses.

Ten feet away from the kitchen door, I turn back to look at Lindy's progress.

And bump into a solid wall of boy.

"Oh! I'm so—"

Jared glares down at me.

"—sorry." I move to get out of his way, but he steps in front of me and blocks my escape.

"Wait . . . Bella. I . . . um . . . wanted to tell you that I'm sorry."

I lift a questioning brow as a couple bumps into me, totally oblivious to anything but each other and the song. He takes a step out of their way. We both smile.

Jared reaches for my hand. "Come on. We're going to get mowed down if we stand still."

And before I can say, "Let me count the ways my boyfriend Hunter is the best guy in the whole wide world," my arms wrap around his neck, his slide to my waist, and we're moving in perfect tempo.

We dance in silence for a few moments before I am compelled to speak. "So . . . whose house did you say this was?"

He frowns. "I didn't."

"Oh." *That usually works on TV.* "Then whose is it?"

He shrugs. "Doesn't matter."

"Are we still in Truman?"

"Just shut up and dance."

"Wow, if you talk all romantic like that all the time, no wonder you have Brittany falling all over you."

"What?"

He's absolutely clueless. "Um, nothing."

"Bella . . . I just wanted to tell you that I'm sorry for the way you were treated after . . . um . . ."

"The nuclear fallout from my blog going public?"

"Yeah. That. What you said about us wasn't cool, but I don't think anybody wanted you dropped to total pariah status or anything."

My eyes travel the room and land on Brittany Taylor, who looks as if she's trying to wish me away with mind power. "I'm not so sure about that." Her eyes are slits, like those of a snake about to strike.

"I know the girls can be mean. But they'll get over it in time. I'd love for you to hang out with us again."

"I . . ." What does that mean? Like a friend or as in he's interested in me? Why are boys so hard to read? "I think it's going to be awhile before Emma and Brittany are ready to talk to me. But I can use all the friends I can get." I tune out the weight of Brittany's stare. "I really appreciate your breaking away from the pack and talking to me."

He opens his mouth to say something just as a large football player appears beside him. Jared and I step apart as the intruder leans down and mumbles low.

At Jared's nod his friend retreats.

"I better go."

"Trouble?" My nosiness kicks into overdrive.

"Nothing serious. Just need to make a sweep of the grounds and make sure nobody's got a lamp shade on their head or is peeing on the petunias. But I meant what I said—or what I was trying to say. I would like to be friends."

I smile broadly. "Friends it is, Jared Campbell." I shoo him away with my hands. "Better go check for lamp shade violations."

Joy flutters in my heart at the sight of Matt and Lindy still dancing, though both look fairly uncomfortable. But we can work with uncomfortable.

Left with no one to hang out with, I decide to return to the kitchen, where I reunite with the Fritos and graze like a grass-starved cow.

Fifteen chips and another Sprite later, my mind drifts back to Moxie. *God, life is so unfair! What could possibly be the purpose of taking away my cat? Punishment? What did I do?*

"I'm onto you, you know."

I freeze mid-bite. Mid-prayer.

Brittany Taylor advances on me like a vulture.

"Hello to you, too, Brittany." There's no way she could know I'm here to sniff out a story.

"You think you can come in here and just move straight to the A-list? It doesn't work like that."

"Yeah, I guess it wouldn't when I have people like you trying to sabotage any efforts at making friends." She flinches. "I *know* it was you who leaked it to Tiger TV about my *Ask Miss Hilliard* blog."

Her pink lip curls. "So?"

"I don't care anymore. The stuff I said was wrong, and I probably needed that little slap in the face to wake me up. Besides . . . I've been at the top of the popularity chain all my life. I didn't realize I had grown bored with it." I pop another chip in my mouth. "Thanks for helping me branch out."

Clutching my can, I flounce past her, onto the back porch and into the darkening night.

Two kegs stand at attention on the deck, but surprisingly nobody is around. Which is odd. Because if there's a spot that never gets lonely at a party, it's next to the keg. Not that I drink. Because I don't. But I've been around it enough.

My mood takes another nosedive as I think of my cat *and* my boyfriend. I texted him a million times to talk to him about tonight's party. It just makes a girl feel good to have her man care where she is—and to at least give her the chance to assure him she only has eyes for him no matter how many tall, buff guys she'll be mingling with. But Hunter never called me, and not only did I not get the privilege of answering twenty questions about the party, all I did get was a text that said "okay." Okay? I tell him I'm going to an event at which there will be alcohol, dancing, and most of the Truman football team, and all he has to say is okay? I think part of me wanted him to ask me not to go. Or at least a "Call me when you get back so you can tell me how you *didn't* make out with anyone." I've already lost Moxie. Am I losing Hunter too? What next, the apocalypse?

My eyes cloud over with tears for the millionth time tonight. I'm like a leaky faucet, and I can't seem to turn it off. Inhaling deeply, I swipe at my face.

Then freeze.

Three shadowed figures at the edge of the property run into the surrounding woods.

Two more follow.

They move silently, stealthily.

Where did they come from?

And where are they going?

Setting my can on the wooden railing, I watch them for another few seconds then descend the steps of the deck and walk toward the woods, following the disappearing shadows.

chapter twenty-five

My heart pounding and my ears peeled like a dog on point, I slow down my steps, careful not to make a sound that the disappearing partygoers can hear. I follow the path of their voices, hanging far behind. We walk deep into the trees, and every ten paces I can't help but sneak a look behind me. I'm officially weirded out.

Just as I'm about to give up because of my really poor shoe choice, they stop.

I'm still too far away to make out the words of their conversation, so I inch forward and move off to their left, seeking cover behind a pair of trees. The moonlight shines down upon them, but I cannot distinguish their faces.

"What's this about, guys?"

Matt! That's Matt Sparks.

"Do you trust us?"

"Dante, just say what you have to say." Matt's voice is weary, cautious.

"You were invited here tonight to become one of us."

"If you're asking me if I think we should all get matching tattoos, the answer is no."

Somebody laughs. "Matt, over ten years ago, a group of football players met after practice. They decided they were sick of losing."

"And?"

"And those players made a pact that they would do whatever it took to see the Tigers become the strongest team in the state. They became more than teammates—they became brothers. And the tighter the team became, the better they played. They were unstoppable."

"What does this have to do with me?"

Good question, Matt. Keep 'em coming.

"Aren't you sick of losing? Don't you want to see us have a winning streak again? Take the state championship?" I recognize one of the voices from the Dumpster.

"Of course I'd like to win, but I'm not following any of this."

"Let's just say that since last year we've been working on our team-building skills. The Brotherhood lives again—with us. Whatever it takes to get to those glory days—that's what we do."

"We think the stronger our bond, the stronger our team becomes. And with strength must come fearlessness. Fear draws us closer. These guys here"—a shoulder is slapped—"these guys are my brothers. I'd die for them. I'd step through fire for them. That's what a real team is."

"What is it you want from me, Dante?"

Get me another name, Matt.

"First of all, what we tell you tonight is private. You discuss it with no one. Do you promise?"

"I don't know. I guess."

One of the football players does not appreciate Matt's casual attitude. "Tonight we are introducing you to the Truman Brotherhood, man. It's all about risking everything—to win. It's about a dare we hope you can't refuse. Because your skills could take us to state this year. Your skills, combined with ours, could get us all a full ride to any college in the state. But we need our strongest players united on this."

"And the coaches are behind this?"

"Oh, Coach knows all about the Brotherhood—and he definitely wants the legacy to continue. The legacy of winning. But we need to know we have your full loyalty, Sparks."

"I don't have to drink any goat's blood or dance naked in the moonlight here, right?"

"This is serious," snaps Dante. "Are you ready to be a warrior?"

"Yeah."

"Care to prove that?"

"How?" Matt asks.

Above me a bird coos in the night. I shiver, even though the air is sticky hot.

"Do you like any extreme sports?"

"Yeah, I like to dirt bike and skateboard. So?"

"Then you're gonna like our idea of an initiation. Are you with us?"

Coo! Coo!

My head jerks up as a bird barrels straight down, its wings mere feet from my face.

I cover my head, open my mouth, and prepare to squeal—

Until a hand closes over my lips.

"What was that?" one of the guys yells.

"Don't move a muscle, Kirkwood," a voice hisses near my ear.

"See if somebody's over there." Someone stomps our way.

I tremble as Luke Sullivan plasters his body to mine. His breath waves over my neck, and his hand still covers my mouth.

Then he cups his free hand and calls into it, making the most perfect shrill cry of a wild bird. He does it again. I hear the footsteps stop.

And as if inspired by God, the bird returns and makes two swoops around the tree, its distressed sounds almost matching Luke's.

"It was just a bird," Matt says.

"We better get back. We've been gone too long. Sparks, you and Dante will go to the house first. The rest of us will follow in a minute."

"We have more to discuss, but we'll be contacting you." My ears perk at a new voice. This one familiar, but too low to really distinguish. "Remember, you know nothing. If any of this leaks, there are consequences. You support the team, or . . . we make sure you get *off* the team."

Matt's response is muffled by shoes crunching on the ground as he and Dante leave, pointing their flashlights on the path.

Satisfied that there's enough noise to move, I turn in Luke's arms and find we're nose to nose. He shakes his head and places his finger on my lips.

Yeah, like I was going to talk at a time like this.

Well, okay, I was. But I was going to be really quiet about it.

I can't make out much of his face, but I can feel his heart beating as spastically as mine.

Finally the rest of the team leaves, but not before shining flashlights near our area of the woods. Luke pulls my head to his chest and covers me with his arms.

The players walk on, their beams hitting trees and bouncing off of Luke's dark clothes.

"You're in pink, for crying out loud," he barks when we're safely alone. "You come out here to spy and you weren't even smart enough to dress inconspicuously."

I rear my head back. "Oh yeah, because wearing camo to the party *wouldn't* have been conspicuous?"

"What were you thinking coming out here by yourself? Do you have any idea what could happen to you?"

"A bird could attack me? My editor could body-slam me into a tree?"

"I saved you. I saved your ungrateful neck."

"I was doing just fine out here on my own. I don't need you or your help."

"Should I review the last five minutes for you? Because I seem to remember saving your completely blown cover."

"You're a pompous, arrogant jerk."

"You're a spoiled, ungrateful prima donna."

"I can't stand you."

"I don't care."

My ragged breathing mingles with his. I feel his biceps bunch under the hands that I've placed on his arms at some point. "Luke?" I whisper.

His head lowers until his mouth rests near my ear. "Yes?"

"Let go of me."

He pushes me away like I'm strapped down with explosives and begins to pace. "You really could've been hurt out here. Those guys are up to something."

"You think?" I lean into the tree and take some deep yoga breaths. "I've been *trying* to tell you that. I *told* you I heard some sort of conspiracy that day at the Dumpster."

"Yeah, but you also inhaled a lot of old burritos that afternoon too."

"Something's up, Luke. Something with the, uh, starting lineup. And now Matt Sparks is getting involved."

"I know. I heard." He clicks on a small flashlight, and I can see the contours of his face.

"How long were you standing there?"

I make out a faint smirk. "The entire time. I followed you from the house. Anybody could've seen you leave, by the way. Remind me to lecture you about discretion later."

"I'm writing myself a note right now." I roll my eyes in the dark. "I didn't know you got an invitation to the party."

"I didn't. I overhead you talking to your friends about it."

"And you *followed* me? Could you get any more pervy?"

The ground crunches as he pivots, and he plants himself in front of me. "You deliberately went against my orders to stay out of this situation. You have a story. This situation is none of your concern."

I jab my finger in his shirt. "You came out here to get information so *you* could get this story, didn't you? Now you're a perv *and* a story stealer. I can't believe you, Luke."

He wraps his hand around my finger. "Keep your voice down," he hisses. "That is not true and you know it. I just crashed the party to see if there *could* be anything to your hunch. I figured I'd be here less then ten minutes—just long enough to ascertain that there was nothing to your idea."

Ascertain? I need a dork dictionary just to keep up with this conversation.

"And just as I was about to leave, I saw you walking into the woods—by yourself." Luke looks at his fist closed over my hand and drops it. "You can't just go walking into a situation—especially at night. In the dark. Alone. Like an idiot."

"Idiot?" I hiss. "This *idiot* has found proof that there's something brewing with the athletes. This *idiot* tried to tell you from the beginning that I had overheard something significant. Maybe I wouldn't have *had* to go off by myself had you believed me in the first place." The bird coos again overhead. "Nice bird distraction, by the way. Somebody's obviously spent a lot of time researching mating calls."

Despite my hot tone, he smiles. "I watch a lot of *Animal Planet*. Look, Bella . . . I'm sorry."

"Do you acknowledge that there's a story here?"

He sighs. "Yes."

"And I can put aside the stupid trash article and work on it?"

"No." He holds up his hands to fend off my verbal attack. "The article is still due first thing. We don't drop one assignment just to work on another. You wrap up your current deadline, and we'll discuss the football situation."

Good enough.

"Bella, this could be huge."

I grin like I've hit the keg a few times myself. "I know."

"What I mean is, you're not experienced. I can't let you work this story. We have a hierarchy at the paper."

"What? No!" I punch his arm. "I'm already neck-deep in it. I let Dante blindfold me and stuff me in a car to be here. I *deserve* this story, Luke."

He runs a hand through his wavy hair. "On one condition."

"I won't share my story with the rest of your staff, Chief."

"Okay. You won't share it with them." He nods then walks away. "You'll share it with me."

chapter twenty-six

"What time did you get in last night?"

As I pour Cheerios into a bowl, I catch the warning in my mom's voice, like she's asking a question she already knows the answer to. "I don't know . . . around midnight."

"You know your curfew is eleven on school nights."

I pull out a chair and sit down. "Sorry. I guess I was so distraught over you giving away my cat that I lost track of time."

Mom puts down her book, *Parenthood Is a Battleground*. "You're grounded."

"What? I said I was sorry."

"That's not good enough, Bella. We have boundaries here—rules."

"Since when do you care about my curfew?" The words fly off my tongue like rocks from a slingshot.

Mom pins on her Sugar's nametag. "I know I've been an absent parent."

Really? And which book did you read that in?

"And I know that I relied on the nanny to do what I should've done myself. And I realize that I spent too much time away from home, taking care of things that might've been important, but weren't as important as my family."

I study my lap and wonder if we could perhaps channel her guilt into the return of my cat.

"But, Bella, if I say be home at eleven, then that's what I mean. I *am* your parent and you will obey me. Now the book I read last week said to start out with small doses of punishment . . ." Mom thinks on this. "So I believe you can forget about going to the game tonight."

"I have to be there for school—an assignment for the paper. I'm not going for the joy of stale popcorn."

She considers this. "Fine. Then cancel whatever you have going on Saturday night. You can babysit Robbie while Jake and I are at a wrestling match in Tulsa."

I swallow a bite of cereal and the ten jokes that immediately pop into my head. I cannot believe she is actually supporting this guy's wrestling dream. How can she not be suspicious of any grown man wanting to wear tights?

My phone rings on my way to school. Hunter.

"Hey." My tone could freeze an Oklahoman pond.

"How's my girl?"

I laugh bitterly. "Your *girl* hasn't heard from you in days."

"I'm sorry. I've been busy."

"With who?"

"Aw, now that's not fair. You know I only have eyes for you."

"Do I?" I swerve past the neighbor's old cow, who seems to spend most of her time in the middle of the dirt road. "You don't return my calls. You ignore my texts. Remember when we said that we'd go above and beyond to make this work? Remember when you said distance wouldn't matter?"

"Hey, back off. I said I had things to do. Do you even care?"

"Of course I—"

"Because every time you *do* call, it's all about you, you, you. *Your* world is ending, *your* cat got taken away. *Your* stepdad's a wrestler. I have problems too. But do you even think to ask me about them?"

"Move it!" I blast my horn. "Stupid pile of feathers."

"Excuse me?"

"No, not you. There's a chicken in the road. Hunter, I'm sorry. I know you have a lot going on. And I apologize if I've been self-absorbed. Why don't you tell me what's been going on with you?"

"You don't really want to listen."

"Yes, I do." Was he always this difficult to have a conversation with?

"Well . . . there is this one thing that's been eating at me. Like I can't sleep and I think about it all the time. It's like I can't get out from under the dark cloud."

"I so relate. Go on."

"We're already working on the Autumn Ball with Hilliard, and they want a Victorian theme while we want to totally do the sixties. As president of the student social committee, do you realize what kind of pressure this puts me under? It affects every detail. If we go Victorian, the punch will need to be pink, but if we have a sixties theme . . ."

I halfheartedly listen to my boyfriend drone on and on about cucumber sandwiches and the recently established napkin selection committee.

"So you can see it's not just you who's under a lot of stress."

"No," I say, turning into the school parking lot. "I guess my problems barely compare to yours."

"Forget it. You're obviously not in the mood to have a conversation. I remember a time when you used to enjoy listening to me."

Do I really find this part of his life interesting? I worry about my stepbrother smothering me with a pillow in the middle of the night. He worries about whether to leave the crusts on the sandwiches or not.

"Hunter, I'm sorry. I don't want to fight. I know you're stressed."

"Bella . . . you know as activities coordinator, I have to escort a Hilliard girl to the dance. It's a tradition."

"I know." I swing open the door of the Bug and climb out, my skirt waving in the summer breeze. "I wish I could be there for it."

"I don't know who to ask. It has to be someone who will know that it means nothing. Somebody who knows that I'm seeing you."

My pulse quickens at the sight of Dante walking with Matt Sparks into the building. "What did you say? Oh yeah, um, why don't you just ask Mia? You guys will be hanging out anyway."

"Are you sure? That would work out perfectly."

"Yeah, you should call her about that. And tell her to call me. I haven't talked to her in days. Hey, Hunter, I gotta go. Call me later." I drop my phone in my purse and power-walk up the steps and through the doors.

When I'm about three people away from Dante and Matt, I take out my phone again like I have a call. I stick it to my ear and act totally engrossed in a riveting conversation. I'll just imagine Hunter's discussing a balloon and streamer dilemma.

"Dude, I just don't know," Matt says, his voice barely audible.

Dante looks around, and I avert my gaze, as if I'm oblivious to everything but the call.

"I need to know soon. People are counting on us."

"Like what people?"

"Just people, okay? There's nothing more to tell you until—"

I can't hear them. I move closer, my ears straining to—

"Hey!" Suddenly I'm pulled out of the flow and into a classroom. "Luke! What are you doing?"

He grabs my phone, presses it to his ear. "Yeah, Bella's going to have to continue her pathetically fake call later." And snaps it shut. "Could you get any more amateur?"

"Could you get any more obnoxious?" We're nose to nose.

"You could blow this whole story."

"Oh, the story that wouldn't have happened if it weren't for *amateur* me?"

"You do nothing unless it's cleared through me. You got it, Bella?"

"I know what I'm doing. You're like a rabid bulldog."

"You need to slow this down and follow my lead."

"You need to . . . jump off a cliff." I huff past him, but he catches my arm, blocking my exit. My cheek is inches from his.

I feel his chest rumble with laughter. "Is that really the best you could do?"

"I know. It was weak." I bite my lip on a smile. "I'm just not on my game today. I'll try to have some better insults by second hour."

Something besides contempt glows in his eyes. It holds me in place, and I can't seem to look away.

"Big news," he says, and I struggle to focus. "Reggie Lee got escorted out of early morning football practice—by the police."

"What?"

Luke nods. "They found drugs in his locker at the field. He's been suspended."

Pieces of conversation from that day at the Dumpster float back to me. It has to be connected.

"Bella . . . I have something else I want to tell you." He leans closer.

"Yes?" I breathe.

"I need you to . . ." He pauses, the eyes behind his tortoise frames still fused to mine.

Like there's a magnet pulling me in, I lean closer.

"I need you to be a water girl for the football team."

I blink. Spell broken. "What?"

"Keep it down." He takes a comfortable step away from me. "I thought about it last night. We have to get you on the inside with the football players. Your friend Lindy is a water girl, so have her pull some strings and see if you can't help pass out water or towels or whatever it is you might do."

"That is a dumb idea."

"It beats chasing after some guys into a dark forest."

"Have you ever seen a football player up close? They're . . ." I search my brain for a visual. "Hot and sweaty and they spit a lot."

"I thought you girls liked hot and sweaty."

"From a distance!" *Duh.*

"If you want this story, you have to be willing to do a little undercover reporting—my way."

I blow out a frustrated breath. "I'm about ready to tell you where you can stick *your way.*"

"It's my paper."

"Seriously, are you five?"

Instead of giving a snappy retort, he laughs again and guides me back into the crowded hallway. These flashes of a kinder, gentler

Luke are totally throwing me off. Maybe he really isn't a tool of Satan.

Could it be I won his respect last night?

"Talk to Lindy. I'll see you at the game." And with his hands in his pockets, he saunters down the science hall, confident I'll do his bidding.

<hr />

"You want to do *what?*" Lindy fills the water bottles at halftime. I can barely hear her over the marching band's version of "Hang On, Sloopy."

"I said I want to do this." I gesture to the stacks of towels and the coolers. "I want to be a water girl. You know, help the team. And why are you wearing a ball cap tonight? Didn't we agree in New York no more hats and no more ponytails?"

"I'm working, Bella." She heaves a tray of water bottles onto a bench and begins to fill another set.

"Looking hot is a twenty-four-hour job."

She looks up from the cooler. "Wow, that would make a great tattoo. Right on your—"

"I'm serious. You said you wanted help looking more feminine. I don't think I'll find a Tigers t-shirt, a pair of basketball shorts, and a dirty hat in my latest issue of *Teen Vogue.*"

"And look where your doll clothes have gotten me—nowhere. Do you know what he said to me at the party when we were dancing?"

"That you're the sun he wants to orbit for all his days?"

She wipes her own sweat with a towel. "He asked me when this phase of mine would be over. He said it's like hanging out with Malibu Barbie." She laughs ruefully.

"She did always have good shoes." I plod on as Lindy rolls her big eyes. "Don't give up yet. Okay, so maybe we change our strategy. If I'm here on the sidelines with you, then I can help out your cause even more."

She focuses on the remaining minutes of the scoreboard, only halfway listening to me. "How?"

"I can see Matt up close, you know. See what really makes him tick. Notice how he interacts with you in this setting."

"And what do you get out of it?"

"I . . . um . . . get to write an article for the paper. Yeah, I want to write an article on the team's season. You know, their bid for state and all." I would throw in some football jargon here, but I don't know any. I am *so* gonna have to start watching *SportsCenter* like my stepdad. "See how they score with their fumbles and do that thing with the flags."

"You have no idea what you're talking about, do you?"

"That's why I need you! You can teach me what I need to know about the game, and I'll help you down here with the water . . . and with Matt. Perfect!" I hug her close. "Thanks, Lindy!" And though I can't see her face, I know she's rolling her eyes again.

She steps back and shoves a set of towels in my arms. "Here. You can start tonight."

"What?" I gesture to my skirt and patent leather flats. "But I'm not dressed for it. How about next week?"

The football boys trot onto the field and head our way. It would be nice to have a bird's-eye view of their interaction with the coaches. I think at least one of them could be involved in this Brotherhood business. See, this is what happens when you stick a bunch of guys in too-tight pants. It cuts off the oxygen to their brains, and next thing you know they're calling themselves a brotherhood, slapping each other on the butt, and meeting secretly in the woods.

About five minutes into the third quarter, I get into the groove of running water bottles to the guys. I have to dodge lots of towels and spitting, but so far my shoes are still intact. My dignity, not so much. If any of them find it odd that I'm passing out refreshments, no one says anything. They're so focused and intent on the game, I think Jessica Simpson could be handing out Gatorade, and they wouldn't so much as turn in her direction.

The Tigers barely hold it together during the fourth quarter, and we're pushed into overtime. With seconds to go, Dante passes to number twenty-four, who promptly dives for the ball. He lands in a heap of arms and legs. But arises, mere feet from the goal, with nothing in his hands but regret.

And the Truman Tigers lose the first game of the season.

"Here's a towel. Good game. That was some fine . . . um, football stuff." I hand Dante some water. I start to spout off more positivity, but Lindy shakes her head in warning. Okay, shutting up now.

I hand out the last of my water bottles and bend down to pick up the empty ones thrown on the ground. I suppose now would not be a good time to remind the team that I am *not* their maid?

"Our team's unraveling, Matt. You saw it out there tonight. No wins, no college scholarships. Dude, if we keep that up, we won't get recruiters out here to even look at us."

I stay stooped down within earshot of Dante.

Matt pulls his helmet off. "Maybe. I don't know."

"I *do* know. The Brotherhood. That's the answer. We need you in. We need to be a team off the field in order to be a team *on* the field."

"You gotta give me more information, Dante."

"You either trust me or you don't. We're your family, Matt." Dante stops. "Do you need something?"

From my bent position, I glance up. His steely eyes are fixed on me. "Um . . . just picking up water bottles." I giggle. "Gets a little messy down here." I twirl my hair around a finger. "Sorry about the game." I offer a friendly wink, grab Matt's towel, and walk away.

A few minutes later, after I've helped Lindy pile all the equipment, I grab my notebook and plant myself in front of the first coach I find.

"Coach Dallas, can I have a word with you?" He's definitely the youngest of the coaches. If anyone is more likely to be hanging out with the players, it's him. "I'm Bella Kirkwood with the *Truman High Tribune.* I was wondering if I could ask you a few questions."

His eyes move swiftly to his players as they gather around the head coach. "I really have to go, kid."

"I'll just take a few minutes of your time." I begin my questions, not waiting for permission. "Last year the Tigers were so close to winning state. Does that make you even more intent on capturing the title this season?"

"Uh . . ." The coach struggles to focus on me as his colleague begins yelling at the team in various tones of mad and furious. "Sure, yeah. We really want to make it to state this year. We have a long history of being champs, so we'd like to recapture that."

"And do you think last year's loss of two players has hurt the team morale?"

His expression freezes and he pins me with his full attention. "No. And we didn't lose two players. Zach Epps is still alive to us. Still a part of this team."

"From a nursing home bed?" I continue my barrage. "Were you here last year? What can you tell me about the night Zach was hurt?"

"I've got work to do, Miss Kirkwood. That's all the time I have."

"Coach, I want to drum up some school enthusiasm for the team through a series of articles. I'm just trying to get a little background info."

He sets his jaw. "Last year was my first year. And I know nothing about Zach's incident besides what the paper reported. Why?"

I fire off some mundane questions, trying to sound less intrusive and soothe any suspicions he might have. "What college did you go to?"

"Ole Miss."

"Is that home, then—Mississippi?"

"Of course not. I was a Tiger." He swats a player on the shoulder. "A Truman Tiger." His sleeve rises. And I see a tattoo.

Truman Brotherhood.

"I have to talk to my team now." Coach Dallas walks away, catching up to Dante to talk.

I close my notebook and grab my purse from the ground. Two familiar-looking shoes appear beside mine, and I jump up. "Luke, thank God you're here. Big news."

"Walk with me." He gestures toward the exiting crowd. "You must've worked pretty hard tonight. You have a hair out of place." He reaches out and tucks a wilted strand behind my ear and my mind completely empties. "Can't have my staff looking disheveled. So how did it go? Come up with anything? Did Jared Campbell's brother give you any information?"

"Who?"

"Coach Dallas—that's Jared's stepbrother."

"What? Why didn't anyone tell me this? So Coach Lambourn is Jared's stepdad?" At Luke's nod, I check behind me to make sure no one is tuned in to our conversation as we stroll across the field. "I overheard Dante talking to Matt again, but just more of the same. Still wanting him to join their group. Matt sounds closer to caving in."

"Any ideas on what this Brotherhood is?"

"No. But Dante won't tell Matt everything about it until he commits, so it's a heavily guarded secret."

"One we need to uncover."

"Right." I thrill a little at his use of "we." Like we're a team on this. Like he finally takes me seriously. I grab Luke's arm. "Oh, get this—guess who has a Brotherhood tattoo?"

"Your mom?"

"Coach Dallas—on his upper arm. *And* he was very cagey when I asked him about Zach Epps." I fill him in on my brief interview.

"And your theory?"

I can't believe Luke's asking my opinion. I wonder if he's fevered. He is *not* acting like his usual snarky self. "Um . . ." I try to focus on the issue at hand as we weave through long-faced Tiger fans. "I think it's pretty obvious Coach Dallas wants to reignite that long history of winning he mentioned. In his day, the team was a brilliant success. Maybe he wants to win so bad that he's formed this supergroup of players that he trains really hard and . . ." And here's where my theory dead-ends. "And who knows what else they do."

"It has to be more than additional training if it's so secret."

"Yeah, I guess the players wouldn't need to meet in a dark field to discuss some extra bench presses."

"Keep thinking on it. Maybe pray about it, if you're into that sort of thing."

I stop and an old lady with a giant foam finger rams into me. "What did you just say?"

Luke smiles. "You know—pray or something. A good reporter can't do this alone. We need some help. That's your assignment for tonight—see you later."

He leaves me standing in the center of the field with gaping mouth and whirling brain. The president of the Jerk Club of Truman High just told *me* to pray about it? He's the one who probably has to add "Be nice" to his daily to-do list. Who does he think he is? Like I wouldn't do that? As if I'm such a weak Christian I need that reminder?

Okay, so maybe I needed that reminder. Whatever.

Maybe God and I have been living in different stratospheres lately. It's like I can't get a grip on anything anymore. Nothing is going how it's supposed to. I have an evil stepbrother, my mom married a man who likes to play pirate, my cat is gone, my boyfriend ignores me, and Mia has forgotten I exist. And I'm supposed to find faith in the midst of this *how*? What was it that youth pastor said at FCA? That we should look for our Mary moments? What if I don't want to find mine? Maybe it's in New York, but I'm not there to intercept it.

I glance across the field to see if Lindy's waiting for Matt like I instructed her to. Though I don't see her anywhere, my eyes land on a lone figure in the bleachers. Sitting. Covered up as if it's chilly, yet it's at least ninety steamy degrees this evening.

With legs that seem to move of their own volition, I retrace my steps back toward the stands.

Kelsey Anderson. The girl who was at FCA, the one who dated Zach Epps.

My heart pounding with dread, I continue up the steel stairs and walk toward the girl who sits alone, staring out onto the field like it holds her captive, transfixed. Her pale, haunted face tugs at my conscience. *"He might be calling you to a Mary moment . . ."* No, I totally don't want to talk to her. She's all spacey and weird. I don't even know her!

I stop a few feet beside Kelsey. Clearing my throat, I rest my hand on her shoulder. "Hey, Kelsey."

She jumps. But says nothing.

"I, um, just wondered if you noticed the game was over." *Oh my gosh. I need a script. Why do I say these dumb things?* "I mean, of course you know the game's over since you're all alone out here and all, oh, but not that anything's wrong with being alone. I like to be alone sometimes too. Well, maybe not as alone as I have been in Truman, but in Manhattan I liked nothing better than to be by myself and with some Ben and Jerry's and—"

"Zach would've done anything to have been here tonight." Her fragile voice stops me like a shotgun blast. "He would've done anything for the team."

I take that as an invitation to sit down. "So Zach . . . was he a good player?"

She slowly nods her head. "One of the best. He wanted to go pro." Her lips curve at some memory. "Coach told him he had it in him too."

"And which coach would that be?"

"All of them. They knew Zach was really gonna be something. He was their hope for state. Their star quarterback." Kelsey lapses into silence again.

"Is there someone I can call for you? Do you have some friends you could hang out with tonight?" I can't just leave her here alone.

She shakes her head. "They've kind of moved on, you know?" Her hollow brown eyes finally meet mine. "I know I'm different—I'm not the same. They want to go to parties and shop and laugh. They care about clothes and boys."

Maybe you could introduce me to them?

"But when the person you love the most in the world lies in a nursing home and dies a little every day, none of those things matter."

"No, I don't guess they would." My words sound flat and useless. "Hey . . . um, Kelsey, you mentioned that Zach went to a party the night of the accident. What do you know about that?"

She shrugs and returns her stare to the field. "Just another party with the football guys. Usually he got an invitation for me, but not the last few times he went. Not that night."

"And he always had a ticket, an invitation, to get in?"

She nods. "They would always pick us up somewhere then blindfold us. It was fun at the time. Mysterious."

"Did Zach ever figure out who threw the parties?"

"I don't know."

"Kelsey, was anyone with Zach when he crashed?"

"No, but I should've been."

My hand covers hers. "You can't think that."

She sniffs. "We had gotten into this huge fight. I thought he was cheating on me, going to the parties by himself, without me. When

I'd press him for details, he wouldn't say a word. Just got mad and said I didn't trust him." Tears spill down her cheeks. "Maybe if I had trusted him, he would've let me go to the last parties with him. Maybe I could've saved him."

"Did anyone see the crash? If it was on the night of the party, where were his friends?"

"I have to go." She draws the blanket around her. "I want to go tell Zach about the game tonight."

"Kelsey—" I stand up with her. "Don't you think there are some things that don't add up here?"

She lifts a shoulder and walks past me. "That's life though, isn't it? Bad things happen—things don't make sense. Like Carson Penturf."

"Wait—who's that?"

"Carson played center. Until last fall."

"And then?"

"Then he stepped off a cliff and broke his neck."

"The guy who killed himself last year, right?"

She lifts a thin brow. "That's what they said. I have to go. Visiting hours will be over soon."

"Wait, I just have a few more questions."

"They don't like questions around here, Bella. They'll just call you crazy like they did me. Besides, you can't argue with a police report. Or the football team."

"Is that what you did?"

"I have to go."

And she runs away on toothpick legs, her blanket flying behind her like one of Robbie's capes.

chapter twenty-seven

~~~~~~

We left a list for you. And I'll have my cell phone, but Jake says it gets so loud in the arena that I won't be able to hear it. But remember, no Coke after seven. He needs to be in bed by ten. And I printed off instructions for the Heimlich and CPR, and—"

"Mom," I interrupt. "Seriously, just go. Robbie and I will be fine. I won't let him choke *or* OD on caffeine."

"I know it's only four o'clock, but we've got to be in Tulsa by five." Jake scoops his youngest son into his hulkish arms. "We won't be back until you're asleep, so that's a long time to stir up trouble for Bella. You won't do that, right? You don't want to be banished to the poop deck, do you?"

Robbie giggles. "No, Captain Iron Jack. I'll keep an eye on the ship while yer gone. Arghhh."

Pirate jokes. Perfect. This makes me want to hurl myself off the poop deck.

The doorbell chimes as Mom and her wrestler walk to the foyer.

"Flowers for Bella Kirkwood." Mom closes the door and hands them over to my waiting arms. "Roses. Very nice."

With a big goofy smile on my face, I rip into the card.

I'm sorry for my distance lately. Being without you makes me kind of crazy. Can't wait until we see each other again. Love, Hunter.

"They're from Hunter." I clutch the flowers to my chest then peck my mom on the cheek. "Don't worry about a thing. We'll be fine here. And, Jake, um . . . good luck or break a leg or whatever it is you people say."

Jake grins and pats me on the back. "It's definitely *not* break a leg."

Break a skull? Don't bust a seam? Have a concussion-free evening?

I shut the door behind them as Budge stomps down the stairs. I turn my head so he won't see the giggle that his Aladdin-inspired uniform always sets off.

"What?" he growls. "You think you're too good for the Wiener Palace?"

I swivel to face him. "No, of course not." My eyes narrow in on his name tag. "I can only hope to one day be called a Sultan of Pork."

"Not everybody has a dad who gets rich off of boob jobs."

"Not everybody cares what you think." Immediately I feel bad. I know I shouldn't talk to Budge like that, but he totally pushes my buttons. "Actually . . . Budge, there is something I've been wanting to talk to you about."

He crosses his arms over his velvet vest, wrinkling his puffy sleeves. "You said you didn't care what I thought."

"When it comes to your hot dog career dreams." *And your genie pants.* "But I would like to hear your take on some stuff that happened at Truman High last year."

His face freezes. Then reddens. "What's it to you?"

"You know what I'm going to ask you about, don't you? About the football players?"

"I don't know anything."

"Did you know them? Zach Epps or Carson Penturf?"

"I said I don't know anything." Budge crams on his sultan's hat, a tall silk thing with an enormous ruby sprouting peacock plumes.

I follow him into the kitchen where Robbie sits with a coloring book. "The school isn't *that* big. Just tell me what the talk was when things started going wrong last year."

Budge jerks open the door and it slams against the cabinets. "Things went *wrong*? One guy jumps to his death and another's a permanent vegetable, and you call that things going wrong?"

"Budge, wait. I'm sorry, I just—" *Slam.* The glass panes rattle in the door.

"Everybody knows not to talk to Budge about Zach."

Robbie's words go off like cannons in the kitchen. "What did you say?"

He sticks out his tongue and selects another crayon. "My daddy says there are three things you don't bring up to Budge—my mama, girls, and his friend Zach."

I pull out a chair and sit next to my stepbrother. "So Budge and Zach Epps were friends?"

Robbie rolls his eyes like I'm simple. "Yeah, for like forever. And you can't ask him about it."

"Has Budge ever mentioned Carson Penturf?"

Robbie shades in a puppy's tail with a pink crayon. "Nah."

"Oh." Dead end.

So Zach and Budge were friends? But Budge is . . . Budge. I mean he's all about computers and video games and . . . eating

Twinkies. And Zach must've been a star athlete. A jock. What could they possibly have had in common?

"What are we having for dinner, Robbie?"

He folds his fingers and shoots invisible webs toward a cabinet over my head. "SpaghettiOs."

"Coming right up, little caped crusader."

My phone sings and I press it to my ear. "Hunter! The flowers are amazing." I tap my stepbrother on his caped shoulder. "Why don't you fly off into the living room. I'll make dinner and call you when it's ready."

He nods. "I might have to take a coloring break and go save a few people. Is that okay?"

"Only a few people. You have to be home by the time your dad gets back." I ruffle his red hair, and he scurries out of the room. "So . . . it was a sweet surprise. I loved the card too."

"I've missed you, Bella. When do you come home next?"

"It's going to be a few weeks. Seems like forever." I dig for a can opener in a drawer. After asking Hunter about his day, I update him on the Brotherhood.

"You be careful around all those athletes. I don't want to see you get hurt."

"Oh, you and Luke. I can take care of myself."

"Luke?" Static crackles on the line.

"My editor."

"Is he old and ugly?"

"Um . . . not exactly." He's tall, muscular, and gorgeous. If you like the nerdy, intellectual, rude sort.

"Do I have any reason to be concerned?"

"Of course not!" *Puh-lease.* "He's nothing like you. He's obnoxious. He's insensitive. He treats me like a total idiot. I would rather run my tongue across Jake's cow pasture than date Luke."

"I just wanted to make sure. This long-distance thing really is hard, isn't it, Bel?"

I sigh into the phone. "It's only been a week, but it feels like forever since I've seen you." The microwave dings. "I better go. I'm babysitting Robbie tonight while my stepdad whups up on some grown men."

"Miss ya."

"Miss ya right back." And I slide my phone back into my jeans. "Robbie! Your gourmet pasta meal is ready!" I walk into the living room, where Superman flies across the television screen. "Robbie?" His coloring books lie open on the floor. I walk to the stairs and call for him again.

No answer.

Running up to his bedroom, I find cars scattered, action figures strewn, and Legos arranged in piles. But no Robbie.

After two minutes of searching and yelling, I race outside, bellowing his name. I check the barn, the old truck, my car, the trees, the pond. Everywhere.

I stand in the center of the pasture next to Betsy the cow, squeeze my eyes shut, and beg God for help. *Please, Jesus. I seriously need a hand here. When I walk in that house, let Robbie be there. If something happens to that kid, I will die—throw myself in front of a tractor and die.*

Fifteen minutes later I collapse onto the couch, hoarse from yelling Robbie's name. My pulse races as I pick up my phone and call my mother.

No answer.

I hit redial until my finger aches.

I text her an urgent message then watch the phone for a reply.

What do I do?

Long moments pass, and fighting the urge to throw up, I press the three dreaded numbers.

9-1-1.

"I need to report a missing child."

By ten o'clock, I've puked twice, talked to the police three times, and tried to call Mom a million times. And nobody at Wiener Palace will pick up the phone.

At 10:05, the picture I gave the police from our mantel flashes on the evening news. The blonde reporter describes his last moments in the house, mentioning the fact that his stepsister was in charge of him for the evening. Great, way to paint me a loser.

I've called Hunter and Mia both, but like everyone else, they don't answer. It's like I'm totally alone in the world tonight.

An hour later, I jump off the couch when headlights shine through the windows. My heart sinks when I see it's Budge. He is going to rip my head off and feed it to the cows for a late-night snack. *Um, hi. Remember your brother? Yeah, I lost him.*

The back door slams, and swallowing back equal parts bile and dread, I meet Budge in the kitchen. "Budge, I lost your brother. I mean he's gone." Snot drips out of my nose like water from a faucet. "I don't know what happened. One minute I was fixing him SpaghettiOs, and I don't know what's in those meatballs, but the next minute the cow and I are walking the fields yelling for him, but he wasn't there. And the police came and one was really short and I kept looking down at him and thinking, 'Wow, he's almost like a midget,' and then they took down all this information, and you just missed him on the news." I wail my last few words.

Budge doesn't even blink. "You lost me at meatballs."

I take deep, shuddering breaths and wipe my eyes. "I said"—I pause as a sob closes my throat—"your brother is   "

The door flings open again and Robbie waddles in dragging his red cape. "S'up?"

"Wh-what?" I point at the six-year-old. "It's Robbie. That's your brother." I rush to Robbie and wrap him in my arms. "Thank You God, thank You God, thank You God."

"Stop squeezing me. Lemme go. You can't kiss superheroes. You're going to suck my powers out!"

"Bella," comes Budge's deep voice. "Step away from the child."

I look up, still clutching my stepbrother. "Where have you been? I've looked for you everywhere. The *police* have looked everywhere."

Robbie shimmies out of my grip. "I went to the Wiener Palace."

"What?" I pin Budge with my evilest glare. "He was with you the whole time? I've been entertaining the Truman PD and watching your brother on the Tulsa news, and *you* had him with you at work? Are you kidding me?" I'm yelling.

"Yeah." Budge picks a piece of lint from his vest. "Good job keeping an eye on my brother."

"But how did you get to Budge's work? Why would you leave and not tell me?"

"I rode my bike. It took a really long time, but I'm pretty strong like my dad. And I *told* you I was going to go save some people."

"*I might have to take a coloring break and go save some people.*"

"I thought you were teasing!"

Robbie frowns and shakes his head. "Being a superhero is not something to joke about. It's my responsibility to the world."

I kneel down to get in his face. "Unless you were there passing out antacids like a Rolaids fairy, I can't imagine why you went to the Wiener Palace."

Robbie scuffs his toe along the linoleum floor. "Budge needed me. You made him sad, and he needed me to cheer him up."

I jerk my head toward Budge. "And you couldn't have called? What kind of crap is that? I've been out of my head with worry."

He shrugs. "Not my fault you couldn't hack ten minutes alone with my brother."

I clench my fists at my side. *Do not punch your fist through his nose.* "You've got issues, you know that, Budge? You're mean, you're thoughtless, and you don't care about anybody but yourself."

The front door opens and closes. Anxious voices call from the living room.

Mom and Jake.

Budge laughs and pushes past me. "Looks to me like *you're* the one with the issues."

chapter twenty-eight

The Holy Church of the Sacred High School has a great choir. It's like watching *Sister Act*. Well, minus the nun outfits. But these people know how to sing some Jesus.

I sit next to Lindy and Matt, opting for some time away from the family. While I didn't really get in trouble last night over Robbie's disappearance, Mom wasn't exactly what I'd call happy with me either.

As I clap along to the up-tempo song, I watch Budge sitting with his friends. He stands with his arms crossed, not singing, looking like he wants to be anywhere but church. Jake totally grounded him for not calling me last night when his brother showed up at the Weiner Palace. And of course, Budge is furious with me. Like it's my fault. If this is the kind of stuff I've missed not having siblings, I can't say I feel deprived.

"What do you say we pick up a pizza and go hang out at the city park?" Matt asks after the service. "Do you want to go?"

"I'm in a dress." I turn to Lindy. "You're in a dress."

"Oh. I guess I'll have to pass. I would hate to muss up my skirt." She flips her hair and her perfume floats between us. "It's Moochie, you know."

I cough. "Gucci."

Matt's face falls. "Come on, Lind. We haven't thrown the football around in forever. You're always too busy doing your nails or worried about messing up your pedicure or something."

Lindy looks to me, waiting for me to throw her a life preserver.

"Maybe a day at the park would be fun. Get a little sun while we eat. Sure, why not?" I link my arm through Lindy's. "Maybe you can do some boy-watching too. A nice day like this—who knows who'll be out there?"

"I'm not going out there so you two can gawk at the guys. Let's just go hang out and have a good time, okay?"

We step into the aisle, and I lean close to Lindy's ear. "He sounds jealous, doesn't he? It's totally working."

Her smile doesn't quite reach her eyes. "I hope he gets the idea soon. I'm sick of dressing like a princess."

"But this is the new you, Lindy. It's not a phase. You've been totally transformed. Lots of girls would kill to have those Chanel shoes you have on right now. You went from looking like a sports warehouse model to a runway model. And he's into it. I've seen him looking at you."

"Yeah, like I'm a psychopathic shopping freak."

"Just trust me." I pat her arm and join my parents.

"Hey, I'm going to the park with—" I choke on the rest of my sentence as I notice a familiar bald man in the family huddle.

"Bella, you remember Mickey." Jake pats his trainer's back.

Yes, how have you been since I broke into your gym and found my stepfather throwing himself on another man?

Mickey takes his eyes off me and focuses on Mom. "Jillian, how's work? Are you adjusting to life at the diner?"

"It's getting better. I never realized what a hard job it was to be a waitress."

Um, probably because you weren't made to be one. My mom used to serve on the boards of directors for charities. Now she's serving anything that comes with fries.

Mickey clasps his hands behind his back, making his chest muscles pop through his oxford shirt. The guy may be pushing fifty, but he could probably take on any member of the Truman football team. "And how is Dolly?" He turns his attention to the floor.

"She's fine, Mickey. Maybe you should come by the diner for a piece of pie someday next week." Mom's face is hopeful.

"I haven't . . . um . . . had any of Sugar's banana cream pie in years."

Mom wraps her small arm around Jake's ox of a trainer. "Sounds like it's been too long. Come in to the diner, Mickey. Things might've changed in there."

Mickey scratches his head. "Oh, did they redecorate?"

"She means Dolly," I blurt. "Not the wallpaper." Boys. They're so dense. "So I'm going to the park with Matt and Lindy, okay?" I give my mom a quick squeeze.

"Why don't you ask Logan to go?" Mom asks as my least favorite Trumanite joins us. She jerks her blonde head toward him. "Bella, wasn't there something you wanted to ask Logan?"

I pry my clenched teeth apart. "Budge, would you like to accompany me and some friends to the park?"

"I'd rather eat hot lava."

"Okay then."

"Bella, go get him." Mom pushes me into the flow of the crowd as my stepbrother walks away.

"Budge, wait." I catch up with him in the school lobby. "Look, you and I have gotten off on the wrong foot, and I'm sorry. Let's—"

"I don't need you, Jillian's attempts to be my mom, or this stupid church. I'm out of here."

"What is your problem?" I catch his arm. "I know losing your best friend had to hurt a lot—still does, I'm sure. But being mad at all of us isn't going to accomplish anything."

"You don't know jack about my life, so butt out." He busts through the lobby doors out into the yellow sunshine, his dark mood like a cloud trailing behind him.

"I'm going to pray for you, Budge," I call out.

At the park I turn off my bad thoughts about Budge and sink my energy into the pepperoni pizza Matt places in the middle of the blanket.

After Lindy leads us in a quick prayer, my mouth closes around my first bite.

And it's everything I can do not to spit it out.

"I see that face." Lindy points her finger. "Do *not* tell us how they make pizza in New York. This is Truman, Bella. Don't be a pizza snob."

"I'm not!" I wipe a string of cheese off my chin. "It's getting better." I chew and smile. "Mmmm." It's like eating cardboard encased in mozzarella. "So, Matt, what did you think of the party Thursday night?" It's the first chance I've really had to talk to him about it.

"It was okay." He stares off toward a giant sandbox inhabited by squealing toddlers.

I so want to just come out and ask him about the Brotherhood, but I can't. I don't know him well enough. And what if he alerted the other guys that I'm onto them? I'd never find out anything else.

"You and the team seem pretty . . . close."

"Yeah, I guess we are."

"It's so crazy," I laugh. "I mean we were there for hours, and I never found out whose house we were at. Do you know whose cabin it was?"

"No. That's the fun of it." Matt wipes his mouth with a napkin.

"Yeah, well, it's not my kind of party," Lindy says. "I don't think we'll be going back. Right, Matt?"

He continues his study of the sandbox.

"Right, Matt?"

"I don't know, Lind. It's good to get away from it all sometimes. None of us drank, so what's the harm?"

Her eyes narrow to slits. "Because we don't *need* to be around that stuff. You've always been adamant about that."

"Lighten up, Lindy. We had a good time."

"Yeah." I nudge her in the ribs. "You said you had a great time dancing. Didn't *you*, Matt?"

His eyes linger on Lindy for a brief second. "You do have some new dance moves I've never seen before. I always thought you hated dancing, but you totally held your own Thursday night."

"Thanks." She bats her curled eyelashes. "Bella introduced me to this guy in New York, and we danced . . . a lot."

I hold my breath, waiting for Matt's reaction.

"I brought a Frisbee. You ladies want to toss it around awhile?"

That's it? No jealousy? No declarations of love?

"I'm game." Lindy forces a smile and jumps up, her skirt swishing around her.

We keep the Frisbee going for a few minutes when my girl radar picks up on something. Yes . . . I'm almost certain . . . I do believe there might be cute boys somewhere close.

"Is that the Truman soccer team?" Just beyond Matt's shoulder a group of guys pile out of cars and onto an adjoining practice field.

"Yeah. They're pretty good. The captain's a little cocky though." Matt spins the Frisbee to Lindy.

A guy balances the soccer ball on his knee. I struggle to bring him into focus, but something tells me—

"Luke Sullivan." And my editor in chief moves closer in our direction and comes into full view. "He's cute." The awestruck words tumble out of my mouth before I can reclaim them. Preppy, uptight Luke has leg muscles any quarterback would envy. And biceps. I had no idea. I just had no idea.

A Frisbee bounces off my forehead. "Ow!"

Lindy laughs. "See something over there you like?"

"What? Me?" I fling the disc and rub my head. "No, of course not! I was . . . um . . . just seeing if anyone of interest for you was over there." This time I catch Lindy's pass. "I know you have your heart set on one guy, but it doesn't hurt to keep your options open." And I release the Frisbee, sending it flying between Matt and Lindy.

They both dive for it, falling into a tangled heap on the grass.

Matt rolls away, shaking with laughter. Lindy jumps up, her skirt stained with green. "Good job, Matt. Look at my outfit." She brushes it with frantic hands. "And my hair."

His freckled face falls. "What's into you lately? It's like you've changed."

"You're just *now* noticing?"

"I'll be glad when this girly phase of yours is over."

"This is me, Matt. This is who I am."

"And I don't like it." His voice rises above the slight breeze.

"I can't stay one of the guys forever."

"I never thought of you as one of the guys!"

"Um, I don't see you burping rap songs in front of any other girls, do you?"

Matt scoops up the Frisbee and the pizza box. "I'm out of here. Let me know if you run into my old friend Lindy. I miss her." He dunks the box in the trash and stomps away.

Lindy's shoulders sag. "This isn't working, Bella."

"Of course it is." I can hardly keep from rubbing my hands together in giddy satisfaction. "Don't you see? He's *finally* noticing you."

"Yeah, noticing that he can't stand me. Fat lot of good *that's* doing."

"Lindy, be patient. He's going to go home, and you are going to invade his every thought. Obviously you've gotten under his skin. If he's unsure about this new you, it's because he's afraid of what he feels." I totally saw this same thing on *Tyra* last week.

"I've got basketball practice in a few hours. I'll see you later."

I watch Lindy go and feel a hitch of nerves. What if I'm not bringing Matt and Lindy together? What if I'm detonating their friendship? But he has to fall for the new Lindy, right? She dresses better, she smells like a girl, and she has killer highlights. Who could resist that?

I stroll across the grass, past a row of swings and an old wooden teeter-totter, lost in thought.

A whistle blows, jarring me from my trance, and I realize I've walked to the soccer field. My eyes locate Luke instantly. He shouts commands to his teammate, then high-fives him. He runs down the field, the chiseled muscles above his knees flexing with every step. The wind sails through his hair, and he pushes the ball toward the goal. I can't help but smile as I see his expression when he sinks the ball in. A grin lights up his face, and his teammates pile around him. Gone is the editor mask. No arrogance. No overblown ego. Out here, he's just a boy.

I reach for my cell and try Hunter.

Right to voice mail. "It's Bella. Remember me, your girlfriend? Give me a call."

A shadow falls across my arm. I look up and Luke smiles.

"Did you come out here to cheer me on?"

"No." Can't. Think. "I was just here with some friends. I'm leaving." I continue my walk, my face red. He'd *better* not think I was checking him out.

"Bella—wait." Luke runs toward me. "Have you found anything else?"

Just my totally buff editor glistening with sweat. "Er, no. You?"

He lifts up a Gatorade bottle and drinks. "Did some research and found out the lake cabin does belong to Coach Dallas."

"How'd you get that information, Detective Sullivan? Did you break into his office? Hack his computer?"

He wipes the moisture from his brow. "Googled the address. Much more legal."

Oh. How unimaginative.

"Now we just have to find out how Carson Penturf's suicide and Zach Epps's wreck are all connected to what I've overheard lately."

"*If* they're connected."

"You know they are, Luke. What does your reporter's gut tell you?" *You know, the one beneath your six-pack abs.*

He slowly nods. "They're related. Just not sure how."

"We have to get more information somehow. And your idea to have me be a glorified waitress at the football games isn't cutting it." Plus I broke a few nails. So not cool.

Luke's tanned fingers tap a rhythm on the bottle as his mind works. "Find out from Matt if there's a party this Thursday night. If so, you have to get an invitation."

"Okay." If my mom will even let me go.

"And why don't you pay Kelsey Anderson a visit?"

"She's hardly ever at school."

"You know where she spends her time, Bella."

I shudder with dread but know the girl could be a source of more information. "I'll go see her tomorrow night."

Across the field the whistle blows again, and Luke's teammates reassemble.

"See you tomorrow. Oh, and, Bella?" He flashes me a wicked grin. "Good luck with your boyfriend."

chapter twenty-nine

~~~~~~

*Y*ou want me to do *what?*"

On Monday I sit beside my mother at Sugar's as Dolly slams down a mug and pours herself a shot of Folgers.

"Cater Jake's party. It will be a fairly small affair at the house." My mom fills a shaker with salt.

Dolly arches an eyebrow. "Who will be there?"

"Jake, some other wrestlers in the amateur circuit, a few select people from the media, and the family."

Dolly juts out a hip and parks her hand on it. "And?"

My mother blinks rapidly, a sure sign she's withholding information. "And a few other random people I've invited. Can't remember who."

"Jillian Finley, I am not going to cook up a spread for the likes of Mickey Patrick."

"I need your help. I don't know how to cook. I can't even manage to squeeze cheese on Triscuits."

"It's true," I say. "She can't."

"It's not that I don't want to help you. It's about . . ."

"Dolly, I think you need to—shoot, there's old man Hodges holding up his coffee cup *again*. That man's going to run my legs off."

Mom bustles away to check on her customer, leaving Dolly, me, and a few questions I'm dying to have answered.

"None of your business."

I blink at Dolly's tone. "What? I didn't say anything."

She smacks her gum and runs a fingernail through her teased hair. "You were going to. I saw it in your eyes."

"Come on, tell me what happened with you and your ex-husband. I mean, if the guy's a jerk, then maybe my stepdad doesn't need to be working with him."

She takes a rag and begins scrubbing the counter with a fury. "He left me, that's what."

"For another woman? Is that what bonded you to my mom so quickly? You know she totally relates to that."

"No, he didn't leave me for another woman. Don't you have somewhere to be?"

"Oh, shoot. I do." I sling my purse over my shoulder. "But we're not through discussing this."

When I pull into the parking spot at Truman Manors nursing home, dread expands in my stomach like a balloon on helium. I turn off the key then rest my head on the steering wheel and offer up a small prayer for fortitude. I do *not* want to go in there. I don't want to see old people in the last stages of their lives. I don't want to inhale the smell that could only belong to a nursing home. And most importantly, I do not want to discuss the football team with Kelsey over Zach's lifeless body.

Five minutes later, I finally talk myself out of the car and into the lobby. On each side of me are seating areas and big-screen TVs. On my right is a glass case that houses ten or so chirping birds. Trapped and on display. Is this supposed to cheer the residents up?

It makes me want to grab a fire extinguisher, bust through the glass, and yell, "Fly away, birds! Go! Go!"

I turn my head from the captive pets and focus on the other side.

And there sits Luke, playing checkers with an elderly man.

"And that's the game! I win again." The man holds out a wrinkled hand and Luke places cash in it. "You want to play another one?"

Luke sees me and stands up. "No, you cleaned me out, Mr. Murphy."

"You can't handle this, can you?"

"Nope." Luke laughs and ambles to my side.

"When you're man enough to face me again, I'll be waiting."

"See you next week, Mr. Murphy." Luke places his hand at the small of my back and leads me through the lobby and past the nurses' station.

"What are you doing here?"

He shrugs an arrogant shoulder. "Waiting on you."

"Really? Because it sounded to me like you're a regular here."

"I don't know what that man's talking about." Luke taps his temple. "He's a bit senile."

I punch his shoulder. "Luke Sullivan, you *do* have a heart."

"Tell anyone and I'll kick you out of the class and send you to—"

"Tire Changing 101?"

I follow him down a hall, passing door after door. Some rooms I have to look away. The residents remind me too much of the trapped birds. Some sit alone in their rooms, empty eyes staring at flashing TV screens. Others yell and call out in barely decipherable words.

"It's not easy being here, is it?" Luke stops before room 202.

I shake my head. "Is this his room?" Unlike the others, this door is closed.

"This is it. Are we ready?"

"You're going with me?"

"Of course." His head tilts and his voice lowers. "You didn't think I'd let you go alone, did you?"

"Because you don't trust me to get the information?"

He opens his mouth, pauses, then starts again. "Let's just do this."

Luke knocks softly, then pushes on the door.

Kelsey sits in a chair shoved next to the bed. The bed where her boyfriend lies, unmoving, with machines pumping and tubes weaving a pattern around him. I swallow hard.

She looks up from her vigil. "Hi, Luke." Her pale eyes dim a little as I step out from behind him.

"I brought you some snacks." Luke reaches into his messenger bag and pulls out some crackers and a bottle of water. "Nurse Betty at the front desk said you've been forgetting to eat lately."

She takes the food and manages a smile. "His color's good today, isn't it? He looks kind of peaceful."

My eyes are drawn to Zach, who looks anything but peaceful.

"Kelsey, I have a favor to ask," Luke says as I sit down in a vacant chair. "I know this is the last thing you want to talk about, but Bella and I have reason to believe that any information you can give us about Zach's wreck would be helpful to something we're working on."

She bites into a cracker. "Are you gonna tell me what this is about?"

Luke sighs. "No."

Seconds pass, the only sound being the push and pull of Zach's ventilator.

Kelsey considers her fingernails for a moment. "Okay." She reaches for her water bottle. "What do you want to know?"

Luke doesn't hesitate. "Why do you think Zach didn't let you go to the last few parties with him?"

She stares at her boyfriend and smoothes a piece of hair from his cheek. "I don't know. I guess I'll never know."

Luke sits on the arm of my chair. "Which players was Zach closest to?"

"That was kind of odd last year. He was always best friends with Budge." She looks directly at me. "Your stepbrother and Zach were inseparable. But during the fall semester Zach and Budge just went their separate ways. Zach started spending more and more time with the team. He mostly hung around Dante and that guy who got suspended this year—"

"Reggie Lee," Luke supplies.

"Yeah . . . Sometimes he hung around Jared Campbell. There were some others."

"These parties—were they at a cabin?"

She shrugs at Luke's question. "A few—they'd change up the location I think."

"Did he ever mention anything unusual going on there?" I ask.

"No. He got really tight-lipped about their get-togethers in the end. Said I would've just been bored, that they were just talking football and planning for the next night's game."

"Why would they drink the night before a game?" I wonder

aloud. "If they are all so obsessed with winning, how stupid is that to wake up on game day with a hangover?"

"Did you see anybody drunk out there?" Luke lifts a dark brow. "I didn't see any signs of people getting hammered. At least not the players."

Kelsey stretches her back and yawns. "I remember the last few parties I went to, Zach would drink a single beer. It was so unlike him. His daddy's a drunk, so Zach couldn't stand alcohol much. And when I'd ask him why he was drinking, he'd say, 'Liquid encouragement,' like he needed bolstering or something."

"Encouragement for what?" Luke asks.

"I don't know."

"You mentioned that you had asked a lot of questions, Kelsey." I lean around Luke and catch the fading scent of his cologne. "What sorts of things didn't add up to you?"

"His car. The fact that he was driving it so fast—and so crazy. That wasn't Zach at all. He loved that Camaro. It was his baby. Washed it every Sunday by hand. He didn't use it like a hot rod. He was always so careful with it."

"It's only natural to want to show off at least once if you have a car like that—see how fast she'll go."

"Not Zach. He was fanatical about that car. Wouldn't let anyone else drive it. He wouldn't have done anything that might've so much as put a scratch on it."

"Accidents happen," I say.

Luke twists around. "But the police report says that some of the players witnessed Zach bragging about his car. Said he wanted to prove what it could do."

"He was at one of those parties. The guys denied it was a party to the police, but that's what it was. Zach hadn't let me go. When the police checked out the scene, everyone had cleared out. Only a few of the guys remained, like they were just hanging out for the evening or something. Reggie told the police that Zach left, tires squealing, his engine roaring. Reggie said they tried to talk him out of it. It was raining that night." She shudders. "So dangerous. And stupid."

I take a deep breath and try to align the facts. "Kelsey, I understand your reservations, but as someone who's not as close to the situation, it kind of all makes sense. It was an unfortunate accident, but it sounds like your boyfriend just overdid it and lost control of the car. What's suspicious about that?"

"Nothing." She runs a hand over her tired face. "But the phone call certainly was."

Luke sits up straighter. "Call?"

Kelsey's hand begins to tremble. "Zach called me from the car—during that joyride. He was panicked, talking nonsense. He kept saying, 'I didn't want to do it. He made me do it. He made me.' Told me he couldn't see a thing, and if he scratched the paint his dad would kill him. Then he said something I'll never forget."

Kelsey sits down on the bed beside her boyfriend. I hold my breath and wait for her to speak.

"He said, 'Stupid coach's son. Trying to make us into something we're not.'" The tears flow freely down her cheeks. "Then I heard it. The crash." Her voice gains in intensity, grows stronger. "You find out what happened. The police wouldn't listen to me. And every time I tried to talk to the players, they'd tell me to let it die. Something isn't right here, Luke. Something happened that night, before the wreck." She chokes on tears.

Luke goes to her and wraps her in his arms. "We'll find out what happened." He rests his head on hers, and his eyes lock with mine. "And I think our Coach Dallas is the guy with all the answers."

chapter thirty

By Wednesday morning, Luke's kinder alter ego is as dead as my MasterCard.

"Absolutely not."

"Why?" I ask him for the tenth time. My temples pound with a stress headache that Tylenol can't touch. The only prescription is Luke getting out of my face. "We need answers."

"You are not going to ask Jared Campbell if he knows his step-brother is evil."

Okay, so it doesn't sound so good coming out of Luke's mouth, but in my head it made a lot of sense. Jared's so nice, so innocently naïve. I really think he'd tell me if he knew Coach Dallas was up to no good.

"What did the coach possibly stand to gain by pressuring Zach to drag race his car?" Luke taps his pencil to his chin.

"Maybe when he was in high school a girl stomped on his heart, cheated on him, and the other guy drove a Camaro. And so he wants to see all of them turned into scrap metal."

"This is not some low-budget horror movie we're working with here."

"It could happen," I mumble.

"Have you talked to your stepbrother? Does he know anything?"

"Budge won't even talk to me about it. For that matter, he won't talk to me, period." Which would be a total gift from the heavens if I didn't need information concerning his former best friend.

"What about Reggie Lee? Kelsey said he gave a statement to the police about Zach on the night of the accident. We need to work on that angle."

"I heard he moved out of town. When are we ever going to see him?"

"He still goes to my church sometimes. We could talk to him Sunday."

"If he's there." I sit on the table and swing my legs, admiring my last new pair of Michael Kors flip-flops. "Sounds like a long shot. We need to be more aggressive than that."

The bell rings, and I hop down.

"Bella, leave the *aggressive* stuff to me."

My heart quirks in my chest. I may not like this guy, but that sounded so hot. "Um . . ." *Focus, focus.* "What?"

His eyes sear through mine. "Your days of taking off alone to trail some guys into the woods are over. No more careless moves. We work together on this or I pull you from the story."

My headache pushes tight on my skull. "I don't need you to watch out for me, Luke. I can take care of myself."

"Yeah, okay, whatever. Think about me saving you in the woods."

Strangely enough, I do. A lot.

"If you go and do something rash, not only will you get hurt or in trouble, but you'll get the paper in trouble."

"Oh, right." My heart sinks a bit. "Wouldn't want you worrying over your paper."

He stands up, planting both palms on the table. "It's not just that—it's . . ."

"Yes?" I lean in.

"The more we find out, the more I'm convinced the people involved in this could be dangerous. It would have to take a lot of intimidation for somebody like Zach Epps to cave in to peer pressure."

At lunch I sit beside Lindy, with a sullen and silent Matt across from us. Neither one of them says a word. The tension is thicker than cafeteria gravy.

"So . . ." I sprinkle sugar into my tea. This stuff grows on a person. "FCA was good this morning, eh? I liked what the speaker said about forgiveness and accepting others as they are."

Matt glares over his sandwich. "I've heard better messages."

"Yeah," Lindy adds. "And the donuts were stale."

"Um, Matt, I was wondering if there was another party this Thursday. I had fun dancing. Meeting people." Not to mention eating Fritos and following people into the woods.

"I'd like to go too."

Eating stops as we stare at Lindy.

"I would. I have a new outfit and there's someone that I want to see it. I think he'll be there." She giggles as she waves to a few guys across the cafeteria.

Oh no. I've created a monster. A flirting, party-going, man-eating monster. While I encouraged this in the beginning, it's not natural for Lindy. It's like asking the football team to wear tutus. Not a good combo.

"Who's this guy you like, Lindy? Just tell me. You used to tell me everything."

She bites into her salad and smiles coyly. "One guy?" She spears a tomato. "I have a few options I'm pursuing, actually. And things are going . . . really well."

Matt looks to me for confirmation. I stretch my cheeks into a stiff smile.

"I'm not going Thursday night, so I guess you'll have to scope out your guys somewhere else."

Lindy cuts him a dirty look. "You're just trying to keep me away from the party."

"Like I care if you're going. You do whatever you want, but I won't be there." He grabs his tray and stomps away.

I grasp a piece of my hair and inspect the ends. "That went well."

"Bella, it's *not* going well. This wasn't part of the plan."

"But he was obviously bothered by the idea of you on the hunt for a boyfriend." Or two. "That's encouraging, right? I really think he's coming around."

She props her chin on her hand. "Then why don't I feel encouraged?"

In English Thursday, I slide into the desk behind Jared Campbell and smile, an open invitation to conversation.

A few seconds later he turns around. "This novel is making me miss Hester and *The Scarlet Letter*." He holds up his copy of *Great Expectations*.

I swat his hand and laugh. "I know, instead of *Great Expectations* it should be called *Crappy Letdown*."

He grins and turns all the way around in his seat. "*Great Expectations—of Insomnia.*"

I smile into his eyes, letting mine linger a little longer than a new friend would. "You know what else is a letdown?" I pucker my glossy lips in a pout. "Not getting the chance to dance with you any more. I had a really good time last week."

"Thanks. Me too."

I lean forward on the desk. "It's been so hard adjusting here. But last week at the party I was able to forget all about my worries and just be me, you know?" I wave my hand. "Anyway, I just wanted to thank you for, you know, talking to me again."

"Sorry we didn't get to talk a lot last Thursday." He rests his arm on my desk. "I like to work the crowd to make sure no one's getting too crazy."

"I think that's great. It's really thoughtful of you." My cooing voice sounds obnoxious to my ears. *Forgive me, Hunter.* "Makes a girl feel safe to know someone like you is looking out for . . . her." I giggle.

"I keep an eye on everyone."

"So is it your party?"

He laughs. "It's the *team's* party. It's all for the team. Everything we do is for that win."

"Jared, if you ever find yourself at another get-together and need a dance partner, here's my number." I scribble on a piece of paper and slide it over.

He holds it between both hands then folds it in two. "Actually . . ."

Yes? Come on, big boy.

"I hear there's a party tonight."

"Really?" I'm all innocence.

"I don't usually do this, but if you'd like to go, I could pick you up."

I clap my hands to my chest. "I would *love* to go! But hey, why don't I just meet you there? I have some stuff to do tonight, so I might be a little late. You could give me directions."

"Wow, I'm sorry, Bella. But the location is top secret."

"So it's not at the same cabin? Do you know where it is?" I purr, like I think this is all totally cute.

"Maybe. But if I tell you where it is, I will be toast."

Because your stepbrother would hurt you? Kick you off the team? Maybe Dante would rough you up? Short-sheet your bed? What?

"Then I guess I'll have to meet you somewhere."

He reaches into his pocket and hands me a purple piece of paper. "You'll need this, even if you're with me. Meet me at the old cemetery. Can you be there by eight?"

I pull the ticket out of his fingers, my hand grazing his. "I can't wait."

"Bella, you can't tell anyone about the party. It's top secret, okay?" He lightens his serious tone. "We don't want the entire high school out there."

I tuck the paper into my backpack as the teacher opens her book to start class.

"Today, students, we're going to discuss what Dickens had to say about pretending to be something you're not . . ."

Stupid book.

chapter thirty-one

~~~~~~

When Jared takes the blindfold off my eyes, I blink a few times to bring the fuzzy surroundings into focus.

"A campground?"

"An old overflow campsite. Nobody's ever out here." He helps me out of the car and leads me toward the festivities. Music blasts from a CD player, and the rest of the partygoers sit on hay bales around a flaming bonfire. Tiki torches are stuck in the ground every few feet, giving the area a dollar-store tropical theme.

Jared high-fives some of the players. He talks to everyone he passes as if they're his closest friends. He's so kind to people. Looking at him, you'd think he would be all stuck up. I mean, he's got it all—Abercrombie-model good looks, Advanced Placement brains, a position as a starter on the football team. It's going to stink when I eventually reveal my theory that his stepbrother's a total psycho.

"Can I get you something to drink?" Jared's hand presses into my back, and we walk toward a car where a cooler sits in the trunk. I peer inside. All alcohol.

"Um . . . nothing for me, thanks."

"Let's keep looking." He takes me to another trunk, reaches into the cooler, and pulls out a Coke. "For the lady."

I thank him with a smile and watch as he grabs one for himself. "I'm not into that stuff either."

But does your stepbrother supply the alcohol for these parties? I want so badly to ask him the questions whirring in my brain. All of Luke's warnings replay in my head.

"I'm glad you brought me tonight." I sigh and gaze into his face. "Whose soiree is this anyway?"

Jared grabs a bag of Ruffles from the trunk, tears it, and holds it open. "It's everyone's party, remember?"

"Is this something you football players throw together?" I can't let this go.

He shrugs. "It's definitely *for* us." Jared's head drops closer to mine. "And anyone special we might want to invite." I giggle but take a step back, putting a little space between us. I can just see me talking to Hunter on the phone tomorrow morning.

"So what did you do last night?"

"Who, me? Oh, went to a party with a guy, flirted with him. Let him think I was interested. How was SportsCenter?"

Another set of headlights shines on the campsite. Jared watches the vehicle until the driver gets out. "Dante's here. I'll be right back." His hand lingers on my shoulder as he passes.

Time to start digging around and asking questions. I grab the Ruffles and turn to find my first interviewee.

And run smack into Britanny Taylor.

"I know what you're up to."

I gasp and a chip lodges in my throat. My cough comes in spasms, and I blink watery eyes.

"Wh-what?"

"You," she spits. "And Jared. I know what you're doing, and I plan to tell him *all* about it."

I clutch the chips to my chest and force myself to take some deep breaths. "What are you talking about, Brittany?"

"He felt bad about how everybody shunned you, and so he's been nice to you out of pity. But you're using it to lure him in."

"Lure him?" What is he, a trout?

"Yeah." Her hateful mouth twists. "So you can get back at *me*. Because you knew I liked him. And now you think you're getting me back for ratting out your *Miss Hilliard* blog. But let me tell you something, Bella. You move in on Jared, and I will come after you with a vengeance. You do not want to mess with me."

Mee-yeow. Is it just me, or are the people in this school just a wee bit violent? Somebody needs to get Truman High some therapy. In large doses.

"Look, Brittany, clearly you've not been to your anger management classes lately, so I can understand why—" I swallow the rest of the words as I look over Brittany's shoulder and see who else gets out of Dante's car.

Matt Sparks.

His face is uncertain, his eyes searching. Then he's swarmed by classmates, teammates, and he perks up. So . . . Matt wasn't planning on coming to the party tonight, huh?

"Are you even listening to me?"

My attention snaps back to the shrew in front of me. "Oh yes. You were threatening me?" My voice is as bland as oatmeal.

Brittany sticks her finger in my face. "Watch yourself, Bella.

Because I'm not going to allow some little rich girl to come in here and take what's mine."

"That's funny—at no point did anyone tell me you and Jared were dating. Because I definitely stay away from the boys who are taken."

She hisses like a venomous snake. "You've been warned." And she slithers away.

That girl is not nice. Let's just hope she stays on her side of the bonfire tonight.

I walk back to the coolers and select another Coke. With dripping can in hand, I approach Matt Sparks. His eyes widen as I stand before him.

"Drink?" I hold it out. He slowly reaches for it.

"I . . . uh . . ."

"You intended to come to this from the beginning, didn't you?"

His eyes flash. "I don't have to explain anything to you."

"Any particular reason why you didn't want us here tonight, Matt?"

"Why don't you go back home and highlight Lindy's hair or something. She's more your friend now than mine. Maybe I thought it was just time to start branching out and hanging with a new crowd."

I'm torn between furious and hurt. "I'm not trying to bust up your friendship. Lindy—" The truth dances on my tongue, but I force it down. "She cares about you. She misses your friendship."

"I think Lindy and I need some time apart."

"So you can hang out with your new party friends?"

"If you don't approve of them, why are you here?"

I open my mouth. Then shut it. "I'm here with Jared Campbell."

Matt looks over his shoulder then back to me. "Look, just be careful out here, okay?"

"What does that mean?"

He starts to say something then retreats. "I . . . um . . . just, you know, the typical party rules—don't set your drink down, don't go off alone with anyone, don't pee on rattlesnakes."

"Don't pee on rattlesnakes?" I lower my voice even more. "Is that supposed to mean something?"

He speaks directly into my ear. "It means if you squat over a rattler, you'll get two fangs in your butt." Matt leaves me to join some friends.

By ten o'clock, I've danced with just about everyone. Truman seems to be forgetting about the Great Blog Disaster. Well, except for Brittany, but if I never regain her friendship, I think I'll still be able to sleep at night.

Great. I am in sore need of a bathroom. Or I guess in this case, a large tree to go behind. I look for Jared to tell him where I'm going. That way if a wild bear comes and hauls me off, someone will know to look for me.

Not finding my date for the night, I suppress a sigh and walk into a wooded area, my cell phone shining like a weak flashlight. About a hundred paces out, I decide I'm far away from view and pick my tree. Oh, the indignity. For the record, I have *never* peed outside. It's unladylike. It's uncouth. And—*ew*—apparently I have bad aim!

All finished and anxious to get out of here, I zip my denim shorts and button the top button.

"Are you sure he's going to do it?"

Who is that? I stop at the voice and plaster myself to the back of the tree. I'm probably stepping exactly where I did my business.

"He's here, isn't he?" That's Dante.

"Between the beer and the music, I think everyone's pretty distracted right now. We should be able to slip out in about an hour. Wait for the signal, then meet at the old bridge."

An hour? I have to be home in thirty minutes due to my new, restricted curfew. It took an act of Congress to talk my mom into letting me out of the house tonight.

"He thinks Sparks is the missing link, that we need him in the Brotherhood to make us stronger."

"I don't know, man," Dante says. "This is getting crazy. We can't afford another disaster."

"Look, you know he won't let you out of this. It's too important that the legacy continues. We'll make sure there aren't any more mistakes."

"Mistakes? Dude, accidents happen. People fall. Drivers lose control. We don't have any power over that. And we also can't stand any more bad attention. I'm not going to any more funerals."

"It's his team. We do what he says, Dante. Now either you're in or you're out. But you think long and hard before you leave the Brotherhood. You *know* what happened to Reggie."

"I'm not backing out. You know I'm in this. Just forget it."

Their voices grow weaker as they walk away.

I know one thing for sure.

I have to get home by curfew—so I can sneak right back out, with Luke at my side. We have some late-night spying to do.

chapter thirty-two

~~~~~~

Jared pulls over and takes off my blindfold when we hit the town square.

I smile prettily, like it's not the creepiest thing ever to have your eyes covered. "Thanks for taking me back early. My mom's kind of a stickler lately on the curfew." I can't imagine why.

He steers the car back onto the road. "I had a great time with you tonight. I always do."

"Thanks." And I had a good time with him. Jared has an amazing personality. But I feel nothing for the boy.

He puts the car in park when we roll up to the unwelcoming graveyard a few minutes later. I mean, seriously, if you want to impress a girl, do *not* ask to meet her at a cemetery.

"So . . ." His arm rests on the back of my seat. "How's that boyfriend in New York?"

We both laugh. "Very subtle," I say. "Um . . . Hunter and I are finding a long-distance relationship to be harder than we thought."

"Bella—" His eyes grow serious in the dark of the car. "I would love for us to be friends—hang out. But if you get to the point where New York is too far away, there are guys here in Truman who would like the opportunity to date you."

My heart constricts. I wish I liked him like that.

My hand covers his on the gearshift. "Jared, if only I had met you a few years ago. Thank you for your friendship. I didn't intend this, but I've noticed a lot more people are willing to talk to me now that I've been seen with you a few times. And if something changes in my life, I'll let you know. But in the meantime, I still want to do things together." Did that sound suggestive? I mean do things as in go to a movie. Not as in get horizontal on the couch.

"Friends it is." He nods, his gaze sliding across the stones in the graveyard.

"You'll invite me to a party again?" I open my door and step out.

"Next week there will be a ticket for you."

I wait until our vehicles part ways at the downtown four-way stop before I call Luke.

"This better be important—it's late."

"Sorry to disturb your beauty sleep, but I have news." I fill him in on what I heard at the party.

"And what do you want to do about it? You've obviously got something up your sleeve, and I have a feeling it's not good."

I should be offended, but I'm not. "How serious are you about seeing this story through?"

He mumbles something then answers. "What do you want, Bella?"

"Be at my house in ten minutes. Park on the dirt road, turn the lights off, and I'll meet you out there."

"You said you were blindfolded. How do you know where we're going?"

"The GPS on my phone."

He pauses so long I think he's gone back to sleep.

"Luke?"

"Wear something dark this time, Kirkwood." And he disconnects.

~~~~~~~~~

"You know we're both probably going to get caught and get grounded for life," I say as I shut myself in Luke's 4Runner.

"I'm okay with that."

He takes in my appearance, making sure I'm not clothed in bright pink. Though I was tempted to wear some sequins just to tick him off.

"How do we know where they'll be out there? And what if they see our flashlights?" I'm suddenly panicked by all these details.

He turns onto the highway, leading us toward Byler, the nearest town. "You should have thought of that before you got me out of bed." His eyes cut to me. "But luckily we have some serious moonlight tonight, so that ought to help some. Let's just hope the wild bears don't get us though. The Oklahoma lakes are just crawling with them."

"What?" And then I see his lips quirk. "Oh, you're hilarious."

"Actually, I think I know which bridge they meant. A train runs through the lake area late at night. It crosses an old bridge. It's so rickety, I don't know how it can hold up a train."

Luke drives on for another few minutes before cutting into a field where a dirt road appears.

"How in the world did you know this road was here?"

Luke lifts a dismissive shoulder. "It's a cool place to take girls."

"If you're a serial killer."

Pulling in behind some trees, Luke turns off the engine and faces me. "Are you ready for this?"

His eyes hold me captive. Why is it easier to look directly at someone in the dark? I blink and glance away. "Let's just get it over with."

We spill out of the SUV, and I follow Luke through knee-high weeds for what seems like an eternity.

Somewhere I hear water lapping, and above us a full moon shines down like a Broadway spotlight just for us.

"We'll have to climb this little hill. Are you up for it?"

I know he's looking at my shoes, expecting me to have worn something totally impractical. I shine my flashlight on my black Diesels. "Don't cry if I beat you to the top, Chief."

Ten minutes later, I'm wishing I had packed snacks. And I need a foot rub. "I think people have climbed Mt. Everest in a shorter amount of time."

"Almost there," he whispers. "We need to turn our flashlights off at this point, Bella."

I flip the switch.

"And you're going to have to take my hand."

"Why?" I squeak.

"Because I know my way around here. You don't. So unless you want to fall down the mountain and give away our cover, I'd grab hold."

I stare at his outstretched hand but can't seem to move.

"Suit yourself. See you at the top."

"No, wait!" I run after him, stumbling on a rock, my body propelled right into his. "*Oomph!*" Ignoring my throbbing ankle and my battered pride, I give him my hand. Which he ignores. "Oh, just take it!" I hiss.

With a hint of a smile, he wraps his fingers around mine and pulls me forward.

I'm out of breath and totally disoriented when he finally stops. "Right over there is the bridge." He points about a hundred feet away.

"And there's some of our fearless football players." I watch as their own flashlights illuminate Dante, his friend Adam, a few guys I don't know, and— "Oh my gosh. That's Matt. What is he doing?"

"Looks like he's drinking."

"He doesn't drink."

"Does he jump off bridges?"

I rub my eyes and strain to get a closer look. "Are they tying a bungee cord to the bridge?" In the distance a train sings a warning. My heart triples in beat. "This is his initiation I heard them talking about." I can't believe he caved in to their pressure. Lindy would die if she knew this.

"That train is really close." Luke's voice is a soft breeze near my ear. "They're insane. I still don't get the thought behind this."

"I don't think we ever will. Oh, I can't watch." But yet I'm powerless to look away.

"They're tying his feet to the cord."

It's everything I can do not to call out to Matt. *Please don't do this. Don't do this.*

God, keep him safe. I don't want to watch him crack his head open or see him ripped apart by a train. We have to stop the football team once and for all—before there's another casualty.

The train's whistle grows louder, closer. Its cry seems to bounce off the water and echo.

Matt stands motionless as his teammates move away from him, walking off the bridge.

"Why are they leaving him? Why isn't he moving?" *Go, Matt!* The train's lights come into view. "Why isn't he moving?"

"It's like a game of chicken. He won't jump until the train's right on him." Luke's so close I can feel his heart beat.

"He could be killed."

"That's the point."

I stare transfixed as the train makes its presence known. The whistle blasts into the night. The wheels beat a rhythm on the tracks. Closer. Closer.

I can't breathe.

Can't move.

Jump, Matt.

He watches it. I can't see his face, but surely he's petrified. I'm about to puke, so Matt's got to be at least a little nervous.

The locomotive barrels down the tracks, its urgent whistle a signal of danger, warning.

Almost there.

Closer.

Feet away from him.

It's going to hit him!

And Matt swan dives off the bridge.

Without thinking, I shine my flashlight on the water. Luke grabs me by the arms and rips the light out of my grip. "We have to go. Go!" He pushes me away from the ledge, toward the trail.

"Did they see us?" I'm panting to keep up with his pace. His hand is a vice on mine.

What if I've blown our cover?

Raised voices float on the wind behind us. They're coming. How did they catch up to us so fast? Did they just leave Matt hanging?

"Run faster, Bella!"

"I can't!" Pushing off the ground with my feet, my calves are groaning for rest. I was made for shopping, not running! I struggle to keep my balance on the downward slope.

Luke's grip tightens, and he pulls harder on my arm. Ow. Does he think inflicting pain is going to magically make me go faster?

He zigzags us through a wooded area, different from the way we came. I know it's a matter of time before I trip over something and fall like a girl in a cheesy horror movie. So unoriginal.

"Bella, we've got some distance between us, but it won't be long." Luke's barely out of breath. It's insulting. I'm sweating right through my Soft & Dri.

Though the guys are still a ways back there, it sounds like a herd of elephants stampeding the hill.

"Don't let up until you're in the car. You got that?"

Can't talk. Sucking air.

"Bella, I'm going to need you to trust me to get us out of this. Can you do that?" He doesn't wait for my response. "Go!" he commands as we break through the trees, his 4Runner in sight. I push my remaining energy into sprinting for the door. We jump into the seats, and Luke locks the doors and turns the key. Pushing buttons on his iPod, he suddenly makes a slow country song pour out the speakers.

"What is that?" I say, holding my panting chest. "Pick your music later. Let's get out of here. They're going to be here any minute."

Luke shakes his head, his expression grim. "No time. It's inevitable they'll see this vehicle. So they can't see it tearing out of here."

In the side mirror I spot three of them, their faces shining in the moonlight. They're running right for us. I grab Luke's arm. "Do something! What's your plan?"

He crushes me to him. "This." His mouth hovers over mine. "You said you'd trust me." And his lips cover mine in a kiss. I tense in shock. One muscular arm slides around my back, the other around my head. He deepens the kiss, and I feel myself falling into it. The voices outside grow louder. Their steps, closer. Yet it becomes background noise, a distant thought, as Luke leans into me.

He shifts and frames my face with his hands. I sigh into his kiss and let my fingers thread through his soft, dark hair.

"It's just a couple making out."

"Who is that?"

"Who knows. Let's go. Keep looking."

Seconds, minutes, hours later, Luke pulls away. He rests his forehead on mine and exhales slowly. "They're gone."

My brain spins. My lips tingle. Heart somersaults. "Hmmm? Who?"

He removes his hands and leans back into his seat. With a curious glance at me, he starts the engine. "Thanks for, um . . . playing along. It saved us."

I blink a few times. "Right." I stare at my lap. "Good plan." *Good kisser.*

"We should probably stay here just a few more minutes to throw them off." He changes the song to some upbeat number about a man and his tractor. "So the Brotherhood has initiations." His fingers comb through his hair—the same hair my hands were in seconds ago. "We know these things happen at parties, when everyone else is occupied. What else?"

"Huh? Oh ... um, we know that ..." *My editor kisses like a movie star.* "These extreme sports feats probably had something to do with Zach Epps's injury and Carson Penturf's death. And there's a pressure to not only join and participate, but to keep your mouth shut." The fog in my head begins to evaporate. "We've got to talk to Reggie Lee. We could have the power to clear his name."

"You could. You're the one who overheard the conversation in the woods tonight."

Luke puts the car in reverse and pulls us onto the path. We continue the rest of the drive in silence, each lost in our own thoughts. I toss the facts around in my head. They're all in pieces, like a jigsaw puzzle. So close I can see the big picture, but still not enough there to completely connect.

And I realize I haven't thought about Hunter in days. There have been a couple calls this week. Some texts. An e-mail or two. But he's been so wrapped up in his world. And I've been wrapped up in—well, a few minutes ago, my editor.

The car stops on my dirt road. Luke turns, holds me with his stare. "Bella, I ..." His eyes look as dark as the sky. "I'll, um ... see you tomorrow."

I nod and fumble for the door handle. "Right." My foot tangles in my purse straps. "Bye." I jump out and run to the porch.

Letting myself in the house, I close the door so quietly even I can't hear it. I tiptoe through the entryway and pass the living room.

A light flares to life.

"Good evening, Bella." Jake sits in his recliner and consults his watch. "Or I guess I should say good morning."

chapter thirty-three

~~~~~~

My alarm goes off, and I shove it to the floor. "Shut. Up." So tired. I've been asleep less than five hours. The events of last night play in my fogged head like a bad movie reel. The party, the bridge, the make-out session with Luke.

Jake's lecture.

I jerk the blankets over my head and try to block out the images. But I'm right back there. Jake sitting in his chair. His face blank but his eyes cautious, untrusting.

"Do you want to tell me what you're doing sneaking in and out of the house?"

"I haven't been drinking. I promise."

"That's not what I asked."

He stared me down with a gaze that he probably reserves for his toughest opponents.

I shook my head. "I had to go back to the party. It's for the paper." I held up my hand to stop him. "No, I'm serious. I can't tell you what it's about, but it's big."

"So's being grounded until you're thirty."

"You could send me back to New York City."

He closed his eyes for a second. "Bella, you know that's not going to happen. Your mother loves you. She wants you right here with her. And whether you care or not, I want you living with our family too."

I twisted my hair around my finger. "I know this looks bad. I just got *ungrounded*, so you *know* I wouldn't do anything to get myself in trouble again so soon." *No, I'd totally wait a few more weeks under normal circumstances.*

"Are you in trouble?"

I considered this. "No. But people are in danger. That's all I can tell you."

"I have to tell your mother."

"You can't!"

"You've put me in a bad position here. Do you realize that?"

"Yes, but—something big's going on at school. People have already gotten hurt. I just need some time. If this situation comes out now, it's over. We've helped no one. Could you wait to tell Mom? Maybe a week or two?" *Or twenty.*

"Sometimes you want to trust a person, but you can't. Right now, you're not in a position to be trusted."

"And you are?" I snapped. "If anybody knows about keeping secrets, I would think you would understand."

"I guess secrets are okay for you but not for the rest of us?"

"Fine, wake Mom up. Let her know what a horrible daughter she has." I walked away, my stomach tied in a triple knot.

His voice stopped me on the first step. "If you know people are in jeopardy, that they could get hurt, you have to tell me what's going on."

I turned back and studied his face over my shoulder. And I felt that pull. That small voice whispering to go against logic and blab it all.

"Jake . . ." I moved back into the light. "I messed up when I first came here. There wasn't a person at Truman High who didn't hate me. But now . . . now I have the chance to change that. I have a purpose for possibly the first time in my life. And I have to follow it, I think . . ." I chewed on my bottom lip and let revelation and acceptance wash over me. "I think I'm in the midst of my purpose here, you know? This is my time. For whatever reason, I've been given a giant task, and I have to see it through. People are counting on me."

My stepdad's silence stretched for an eternity. Finally he nodded. "Okay."

"Okay?"

"I'm going to go against my gut here and trust you—for two weeks. Then we tell your mom and both of us will suffer the consequences."

I would've rushed over and hugged him, but Jake and I—we're not really on hugging terms yet. "Thank you. I know it makes no sense. But you're doing the right thing."

He did not look convinced.

And then four and a half hours later my alarm went off like a tornado siren. I still can't believe he's not going to rat me out. Makes no sense. But then, lately, what does?

Down in the kitchen, Mom reads a parenting magazine while chewing on a piece of toast. Her Sugar's uniform sits stiff and starched on her slender frame.

"What in the world is wrong with you? You look like you've been up all night." She jumps up to pour me a glass of juice.

"Um, nothing. I'm fine. Just didn't get much sleep." I scrutinize every line and movement of her face to see if her husband has spilled the beans.

"Jake said you offered to help with tonight's wrestling party." She wraps her arms around me. "I'm so glad."

"What?" I never agreed to that.

"He told me this morning. Said you two discussed it after I went to bed last night."

My juice hitches in my throat. "Oh. That. Right. Yeah, can't wait to help." He didn't mention there were strings attached to our deal. I have a game I need to go to. Football players to watch. People to stalk!

"Well, this will wake you up." She pulls out the chair next to mine. "I know you've been really upset over losing Moxie."

Still hurts. Thanks for bringing it up.

"So . . ." She shoves a piece of paper across the table. "I got you a ticket to New York. And since you had such a good time with Lindy, I got her one too. You girls leave tomorrow morning."

I hold on to the ticket like it's a Tiffany diamond. "I'm going to New York!" I jump up and down, forgetting my lack of sleep, forgetting my problems. Now I can surprise Hunter at the Autumn Ball. This is perfect. I can see Mia. And Dad.

A plan percolating in my head, I run upstairs to text Mia.

Have big news. Call me later.

~~~~~~~~~~

"Shrimp puff? Cucumber sandwich? Mini quiche?" I glide through the room, carrying a serving tray of hors d'oeuvres to men who could crush me with one hand.

"Thank you, little darlin'. I love the light hint of oregano on the quiche." This from a man whose wrestler name is Breath of Death. "And I love your t-shirt. If I'm not mistaken, that's a Tory Burch, right?"

I think I've stepped onto another planet. "Yes, it is." I walk away before the six-foot-seven dude starts giving me makeup advice.

About thirty wrestlers and their wives mingle with a few reporters from the local papers, plus a journalist from the Channel 5 news. Mom knows how to throw a party. And how to recruit some PR. She did it all the time for her charities.

"What are they saying about my garlic hummus?" Dolly asks as I enter the kitchen for a reload.

"One guy said it's better than a pile driver, but I have no idea what that means."

She shakes her big blonde head. "Wrestler talk." A shadow of a smile passes her face.

"You miss it, don't you?"

"Of course not. I got so sick of hearing about wrestling back in the day. That's all Mickey did was live, eat, and work wrestling. And now that he's a trainer, it's probably even worse."

"He's been watching you all night."

"Has not." Her cheeks burn a suspicious pink. "Well, if he has, it's because I've had a plate of food in my hands every time he sees me."

"You should go talk to him."

"I'm busy, Bella. Now go push the sausage balls. I made too many."

"How long has it been since you spoke?"

"To the sausage balls?"

"To your ex-husband." I sit down and rest my feet.

She rearranges some perfectly lined up fruit on a tray. "The day he left. We let our lawyers do the talking after that. Not that there was much to say. He walked away and left it all behind. And I mean *all*. Didn't fight for a thing."

Including Dolly, I guess.

"But that was a long time ago. We're different people now with different lives."

"You live in the same town though."

"Big enough to avoid someone." She dusts off her hands on her apron. "Speaking of avoiding someone, if I were you, I wouldn't avoid *that*." She wiggles her brows.

I turn around and there stands Luke, leaning in the doorway, his shoulder resting on a cabinet.

"What are you doing here?" I feel my own face flaming. He and I pretty much ignored each other all day, even in class. It's hard to make out with someone at night then face him in the light of day— when it was all for show.

Dolly takes my tray and heads back out into the sea of over-stuffed men, leaving me and Luke. Together. Alone.

"I was invited. Your mom called to see if the school paper would cover it. I saw the other media. She seems to have covered all her bases."

Now that Mom knows about Jake's wrestling, she's his biggest promoter.

"I talked to Reggie Lee. He's agreed to meet us later tonight if you can get away. He wanted to talk Saturday night, but I thought I heard you tell someone today that you're leaving for New York." His chiseled face is expressionless.

"Thanks. I'm glad you did that—included me. I know you could've met him this weekend on your own."

He smiles. "We're partners."

Awkward! Awkward! Why can't I get over this weird feeling? He doesn't seem to be fazed by it. Maybe he makes out with girls all the time in the name of a good story.

"So are you looking forward to going back home?"

Home. I feel more disconnected from my friends and family in New York than ever. Mia has yet to call. Dad said he'd have to work this weekend. It's like I'm slowly transitioning to Truman. I'm not sure if that's a good thing or not.

"Bella?"

"Oh, home. Yeah, I'm excited to see my dad, my best friend." And just in case Mr. Arrogance thinks I now pine for him, take *this* "And my boyfriend, of course. I'm surprising him."

Luke has the nerve to continue smiling. "I'm sure everyone will be glad to see you." He pushes away from the cabinet. "I'd better get to work. Hey, pretty cool your stepdad's a wrestler."

"Yeah, about as cool as him making maxi-pads."

Three hours later, there's not a shrimp puff or melon ball left. I don't know about their skills on the mat, but those wrestlers are champion eaters.

"Iron Skull, are you sure you have to go?" my mom asks the final one making his retreat out the front door.

"Oh yeah, Mrs. Finley. That bean dip ought to be kicking in any moment now."

Nice. Maybe he should go by Noxious Gas. Or the Deadly Farter.

"So, Robbie, what did you think about all that?"

I startle at Luke's voice behind me. I thought he had left with the rest of the press.

Robbie scratches his head. "Well, I think tonight we had an

example of mankind laying aside their differences, not to mention their stage makeup, and coming together in unity. It shows that peace is attainable. They are a model to our brothers and sisters in the Middle East."

I pat Robbie on his scruffy head. "He's had a lot of Mountain Dew tonight."

Mickey balances a stack of plates and heads toward the kitchen.

"Excuse me." I leave Luke's company to seek out Dolly, scrubbing down the table in the dining room.

"Um . . . could you give me some help in the kitchen?"

Her hand pauses. "Sure, kid. What do you need?"

I don't answer but walk away, grateful when she follows.

I hear her intake of breath when she sees her ex-husband standing at the sink. He turns around. Frowns.

"Well, hey, Mickey!" My voice is overly bright, even to my own ears. "What a nice guy, doing the dishes. Isn't that nice of him, Dolly?"

Her overshadowed eyes narrow. "Oh, he's a real sweetheart."

Hurt flashes on his face. He turns around and attacks a platter with a scrub brush.

Dolly plants a hand on her curvy hip. "Get out of my kitchen, Mickey."

"I believe it's the Finleys' kitchen. *You* get out."

Her mouth drops. "I'm the caterer tonight. You're just . . . just . . . the—"

"Manager?" He points a sudsy brush at her. "That's never been good enough for you, has it? *I've* never been good enough."

"You leave me out of your inferiority complex. Don't you put that on me. I always supported you."

"As long as I worked eight to five. You wanted me to have a desk job—admit it. You hated my late hours."

"Late hours?" Her voice explodes in the tiny kitchen. "There's a difference in working late now and then and *never* being home for your family."

Just when I expect Mickey to match her volume and snap back with a comment, he closes his mouth. And stares at the floor. The gross linoleum floor.

"I have regrets, Dolly. Don't think I don't."

"Yeah, well, is leaving your family one of them?"

Thunderclouds roll behind his eyes. His expression is so pained, I find myself stepping back toward the door.

"I killed my family."

Dolly's breath hitches. "*I* was your family too. Maybe I needed you." A tear glides down her cheek. "An accident killed our daughters, Mickey. Pulling the plug on our marriage is what I could never forgive you for." She throws down her rag and rushes out, her heels an angry staccato on the floor.

Mickey watches her go. After a moment his troubled eyes rest on me. "I tend to ruin parties." He forces a smile. "I'm not very good at Scrabble either."

"You were driving the car the day your daughters were killed." It's not really a question. But it's also not something I meant to say out loud.

"Yup." He runs a big hand over his stubbly face.

"Don't tell me that's the first time you two have talked about it."

"I kind of disappeared after the accident." The dishwater covers his arms as he returns to cleaning. "I'm not proud of that. I couldn't stand to look at myself, and even worse, I didn't want to see myself through her eyes."

"It was an accident."

He hands me a bowl and a dry towel. "I was driving. I walked away with barely a scratch. My little girls never woke up." His voice is hoarse, raw. He hands me another dish to dry.

"What happened?"

"Ice. It was a bad winter. An eighteen-wheeler lost control, and I swerved to miss him. We spun into the median on the highway." Mickey laughs, a sound as bitter as a rotten grape. "I had a match that weekend. I was mad because Dolly'd been called into a second shift and asked me to watch the girls and not go to the gym. But training came first, and I put them in the car and drove us to Byler so I could get my workout in. So even if my driving didn't kill them, my priorities did."

"That's not true, Mickey." I feel my *Ask Miss Hilliard* instincts kicking in. "You heard Dolly say she doesn't hold you responsible. She forgives you. Maybe it's time to forgive yourself."

He flings the water off his hands. "Nothing's going to bring them back, Bella." Then he looks at me with that expression that says, *Why am I talking to a kid?*

"Mickey, wait—"

But he's gone. I sigh and rub the tension building in the back of my neck.

"Why is it people want to pour their hearts out to you?"

Luke.

"Why is it you like to eavesdrop on my conversations?"

"My reporter's intuition led me here."

"You heard Dolly yelling."

He shrugs. "Something like that." Luke removes my hand from my neck and replaces it with his own. "Got some tension, Counselor Bella?"

My skin tingles at his touch, and I'm reminded of our lip-locking moment. This boy is so maddening. Frustrating. Confusing.

His magic fingers stop, and he turns around.

When I see his face, disappointment swishes in my stomach. He looks totally bored. Not that I like him, but where's the look of burning passion he's unable to contain? Where's the look that says, *Bella, I admire you from afar—your face, your scent, your growing journalistic abilities that could one day rival mine. Where is that?* Instead his face says, *When my hands were on you, I was doing long division in my head.* How dare he look bored!

"Are you ready to meet Reggie Lee? Bella—did you hear me?"

"Huh? Oh yeah, let me grab my purse." I should be packing instead of talking to former football players in secret. I run upstairs to get my bag. My eyes automatically go to my bed, where Moxie should be lying. But she's not.

Outside Luke waits for me in his 4Runner. He doesn't even glance my way as I snap myself into the seat belt. His car smells like his cologne, and I stop myself from breathing too deeply.

"Where are we going?" I ask when Luke turns toward Tulsa.

"We're meeting him at the Cherokee Waffle House."

"Sounds very classy."

Luke shoots down my every attempt at conversation with monosyllable responses until I'm forced to quit talking. Just to be obnoxious, I try to sing along to each tune on the radio. And since it's a country station, I know absolutely none of the songs. So I just make up the words. He ignores me anyway.

The interior of the SUV is illuminated as he pulls into the restaurant's parking lot. Through the glass windows I see tired truckers and mostly old men taking up the seats.

Inside we're greeted by the smell of twenty-four-hour breakfast. And though the interior leaves a lot to be desired, decked out in every Indian whatnot ever made, the food smells heavenly. I didn't have time to eat a single crumb at the party.

I slide into a booth across from Luke and open a sticky menu.

A slender African-American girl stops at our table. She pops a pink bubble. "Are y'all from around here?"

"Truman," Luke answers.

She nods. "So what can I get you?"

My eyes scan the choices. "Belgian waffles with strawberries, please."

For the first time all night, Luke smiles. "Me too." Guess he didn't get to eat either.

We both watch the door for the next hour.

I pick at my last bite of waffle. "He's not coming."

"No. He's not."

We pay and then walk into the muggy night air toward the 4Runner.

"Hey!" The waitress walks out of a side door. She hurries to us. "You're here to meet Reggie, aren't you?"

"Yes. Do you know where he is?" Luke asks.

She looks behind her, as if she's afraid someone's watching. "He couldn't make it."

I step closer to her. "Who are you?"

"His girlfriend. And I think you guys should leave all this alone. Reggie's been through enough. He just wants to move on."

"But what if we could prove that the drugs in his locker weren't his?"

She casts a wary eye at Luke. "It doesn't matter. They'll come after him another way." She shakes her head. "It's over. It's done. He wasn't responsible for Zach Epps's accident."

I startle. "What? Who said he was?"

"I have to go."

"Wait!" Nothing like chasing someone in a parking lot. "Wait!" I catch her at the side door.

"They're like a high school mafia, okay?" Her breathing is ragged, her eyes wild. "You don't know what they'll do. For your own sakes and Reggie's, stay out of this."

"We can't." I read her name tag. "Marissa, one person's dead, one's on life-support. How many more have to be hurt before someone's willing to speak up?"

Her hand pauses on the door handle. "The Brotherhood has its own MySpace page. Only the members can access it. But every initiation is recorded."

This doesn't surprise me. In fact, I should've thought of it. Even serious gangs post videos of their beat-ins, shootings, and initiations. The question is . . . how can we access a MySpace page that's set to private?

"Reggie was racing Zach Epps the night of the accident, wasn't he?"

Her mad stare is the only response.

"Please, you have got to tell Reggie to come forward and talk to the police. Zach lost his life that night."

She wrenches open the door. "He may not be on life-support, but that night . . . Reggie lost his life too."

chapter thirty-four

～～～～～～～～～～～

J saw you on *E!* last night, Dad. How did the pitch go for the new show?" I lurch forward as my dad slams on his brakes for the zillionth time. New York City traffic—there's nothing like it. I'd rather drive behind a slow tractor in Truman any day over this madness.

He zips into the other lane and honking ensues. "I don't know. Budgets are tight right now. They're not sure if they want to invest in a new show about another high-profile plastic surgeon. I have another meeting with my agent today."

Though she's seen it once, Lindy's nose is pushed against the window like she can't get enough of Manhattan. I know the feeling. It's like a new town every time you see it—even if you live here.

When we get to the house, Luisa crushes me in a hug worthy of a wrestler. "I've missed you, Isabella!" She pulls away, her pudgy hands clasping my face. "Let me look at you. Oh, Oklahoma agrees with you."

"Do I smell homemade chocolate chip cookies?"

"Chips Ahoy! are for losers," Luisa says, ushering the three of us into the kitchen.

"I have to get to my meeting. Here's my credit card." Dad hands over his Visa. "Don't go crazy with it, okay?"

"We do have an Autumn Ball to crash. Might need to buy a dress or two."

He kisses me on the temple. "I'll see you tonight."

An hour later Lindy and I are in shopping nirvana.

Well, I am.

"No, Bella. I don't like the strapless look. Are you sure I can even go to this party?"

"Of course." I throw the pink concoction over the dressing room door anyway. "We're just dropping by. I can't *wait* for the look on Hunter's face when he sees me. Lindy, *why* is this green thing in the try-on stack?"

Her hesitant voice comes from the other side of the door. "I liked it."

"I said no. Green is a color on its way out. You don't want to be *this year*."

"What year do I want to be?"

I hand her another gown. Still so much to learn.

The door creaks, and Lindy steps out into the small hall. I twirl my finger and she spins in front of the mirror.

"I can't wear this." She tugs on the sliding bodice. "I feel naked."

"It's a very conservative dress. Lindy, I know fashion, and that dress is *it*."

She sighs and casts a longing glance at the green dress lumped in the pile. "Green is my favorite color. Matches my eyes."

"But this dress shows off your curves, your toned shoulders. And it's so trendy."

Lindy's gaze meets mine in the full-length mirror. "Are you afraid I'm going to embarrass you? Is that it?"

"No, of course not." Right? I like Lindy for who she is. She simply needs some guidance. "I just think you should leave the clothing decisions to me."

"It's your dad's Visa. Your party." She pulls on her top once more and returns to the dressing room.

Oh, fine. I toss the green frock over. "Try it on."

She squeals, and twenty seconds later she prances before the mirror again, her face beaming.

"How do you feel in that dress?" As if I have to ask.

White teeth sparkle against her tanned complexion. "Comfortable."

"The old green dress it is."

We have lunch at Le Cirque, sitting beneath the big-top light shade hanging from the ceiling. The food is heavenly, but Lindy calls them "snobby" portions. She refuses dessert—the fabulous Le Cirque chocolate—and acts relieved when we leave.

Later that evening, I study my new manicure and wonder how Lindy is getting along upstairs with her makeup. Dad reads through his e-mails beside me.

Luisa enters the kitchen and clears her throat. "Presenting . . . Miss Lindy Miller!"

She sashays into room, almost floating above the marble tile.

The queen has arrived.

The three of us clap for her as she spins, her green dress billowing.

"You girls are going to have a great time." Dad hands me my

clutch from the counter. "Both of you look fabulous. And believe me, I know fabulous."

This is true. He sells it every day.

In the car, Lindy grows quiet beside me. I can feel the nervousness radiating off her like static electricity.

My phone beeps and I check the message. It's from Hunter.

The party is so dull without U. Miss U. Wish U were here.

I laugh and show Lindy. "I can't wait to see him." She doesn't even crack a smile. "Lindy, relax. We're going to have such a good time."

"I love the dress, and I appreciate the hair, the nails. But, Bella, this is your world. Not mine. I'm more of a Yankees-and-hot-dog kind of girl."

"We'll do that next time, okay?" I grab her hand and squeeze. "If Matt could see you now—he'd be speechless. You seriously look hot."

That coaxes her mouth into a smile. "But is it me? Sometimes I look in the mirror—at the highlights, the famous label clothes—and it's like I'm looking at someone else. Like I'm a phony."

"Everyone's got another side to him . . . even your Matt Sparks."

The car stops, and Dad's chauffeur turns around. "We're here, miss."

I pull Lindy out, instructing her all the way on how to depart a vehicle in the most delicate manner. It's like sometimes the girl forgets she's not in basketball shorts. No need to give someone a free peep show, you know?

Music spills out into the lobby of the Broadway Park Hotel. A few of my former teachers greet me, and I introduce Lindy.

Soon old friends swarm, and I lose sight of Lindy in all the chaos.

"How's Oklahoma? Is it hideous?"

"Do you have to shop at Kmart?"

"Have you gone cow tipping?"

"Oh, I can't imagine what you've been going through."

I don't even have time to respond to any of the questions. As soon as I open my mouth to defend my new home, somebody asks something even more ridiculous.

"Lindy?" I shout over the voices. "Lindy!"

I see her hand wave in the back.

"Excuse me—excuse me." She pushes her way through.

"Girls, you remember my good friend Lindy from Truman, right?" Soon Lindy is being peppered with questions.

"Hey," I whisper in her ear. "I'm just going to slip away for a bit and find Hunter. I won't leave you alone for long."

Six songs later, I'm still searching for my boyfriend. Not only are there tons of people here, but at least half of them stop me to catch up.

When I've exhausted every spot in the ballroom, I notice French doors leading outside to a courtyard. The sparkle of tiny white lights strung from the trees lures me outside. I breathe in the night air and look to the sky.

No stars. They must all be in Oklahoma.

I breeze through the courtyard, finding nothing but random couples using the benches to make out.

Time to go back in. Hunter would definitely not be out here.

I stop and catch of flash of something familiar. "Mia?" I can't control my laughter. Mia has a boyfriend and didn't even tell me!

And from the looks of things, it's serious. "Mia!" I'm on limited time here, so I tap my finger on her shoulder, shamelessly interrupting her interlude.

She comes up for air, her face now in the light. "Oh! Bella!" She jumps to cover the object of her affection.

But it's too late.

"Hunter?"

He all but falls off the bench. "Bella, I can explain."

"With the same mouth you used to kiss my best friend?"

He pushes Mia aside and grabs me. "You don't understand. It's been so lonely here without you. And then Mia and I have been working closely on this dance . . . and things just happened. It means nothing though, Bella."

"You're right." My glare could melt a polar ice cap. "It does mean nothing. We're over, Hunter. You never intended to make this work." I turn on Mia. "Neither one of you did. I've done all the calling, all the e-mailing. It took me leaving New York to see how much I really meant to both of you, to see what our relationships were truly made of."

"You didn't make it easy," Hunter says.

"Yes, I can see how rough it's been on you both."

Mia finally finds her tongue. "Every time I did call you, it was Truman this and Truman that. And all about people I didn't know or care about, like that Lindy girl. I mean, seriously, Bella." She crinkles her nose. "You come to see us and you bring *her*. She doesn't fit in with us. And maybe you don't either anymore."

"Of course I fit in here. This is still my home." *Isn't it?* "I walk out in that ballroom and see hundreds of *my* friends. And as for Lindy, she's got more class in her little finger than you've got in your entire *closet!* Just because she doesn't hide behind designer clothes and her daddy's checkbook."

Mia laughs. "Oh, you're a fine one to talk!"

"Um, I think we *were* talking about the fact that my best friend and my boyfriend are cheating on me. So can we get back to the topic at hand, where I was telling you what *skanks* you are?" Voices murmur behind me, and without even looking I can tell there's a crowd gathering. *Good. Bring it.*

Mia stomps closer in her Louboutin heels. "We don't like the new you, Bella." She crosses her arms and looks to Hunter for support. "There. I said it—even if no one else will. You talk about school all the time, you act like our world isn't important, your charity case friend looks like a cabbage in her dress . . . and you have roots."

Giggles erupt behind me. I spin on my heel, only to see Lindy standing there. Tears stream down her cheeks. She shakes her head and runs back into the ballroom.

My fists clench at my sides. "I don't even *know* you people! And if I have changed, I'm glad. Because if the old me acted anything like you, Mia, then thank God He moved me to Oklahoma. I'd rather be real any day than be whatever it is you think *you* are." I take one last glance at my boyfriend. "You can have him, Mia. You two deserve each other." I walk off but throw one final shot over my shoulder. "You should probably know he has a Lifetime fetish. He cries during *Golden Girls.*"

I pick up my pace until I'm running through the dance floor, searching frantically for Lindy. The crowd swallows me, and I shove through couple after couple before I break through and locate the exit.

But no Lindy.

I call her phone, but the only response I get is her voice mail. Where could she be? She can't just leave by herself. This is New York, for crying out loud. Not Small Town, Oklahoma.

I question a few adults in the lobby. Two people think they saw a girl in a green dress leave.

I jog to the parking lot and call out her name. No response.

After a brief survey of the rest of the hotel common areas, I give up and call my dad's chauffeur. I can't wait to get out of this place. And far away from my "friends."

The ride home stretches forever as I sit alone in the backseat. I don't even tell the driver good-bye as I tear into the apartment, yelling for my dad.

"He's not here, Miss Bella." Luisa wipes her hands on her apron, her face wrinkled in concern.

"Where is he? Lindy's missing. She just left the party." I shake my head, trying to dislodge the image of her horrified face.

"She's upstairs. Packing. She took a cab."

My sigh of relief could probably be heard from Jersey. "We've had a horrible night." I take the stairs two at a time, a shoe in each hand. "Lindy!"

Out of breath, I shove open my door and find Lindy throwing clothes in a suitcase.

"I hate them," she says.

"Lindy, I'm sorry. They were hideous."

She glances at my ceiling. "I meant them." She points to the demonic cherubs. "They weird me out. I never told you that. But I thought as long as we're all being honest tonight, I'd share."

I sit down on the queen-size bed. My dress fans around me and covers the ghastly comforter. "I'm so sorry. They don't know you,

Lindy. Please tell me you didn't believe a word of what they said."

Tears glisten in her eyes. "You tried to stop me from getting the dress." She runs a hand over the skirt. "I still like it though."

"Of course you do. And it looks great on you."

"They said I looked like a cabbage."

"You most definitely do not resemble any vegetable. They're just jealous. Jealous of your toned biceps. And jealous of our friendship."

"I'm not your charity case though." She unzips her dress as she stomps into the bathroom. She returns in her sweats and a ball cap, then tosses the dress on the bed. "Maybe you can take it back. Otherwise I'll pay you for it. I'll pay for all of it."

"Don't be silly. You're not paying for anything." I laugh and swallow some bitterness. "My dad loves doing that sort of thing—especially when it gets him off the hook for spending time with me."

"Oh, I feel *much* better." She yanks the zipper around her suitcase.

"Please don't do this. Don't go." I hop off the bed and sit next to her bag.

"I have to get out of here. I want to go back home, to Truman. Luisa got me a late flight. I'm not staying here. I can't be around you people any longer."

"I'm not like them. I'm not."

"Are you sure about that?" Lindy closes her eyes for a moment, then her words come out slow and steady. "I may have embarrassed you tonight, but you know what? I embarrassed myself—for trying to be something I'm not." She heaves her suitcase up and charges toward the door. "And I'm done with it."

chapter thirty-five

$\mathcal{I}$'ve lost my boyfriend. Lost my best friend. Lost Lindy. And the only one worth fighting for is sitting on a bleacher watching the Truman Tigers practice on this Monday afternoon.

"Hey." I sit a few feet away from Lindy, my eyes fixed on the field. "I've been looking everywhere for you." I've spent the entire hour I've been home searching for this girl, praying our friendship isn't over.

"Didn't know I was lost." Her monotone does nothing to inspire hope.

Coach Lambourn blows his whistle. "Jared, snap the ball. Is it really that hard? Do you need to sit on the bench Friday night until you've mastered the fundamentals?"

I wince at Jared's public humiliation. His stepbrother, Coach Dallas, watches the exchange with a smile. Jerk.

Minutes later, the whistle is blown again. "Coach Dallas," the father yells. "Take my starters here and work them over until they're ready to be state champs."

"That's my specialty." Jared's stepbrother escorts them to the other side of the field and shoves Dante forward, and the group begins to jog the perimeter.

I return my attention to Lindy. "I know you're mad at me. And maybe you've decided to totally write me off. But before you do, I have something to say."

"No." She holds up a hand. "Me first. Do you know what I've decided?"

I shield my eyes from the harsh sunlight. "You think a liar like Hunter is bound for a future in politics?"

"No."

"You think I'm the worst thing that's ever happened to Truman?"

"That would be the Miss Truman pageant of 2007. We had our first transvestite in the competition—lots of back hair." She shudders at the memory. "No, I think I'm going back to being me." She reaches down and dusts a speck from her Nike running shoe. "If I have to be someone else to impress Matt Sparks, then I don't want him. I don't want to look in the mirror six months from now and see one of your New York friends staring back at me. I don't want to care whose name is on my shirt label."

I'm guessing it's Adidas.

"I don't want to throw out a perfectly good pair of shoes just because they went out of style two months ago. Or judge someone because they'd rather shop at Payless instead of Prada."

"You're exactly right."

"What?"

"You're right. I tried to make you into one of *them*. And that's not you. Lindy, Matt likes you for who you are, inside and out. I think you should just tell him how you feel and come clean with it. And if he doesn't realize what amazing girlfriend material you are, then it's his loss and he doesn't deserve you. But . . . that doesn't explain why you're out here."

Her eyes return to the field where the boys in the starting lineup look like they could collapse at any minute. "I thought I would catch Matt before practice—talk to him. Tell him how all of this"—she lifts a piece of her highlighted hair—"had been for him. But, Bella, I think I've decided to just leave it alone. More than anything in the last few weeks, I've missed my *friend* Matt. I'm not ready to risk losing him permanently if he doesn't feel the same way."

"Are you sure? I have a few other boy-winning strategies in my repertoire."

A corner of her mouth lifts. "Two days ago you witnessed your boyfriend pawing your best friend. No offense, but your advice isn't worth much right now."

I laugh. "Fair enough."

Though it still smarts. I can't wait until the image of Hunter and Mia disappears from my brain. I've been on a steady diet of Ben and Jerry's ever since. I tried to smuggle it in on the plane today, but security didn't care about my boyfriend cheating on me. They said my contraband pint of Chunky Monkey was a security risk. Like anyone would ever desecrate a holy carton of Ben and Jerry's by sticking a weapon in it. Please.

"Lindy, I'm sorry for trying to change you. I never thought of you as a charity case. Your makeover was fun for me, but I know I got carried away. I don't want you to be like my New York friends." My *ex*-friends. "This weekend I realized how shallow they all are. I can't believe all they care about is shopping and . . . shopping."

"You know that was you about a month ago, right?"

"I wasn't *that* bad."

She bites her lip. "Um, okay."

"Seriously, was I?"

She elbows me in the ribs. "Let's just say you've grown on me."

I giggle in relief. "Still friends?"

"Yeah." She smiles. "I think we are."

Thirty minutes later my butt has fallen asleep. I don't know why I'm still sitting here watching practice. Not sure what I'm looking for.

"Is Coach Lambourn always that rough on Jared?" Seems all he's accomplished with his practice is demolishing his stepson's self-esteem.

"He's hard on all of them, but I think he expects more from Jared."

"It must be hard to grow up in the shadow of his all-star stepbrother."

She shrugs a shoulder. "I guess. He seems okay with it. Jared loves the sport. It's everything to him. We haven't won state since Coach Dallas's day, so I think everybody's just focused on winning right now. It helps the players get scholarships, and it helps the coaches keep their jobs, especially the newer ones."

Yeah, but at what cost? "So you mean if they didn't win this year, some of the coaches might be fired?"

"Yes. It's just how it is. Their jobs depend on winning seasons."

And how far would Coach Dallas go to keep his job *and* restore the Truman Tigers to their former glory?

When practice is over, Jared Campbell finds me sitting on his hood. I hand him a water bottle. "You look like a thirsty boy." Maybe in time I'll like him as more than a friend.

He takes the bottle and scoots next to me on the car. "Could you have picked a hotter seat?"

I consider telling him I prefer my buns toasted, but decide against it. "Rough practice."

He grimaces. "It always is. What are you up to? Didn't see you in school today."

"I was in New York. And I hear you took a bunch of notes today in English. I thought maybe we could hang out and I could catch up on what I missed in class."

"Now?"

"You don't want to?" I need to get into his house and see if he has access to the Brotherhood's MySpace page.

"Well, yeah, but I'm a disgusting, sweaty mess."

He really is.

"I know," I purr. "We can go to your house, and while you clean up, I'll jot down the notes. Then you can fill me in on everything that happened at school today." He looks doubtful. "Don't worry. I won't stay long. I have to babysit my little stepbrother tonight." Surely his password to MySpace is saved. "You'd be doing me a *huge* favor."

"Okay. For you."

"Perfect! I'll follow you." *And maybe your computer will lead me to the proof I need to get Coach Dallas in some very big trouble and end the Brotherhood forever.*

"So I'm going to take a quick shower. Help yourself to the fridge. I'll be out before you can dunk your first Oreo."

"Thanks. I really appreciate it. I'd hate to work on an empty stomach."

He saunters down a hall, and I watch him walk into his bedroom. Tapping my fingernails on the table, I try to take some deep breaths and calm my racing heart. I might not find anything on his computer, but I have to make sure.

When I hear the water start, I get up and tiptoe down the same hall. I stand outside his door and listen. After a minute, I decide he has to be safely in the shower. I peek in his bedroom and, seeing no signs of Jared, I push on the door and creep inside.

My eyes home in on an iMac sitting on a corner desk. *Here we go. Steady now. You can do this.*

I click on his Internet icon and wait for it to load. *Hurry! Hurry!*

When Jared bursts into "Friends in Low Places," I stifle a scream, my heart lodged in my throat, until I realize he's still in the shower. And a really terrible singer.

His home page pulls up, and I see the ESPN logo and a list of game scores. My pulse skittering, I check his favorites. Scanning, scanning. Nothing.

I type in "MySpace.com."

"What are you doing?"

I jump like a cat, my hands clutching the chair.

Coach Dallas stands in the doorway. His meanest coach's stare is trained on me, and I can't seem to form a coherent thought.

"I . . . I . . ." *This is bad. This is very bad.* "Your brother is loaning me some notes from class. I was hoping to"—Snap my fingers and disappear. Jump out the window. Ask God for a swarm of locusts—"save some time and use his computer to type them up." I hold up my French-tipped nails. "A girl can ruin a manicure with all that writing we do in AP English."

"Where is my *stepbrother*?"

Oh, do I detect some fraternal sensitivity?

I jerk my thumb toward the bathroom. "You can't hear his *American Idol* audition in there?"

"So you're in his bedroom while he's in the shower?" His lips quirk.

Yeah. Not only am I a snoop, but I'm a perv too. "I wasn't peeking or anything." *Believe me, all I wanted to see of Jared's was his computer.*

"I guess the rules have changed in this house since I lived here."

Coach Dallas relaxes, and I begin to breathe again.

"What are you two doing?" Jared walks out of the bathroom, a towel knotted at his waist. My face floods with heat. Luke would have a coronary if he knew how badly I was bumbling this.

"I'm sorry, I'm in such a hurry with the babysitting thing," I speak to the general space beside Jared. "So I came up here to see if you had a computer. I was hoping I could type your notes. I can do sixty words per minute." I'm rambling! Boy in towel! Look away! "I think I'll wait in the kitchen." Maybe try to drown myself in the sink. Gouge out my eyeballs with a can opener.

"Don't go anywhere." Jared steps behind the door for a split second then reappears in a pair of shorts. "How did you think you were going to type my notes if I hadn't even given them to you yet?"

I giggle like a space cadet. "I heard singing, and I had to follow the sound. It lured me in here, Jared. Like a siren from the *Odyssey*." Or a scratched CD. "And I thought, 'As long as I'm here, I'll check out his computer.'" My face is as sincere as a TV preacher—though what I'm saying makes absolutely no sense. "If you'll just get me the notes, I'll leave you two alone while I copy them the old-fashioned way in the kitchen." *And get the heck out of here.*

"No, that's okay." Jared's eyes flash for a moment, their usual gentleness replaced with something fierce. "Dallas here was just leaving."

"Actually, I wanted to talk to you for a minute, little *brother.*"

I scoot around the desk chair and pass between the two guys. "I'll just get out of your way."

"No, Bella, wait."

I wave a hand and back out the door. "No problem. Finish your talk." I stop halfway down the hall and listen.

"I have a lot riding on this season."

"That makes two of us," comes Jared's angry voice. "Back off, Dallas."

"If the team goes down, we all go down. The school board will terminate all of the staff, and you won't even get to play as a college walk-on, let alone get a scholarship."

"I know that! You think I don't feel the pressure?"

"Dad's been talking about cutting you from the starters. I've held him off, but I can't much longer."

"Nice to know you care."

"This team's important to me. And to Dad."

Jared laughs, his bitterness obvious. "Winning's important to you two. Not me, not the team. *I* care about the team. *I* care about the players. They're not even people to you—just a means to an end. Quit trying to relive your high school days through me."

I replay this in my head, wanting to store it word for word for Luke. Coach Dallas is so our man. Now I just have to get someone to admit it. To confess and hand over the video files. Maybe one more party with Jared, and he'll let me in. He has no reason to protect a stepbrother he doesn't even like. Especially at the cost of his friends.

Two minutes later Coach Dallas sails through the living room. I wave at him from the kitchen table as he slams the front door behind him. Nice guy, that one.

Jared reappears, this time wearing a shirt. "I'm really sorry about that. Dallas and I aren't exactly best friends."

"So I see. It must be hard to live in a family of two coaches."

"He just doesn't get it. He wants everything to be like it was when he was in school—same plays and everything. He thinks he knows what's best for the team, but he doesn't even know us."

"You know, Jared . . . if you ever want to talk, I'm a great listener." *And snooper.* "And I hear I give some pretty good advice." *And this would all be over if we could go to the police together.*

"Thanks." He hands me a stack of papers. "Your notes *and* an invitation to the Thursday night party."

"You're the best." I smile and clutch the ticket like it's gold. "Is it okay if I just borrow the notes tonight? It's getting late, and I really do need to get home for babysitting duty."

"You seem a little more adjusted with your new family."

I think about this. "I guess I am. Except for one stepbrother. All he cares about is making my life miserable."

Jared nods, a faraway look in his eyes. "Then I guess we have that in common."

chapter thirty-six

~~~~~~

"No friends over. No parties. No leaving for any reason. And keep your eye on Robbie at all times."

"He will not so much as tinkle without my presence," I tell my mom. She and Jake stand on the front porch ready to leave for his amateur wrestling match.

"I do not pee with an audience." Robbie pulls his cape around him, his hero's pride totally insulted.

"Emergency numbers are on the fridge."

"Go, Mom. We'll be fine. Superman here will not escape this time."

"I'm Spiderman tonight."

"What you are is dead meat if you so much as step a foot out of this house." I shut the door behind our parents.

"I know, Dad's already told me. No CNN for a month if I don't obey your every command."

"Oh, really?" I walk into the kitchen, Robbie following my every step. "So if I tell you to clean my toilet with your toothbrush, you're going to do it?"

"I'll clean it with *somebody's* toothbrush."

I grin and open the freezer door. "Mom said you want pizza for dinner." I pull out pepperoni, his favorite. This kid eats nothing that doesn't come from a box.

Robbie grabs a bag of chips off the counter and pulls out a handful as his brother appears. "Hey, Budge." He shoves the whole mess in his mouth. "Want thom pitha?"

"Nah." He runs his hand over Robbie's head. "I gotta go sell some hot dogs. I'm up for a raise this week."

"That's great." I've decided to try with this guy. Maybe I'll win him over with kindness. "You must be the best thing that's ever happened to the Wiener Palace. The, um . . . Chief Wiener must be so proud of you."

Budge takes a potato chip from Robbie's greasy hands. He chews it as he stares at me. "I heard you went to see Kelsey Anderson."

"Yeah. Nice girl." I cut into the plastic wrap on the pizza.

"She said you asked a lot of questions about the accident. What do you hope to gain by digging into that? You can't bring him back." The edge in his voice makes me put down my scissors.

"No, I can't bring him back, Budge." That would take a miracle, and that's God's department. "But I can expose the truth. If he was pressured into racing his car that night, people need to know. And if there are specific people responsible, then they need to be stopped."

His expression is blank, neutral. But for once he's not looking at me with uncontainable venom. Budge nods his red, frizzy head. "Okay."

"Okay?" I have my stepbrother's approval? "Zach never said anything to you about any of the coaches? The football players? Nothing that would help us out?" I slide the pizza in the oven.

"He just talked about being under a lot of stress. People telling him what to do. But then Zach pretty much stopped talking to me last year. He wouldn't admit it, but I think the players made him cut me out. He only hung out with the team—and Kelsey, of course."

"But even she said he had grown really distant."

"You think you can really get to the bottom of this?"

"I'm going to try." I take a step closer to him. "I could use a prayer or two if you want to help."

The anger slips back over his face. "I'm done with that. Take care of my brother." And he walks out, his sultan pants swishing as he goes.

"Bella, there's someone at the door." Robbie chews on a finger-nail. "He looks mad."

That doesn't narrow it down. Who *haven't* I made mad lately?

"Okay, I'm putting you in charge of watching the pizza. Not much longer, maybe ten minutes, and we'll eat."

Robbie throws himself over a chair, his arms drooping to the floor. "I feel my superpowers draining. I need food."

Walking into the entry, I see Luke's brooding face staring back at me through the screen. With a final glance at Robbie, I step onto the porch. "Hey."

"Hey, yourself."

I see his frigid editor ego has returned. Oh, how I missed him. Like a too-tight bra.

"I got your text. You said you visited with Jared tonight and we needed to talk."

"Yeah, I tried to check his computer to see if I could log on to his MySpace." Without taking a pause to breathe, I fill him in on everything that happened. "And that's when his brother stormed out." I finish, expecting to see Luke beaming with pride over my efforts.

He pushes off from the porch railing and plants himself directly in front of me. "You were told not to do anything alone. I meant that, Bella Kirkwood."

He really needs to work on his "atta girls."

"I'm not in any danger. I went over to get notes from Jared. I was in his room for a little while, no harm done. I was there less than thirty minutes."

"And just enough time for Coach Dallas to *catch* you pulling up MySpace."

"He didn't see that. Just saw me *on* the computer. No harm done."

"You don't know that."

"And you don't know that harm *was* done. Get over yourself, will you? You're just mad because I took the initiative. If you had a better idea for getting into Jared's computer, I didn't hear it."

"Here's a scenario I don't want to hear: you snooping in his bedroom, and Jared in a towel."

His blue eyes are liquid intensity. I have to turn away from them. "Okay, so it doesn't sound like the most wholesome situation. But it's Jared, come on."

"He's a guy with a girl in his bedroom. He's not to be trusted."

I lean in until my nose is inches from his. "What are you, my dad?"

"No, I'm . . . I'm . . ." He crushes his hair with a hand. "I'm your editor. And I'm still in charge of this project."

"It's *my* story."

"Not at this rate. I warned you once, Bella."

"I'm not some underling you can boss around. We don't have time to waste. If I have the means, what's wrong with me taking some initiative and getting some information? The sooner we expose Coach Dallas, the sooner names can be cleared, people can heal, and football players are saved from any more catastrophes."

"You *are* a catastrophe—waiting to happen."

"You're an egotistical ogre!"

"You are not to do anything on this story that isn't cleared through me first. You'll hurt yourself. You'll hurt this story. One mistake, and it's all over. Right now the Brotherhood is too cocky to take it underground completely."

"Well, if anyone knows cocky, it's you."

He closes the small space that separates us. "You're off the story."

"No, I'm not."

"There's no party this week, so we have some time. Stay away from the football players this week. I'm working on a few things, and I don't want your interference. It's important."

"So *you* can operate solo, but *I* can't?" I stomp away from him, pace the length of the porch, then return to face him. "You're just jealous because I have an in with Jared Campbell. You want to be the big dog here because that's how Luke Sullivan operates."

"This is about playing it smart."

"This is about playing by your rules. Well, I'm not in this to stroke your pride, so Thursday, there *is* a party. And I'll be there. And I *will* come away with information that ends it once and for all."

"Who told you there's a party?"

"Jared invited me."

"Then how come nobody's talking about it? There aren't any more initiations left." His forehead furrows deeper. "You're off the story, Bella. Stay away until told otherwise."

I toss his words back to him. "Stay away from *me* until told otherwise."

"Bella!" Robbie's shrill voice calls from inside. "The pizza's burning!"

Luke steps off the porch. "Glad you've got everything under control, then."

My face is a picture of serenity and composure as he leaves. Then I run like mad to the kitchen. The fumes are worse than a New York sewer grate.

"What happened?" Grabbing oven mitts, I place the charred remains on top of the stove. "Five hundred degrees? Did you change the temperature?"

Robbie studies his Spiderman belt. "Maybe. I was hungry though. Starving! I just wanted it to hurry up."

Ugh! I turn on the oven fan, but it does nothing to diminish the black smell. "Find some candles, Robbie." I open windows in the kitchen, then the living room, pressing my nose to the screen to suck in some good air.

Fifteen minutes later, with the sun barely visible, I pray over our peanut butter, jelly, and potato chip sandwiches. Candles glow all around like we're holding a memorial for the dead pizza.

After helping Robbie with some reading homework (I read, he made sound effects), we settle onto the orange couch for *The Incredibles*, a movie he's seen exactly one hundred and four times.

By the time the credits roll, Robbie's drooling on my shoulder. I scoop him up and carry him upstairs. He snuggles into me, bringing a smile to my face. Odd as he is, I do like this kid. When he's twenty-five, he'll probably be the inventor of something to rival Google, he'll be a Jeopardy grand champion, and he'll still wear his Superman underwear. He doesn't even stir when I lay him down on his comforter.

I return downstairs to extinguish all the candles and sandblast the pizza pan. The phone in my pocket beeps. A text. From Hunter.

I'm so sorry. Pls call me. Need 2 talk. We can work thru this. Temporary insanity.

Insane is what I'd have to be if I took him back.

Delete.

Only an hour into my own homework, my eyes grow heavy. I didn't sleep a lot at my dad's. I give in to fatigue, peel back the blankets, and collapse into my bed. I dream of standing on the football field. The Brotherhood is there. They build a giant fire on the fifty-yard line. I want to watch them, but the smoke is too strong. It burns my eyes.

Coach Dallas yells at each player. He blows his whistle. "Run through the bonfire! Show your allegiance to the Brotherhood."

I can feel Matt Sparks's fear from where I am. His pulse accelerates. His skin sweats from the heat.

One by one, the football players run through the flames. They come out unharmed, unscathed.

Then it's Matt's turn. He walks away, only to turn around, get the fire in his sights, and sprint toward his target.

I have to stop him. Some way. Somehow.

"Nooooo!" I burst through the dream, my voice dragging me back to consciousness.

Sitting up, I wipe my hands over my face, my heart pounding in fear.

What is that noise?

Our fire alarm!

That smell.

I shoot out of bed. I have to get to Robbie. Throwing my door open, I'm nearly knocked over by the smoke. The alarm screams. Or maybe it's me. Everything's a blur as I run to his room.

"Robbie!" I yell his name over and over.

"What's going on?" His eyes are wide as tractor wheels. He clutches his sheet to his chin.

"I don't know. We need to get downstairs and go outside though, okay?" I force myself to slow down and talk calmly. We can't both be flipping out. I'm in charge here. There's no one else.

"It's going to be okay." I throw out other useless words of comfort as we hurry down the hall to the stairs.

Robbie points ahead. "The stairs are on fire!"

How in the world could the stairs be on fire? I stand motionless and just watch the flames. Thinking. Praying.

"There's no other way out, Bella!" Tears streak Robbie's face, and he clings to my leg. I pick him up.

"I need you to be very brave, okay?" He nods against my shoulder. "You're my superhero, right? It's time to put those powers to use and save us."

Holding my stepbrother, I run back into my bedroom and grab my phone. "I need you to hold this for me, Robbie. It's a very important job. Can you do that?"

His red head bobs.

I set him down long enough to fling open the window and pop out the screen. "We're going to my secret hiding place, okay? You and I are going to crawl out on a big limb and climb down."

"It's too high." He backs away, but I grab his wrist.

"Robbie"—I bend down to his level—"we have to do this." I hear a loud pop from downstairs. "And we need to hurry."

I don't even wait for his response. "God, help us. God, help us." I recite it like a mantra as I hoist Robbie onto my back and find my balance on the window ledge. "Hang on. Whatever you do, don't let go of me."

I climb out onto the roof, my hands flattened to the shingles so I won't topple over. I scoot closer to the edge where the tree meets the roof, then stand to my feet, grabbing the thickest branch I can find.

"Here we go." I step onto a limb bigger than Jake's arm and test it with my foot. Finding it secure, I put both feet onto it and reach above us for another limb to hold on to.

Stopping every little bit to hoist a slippery Robbie tighter to my back, I walk us around the oak, moving as far away from the roof as possible.

Now. Time to descend.

Please, God. Please, God. Please, God.

Don't let me drop him. Keep my feet steady.

The moon shines on the ground below—the cold, hard, far-away ground. *Look at the branches, not any lower.*

My hair clings to my face in wet strands, and I swish it away. But there's no time. I get us farther down the tree. One limb at a time.

Low enough to brave a look down, I estimate how many more feet until we're safely on land. At least six, maybe seven more branches—

My foot slips.

My world tilts.

And Robbie and I go sailing through the tree. Down, down. I twist and somehow pull him to me, desperate to shield his body from the blows of the limbs.

Falling. Hurting. Crashing.

Land.

My back absorbs most of the hit as I connect full-body with the ground. My head bounces once then is thrown back as the force of Robbie's frame hits me. His elbow, knees, head—every bit of him falls into me.

I struggle to catch my breath as everything in my vision spins. Robbie rolls off of me, shaking out the kinks. Not quite ready to move, I suck in the night air, grateful my stepbrother is safe. Stars swim before my eyes.

"Robbie, my phone. Still got it?" I manage to keep one eye open. Pain shoots through my head.

"Yup."

"Call 9-1-1."

"Last time I called them I got in trouble. They said I couldn't call anymore unless I had a real problem." He mumbles something about giving his goldfish mouth-to-mouth.

"Call them *now*."

He punches in the number with one stubby finger. "Yeah, I have an emergency. My house is on fire." I close my eyes and try to hear the dispatcher on the other end. "My stepsister, Bella, just saved me. But you need to hurry up because I don't want to lose any of my action figures."

I rub my brow bone, the recipient of a mean elbow jab from Robbie. "This night could not get any worse."

"Oh yeah?" He points upward into the tree and giggles.

There, five branches above us, hang my pajama bottoms, swaying in the breeze like a sign of surrender.

And that's how I met the Truman Fire Department.

chapter thirty-seven

"Is she gonna die?"

"No, Robbie. She'll just have the black eye for a while." My mother sits on the bed beside me. Mom and Jake came home not too long after the fire trucks showed up last night. After a quick trip to the emergency room, the entire family camped out at Dolly's house.

Robbie squints as he studies my face. "She could get a glass eye. That'd be cool."

"There's nothing wrong with me. You gave me a shiner when we fell out of the tree. Nobody's getting any body parts removed."

But my eye looks hideous. It's a lovely blend of purple, blue, and swollen, and Sephora doesn't sell anything that could cover this up. But the doctor said I was lucky that's all I suffered. I didn't even have a concussion. Just some leaf burns. Some limb lacerations. Bark bruises.

Mom let all of us stay home from school. Budge went with Jake to the house this morning, and Robbie chose to stay with us at Dolly's, not knowing when he would have another opportunity to watch the cartoon channel on her satellite.

We sit in the living room, Robbie inches from the giant TV, while Mom and I lounge on one of Dolly's leather couches.

When Jake and Budge walk into the room, I'm instantly on alert. Jake's eyes dart to me, then to my mother. Budge stands back, looking at no one.

"What's the matter?" Mom asks.

Jake inhales deeply, his frown severe. "The fire chief said the fire was started by a candle left on in the kitchen."

I stop breathing.

"He said it burned until it spread on a plate then caught a nearby towel on fire. It shot right up the wall and eventually caught the stairs behind it."

Mom's face is grave. "Bella, did you burn a candle last night?"

Robbie pipes up. "No, she didn't burn *a* candle. She burned a *lot* of them."

My stomach twists, and I have to fight a wave of nausea. "I snuffed them out—all of them. I know I did." *Didn't I?* It had been a crazy night. A fight with Luke. The pizza burning. Robbie's home-work, then mine. What if I *had* forgotten and left one candle burning?

Mom grabs Jake's hand, and he sits on the arm of the couch. I feel like I've committed a crime. And it's them against me. They think I set the fire.

My vision blurs with tears. "I did put out the candle. I know it. At least I'm pretty sure . . ."

"Bella, you could've burned the entire house down." The edge in my mom's voice is like a thousand paper cuts.

I stand up, desperate to get far away from all of them. "I'm tell-ing you, I didn't do it."

"How bad is it?" Mom asks.

Jake studies their joined hands. "Could've been a lot worse. We'll have to redo the back wall of the kitchen, the stairs, part of the ceiling. The important thing is that everyone's okay. Bella, I know I told you this last night, but looking at the house today, I want to say it again. Thank you for your quick thinking. You and Robbie are alive today because you climbed onto that tree." He watches his son, who has gone back to *Scooby-Doo*, totally uninterested in any near-death talk. "You saved my son."

But killed your house.

"What did the insurance guy say?" Mom asks Jake. He shakes his head and speaks to my mom in a hushed whisper.

I take myself into the kitchen, desperate for some aspirin and caffeine. Instead I find Budge.

I jerk one cabinet open then another, searching for a glass.

"Here." He holds out a blue cup. "You know I—"

"Save it," I snap. "Whatever jerk thing you have to say, just keep it to yourself. I know you're mad at the world, and now I've given you one more reason to be miserable—I apparently just burned down part of your house. So I'm sorry we're stuck here for a few weeks. And—"

"I just wanted to say thanks." He clears his throat. Studies his feet.

Shaking my head, I try to reengage my ears, which obviously cannot be working.

"It sucks that we're kicked out of the house for a while, but Dolly does have a killer pool."

"Did you just thank me?"

"Yeah." He stabs his hands into his pockets. "The whole saving-my-brother thing you did was pretty cool." And he walks past me, where I stand in mute shock at his freakish kindness. "Nice eye, by the way. You look like a Cyclops."

Now that's more like it.

"Tell me again why you dragged me to football practice?" I sit down beside Lindy on the warm bleacher.

"Your mom said you needed to get out of the house. She's worried about you."

I have spent the whole afternoon in my temporary bedroom, hugging a trash can, afraid I was going to hurl at any moment. Setting a house on fire can do that to a girl.

"Accidents happen, Bella."

My stomach clenches. "Thanks for bringing it up. I love the subject of the fire. I could talk about it *all* day."

"I just mean that it wasn't your fault."

"Apparently it was. I'm the one who lit the match that lit the candle, so therefore, it's my fault. I've tried to think of at least ten other people to blame, such as my cheating liar of an ex-boyfriend or my loser ex-BFF, but logic prevails, and it all points back to me once again. I started the fire."

"But you didn't mean to. That's the important thing. Your parents know that."

"Pretty soon the euphoric feeling that their children are alive and well will wear off, and they will begin to look at me as the arsonist I must be."

But if there's one thing I did get out of this, besides a serious need for a manicure, it's that life is short. And I'm going to take the Brotherhood situation by the horns and talk to Jared. I think I've earned his trust by now. Surely he'll open up to me about what he knows.

My head still throbs, and the shouting of Coach Lambourn and Coach Dallas does nothing to help.

Coach Dallas butts up to Dante, his face inches from his star player's. "When I was in school, we were winners. A state championship was a given. And why? Because we *worked* hard! Because we were a *team*." He moves on to his stepbrother. "Your team makes me sick. You have a heritage here, and you're destroying it game by game. We barely pulled it out last week. Uphold the legacy at all costs." His gaze travels to every starter.

I can't wait to blow the lid on this guy's craziness and send him up the river. To the big house. The pokey. The slammer. If he continues killing off all his players, there won't be anyone left to uphold a football, let alone a stupid legacy.

"Well, look at that."

I follow Lindy's stare and see Luke walking toward us. With Kelsey Anderson.

"Hey, ladies." Luke addresses us both, but he watches me.

"Kelsey, it's good to see you out here. You look great." Lindy lies through her teeth. Kelsey looks like a strong wind could pick her up and deposit her in Arkansas with one gust.

"I ran into Kelsey at the home today and thought some fresh air might be nice," Luke says. "How are you?" He turns his attention toward me as Lindy pulls Kelsey in with some small talk.

"I'm fine." *And still mad, thank you very much.* "Couldn't be better."

He lifts his hands toward my face and eases off my oversized sunglasses. And scowls. "That doesn't look fine. You could've been seriously hurt."

I grab my shades back. "Well, I wasn't."

Luke clasps my wrist and pulls me a few steps away from the girls. "Budge said that the fire department claimed you left a candle burning. He said you swore you snuffed out all the candles."

"I guess I was wrong." And the house is short a few walls to prove it.

Luke casts a glance over his shoulder. He steps closer to me. "What if you're not wrong? What if someone else started the fire?"

"Who, Robbie? I put out the candles *after* he went to bed."

"Not Robbie." A warm breeze blows between us, ruffling Luke's dark hair. "Bella, how hard would it be to get into your house? I'm guessing the windows are fairly old. And if your stepdad is like half the people in this town, the doors probably aren't locked much."

It's true. Jake does not believe in locking doors. Whenever I ask him about it, he just makes a joke about his attack cows.

"But I locked the doors that night. That place is so isolated it kind of creeps me out sometimes."

"Dead bolts?"

"No."

Luke watches the team, his jaw set. "You need to stay away from the football players. No more asking questions. No parties. Nothing."

"No! We've already been through this. I have an in with Jared Campbell, and you know it. There is no reason not to take advantage of that."

"Any of those players could have been in your house last night.

We have to play it safe from this point on. The closer we get to the truth, the more dangerous it could get."

"I have to go to the parties. We have no other options. It's our best resource for information. Unless you want me to enlighten Lindy and see if Matt will tell her anything."

"I said no, Bella." His voice is as hard as an oak tree. "Thursday night I'm going with Kelsey to Zach Epps's house."

"What? Why?"

"We're going to search his bedroom. Check his computer. See if we can find anything at all."

"You weren't at least going to ask me to go?"

He shakes his head. "She trusts me. We've known each other since kindergarten. This is kind of a delicate situation."

"I *knew* you would take over! I knew it. That's what this is about. You want to be the hero here. Spare me your fake concern over my safety, Chief. I'm not backing off this story—and we'll see who gets to the finish line first."

He clutches my arm and pulls me to him, his voice a whisper in my ear. "You're off the article, Bella. You were warned. I can't risk the story." Anger swims in his deep blue eyes. "Or you."

"I'm not your responsibility." I take my arm back. "I don't need your permission *or* your protection."

"Need I remind you of the very first party?"

"And if I need you and your birdcalls again, I'll say the word." My eye throbs like a football's trying to sprout out of the socket. "Good-bye, Luke Sullivan."

"I'll have your new assignment on your desk tomorrow."

"An exposé on the poor quality of toilet paper at Truman High?" And I'll know *exactly* where to stick it.

I say good-bye to Kelsey Anderson and walk toward Lindy's car, hoping she'll get the hint that I'm more than ready to leave.

"Bella!" A sweaty Jared Campbell intercepts me as I reach her Mustang. "Hey." His face is red from the heat, but it doesn't hide his concern. "How are you? I heard about the fire today."

I smile and push my sunglasses farther up my nose. "I'm fine. Really." It is kind of cool how I have people caring about me—the same people who last month wouldn't have minded if the whole house caved in on me.

"I'm so glad." He wipes at his dripping forehead. "We're playing our rival Friday night. You should come."

"I'll be there this week." Even though Luke, spawn of Satan, has removed me from the story, he didn't remove me from manager duty with Lindy. I'm totally going to break this case before he does.

"Are we still on for the party Thursday night? I understand if you don't feel like it."

"No, I definitely feel like it!" Okay, right now I feel like some Ben and Jerry's and an ice pack, but I'm sure I'll be in the mood in a few days.

"I saw you guys talking to Kelsey Anderson." His eyes travel across the field to where she still stands deep in conversation with Luke and Lindy. "What did she have to say?"

"We were just talking about Zach—the night of the accident."

"I don't think that's something we'll ever get over."

I rest my hand on his forearm. Which is also sweaty. "I know it's still tough. It's good that Kelsey's getting out some though, right? She needs a break from her vigil at the nursing home. That place is so depressing."

"You've been there?"

"Yeah, I went with Luke once. Just to visit." *And to dig up some information.* "Do you go?"

He shakes his head. "Can't." He bites his top lip as he thinks on this. "It's hard . . . you know? It's nice that you're spending time with her though."

"Jared—" *Tell me everything you know about the Brotherhood. Where are the videos? Help me stop your stepbrother.* "I, um . . . I'll see you at school tomorrow."

chapter thirty-eight

I think waffles with whipped cream make everything better. The entire family sits at a table at Sugar's. Dolly brings me another round of fresh-squeezed orange juice and pats me on the back. "Honey, you eat up now. It's all-you-can-eat Thursday, so get your money's worth."

"And it's payday too." Mom waves her paycheck in the air. "It's my first full check. Haven't seen one of these things in years." And she looks content. My mom, a Manhattan socialite, sits in a grungy diner perfectly happy with her wrestler husband, grab bag of children, and minimum-wage check. God sure has some strange things up His sleeve. And when I say strange . . . I mean weird.

A bell jingles as the door swings open.

Mickey Patrick walks in. All heads swoop in his direction. And the small-town talk begins. Whispers fly over hotcakes and hash browns.

He waves to a few people, gradually making it to our table. "Hello." His eyes greet all of us. All but Dolly. "Hadn't seen you since the fire, Jake; saw your truck here and just wanted to see for myself that everyone was okay."

Jake's arm settles on the back of my chair. "We're great. Thought we'd have some breakfast together before we all went our separate ways for the day. Sit down and have some coffee."

"Nah." His eyes jump—like he *wants* to look at Dolly. "Saw the house yesterday. Not good, but could be a lot worse."

My stepdad's hand rests on my shoulder, and he gives it a small squeeze. "Nothing that can't be replaced. This is our hero right here."

I nearly choke on my bacon.

"You've got yourself a brave girl all right," Mickey says.

"That we do." Jake nods his blond head. "Couldn't be more proud. And blessed."

Even though I've just inhaled ten pounds of waffles, I suddenly feel a hundred pounds lighter. I'm forgiven. Jake doesn't hate me for nearly burning the house down. No grudge. His words thrill my heart, and it's everything I can do not to jump on this table and belt out a happy tune—*High School Musical*-style.

"Nothing's more important than family. The rest is just stuff." Mickey's gaze aims straight at his ex-wife this time. "Only a fool would forget that."

"You gonna start coming in my diner and spouting off like a fortune cookie on a regular basis?" Dolly pops her gum. "'Cause I don't think my gag reflexes are that strong."

Mickey pulls up a chair and sits himself down. His eyes flash fire. And a challenge. "Maybe." He tucks a napkin into his collar. "Yep, maybe I am."

~~~~~~~~~

As I sit here in the dark, staring at the rows of gravestones and waiting for Jared to meet me, I picture Luke and what he must be doing right now. He's at Zach Epps's with Kelsey, and they're digging through dresser drawers. Then they move to his computer. Because life is kinder to him, Luke finds a Word file called "Everything You Could Possibly Want to Know About the Brotherhood." He immediately prints it and takes it to the authorities. They are probably minutes away from naming a street after him and declaring it National Luke Sullivan Day.

Tonight I'm ditching Jared and trailing the Brotherhood like paparazzi on Britney Spears. I've got my camera in my purse and fully intend to do whatever it takes to get my own video for the police and pictures for *my* article.

His headlights spotlight my car, and I step out and wave. "I know the drill," I say when he opens his car door, and I hold out my hand for the blindfold.

Jared takes a swig from a giant water bottle. "My car's acting up. Mind if we take yours?"

I quirk an eyebrow. "What? You're going to let me see how to get to the mystery party location?"

He grins and ducks his head. "You know I can't. Rules are rules. But I thought . . . maybe I could drive your car?"

I tap my finger to my lip and consider this. If anything were to happen to the Bug, I would be in the passenger side of Budge's hearse again. Not a comforting thought.

"I promise I'll be careful with it. Come on." He wiggles his fingers for the keys. "You can trust me."

"Fine."

He spins me around and covers my eyes with a red paisley bandanna. This part always creeps me out a bit. Maybe this will be the last party I have to attend. No more rendezvous in cemeteries, blind drives to the lake, or staying out past curfew and getting myself grounded 'til I'm old enough to need Miss Clairol.

"Tell me about Coach Lambourn and Coach Dallas," I say a few minutes down the road. "What's it like playing for your stepdad and his son?"

I hear Jared snort. "Unbearable."

"They seem to put a lot of pressure on the team—especially on you."

"Yeah." He taps his hands on the wheel to the song on the radio, and I think he's not going to elaborate. "My stepdad doesn't even see me. I'm just a means to a win. I'm not even a real person, just a player. We all are."

I throw out some bait. "From watching practice, I get the idea your stepbrother would do *anything* to recapture the former Truman glory. He seems . . ." I pretend to search for a word. "*Desperate* for a win."

"I guess we all are."

Sometime later the car slows then finally stops. Jared continues his tapping on the wheel though the radio is silent.

"Here we are." His sigh drags out. "Sit tight, and I'll be around to get you."

Warm air replaces the air-conditioning as he gets out and opens my door.

"Where's the party music?" Normally you can hear the bass a good thirty seconds away. But tonight it's quiet. "Are you sure there's a party tonight?"

"Yeah." He pulls me out of the passenger seat, his hands gentle on my arms. "No, don't take your blindfold off yet. I, um, have a surprise for you."

"A surprise?" A smile curves my lips. "Interesting." But time consuming! I need to be where the party action is so I can investigate and get some hard evidence. *Before* Luke does.

"Ready? Watch your step." I hear the grass crunch beneath my feet as he leads me forward. "Not much further." A door opens, then light filters through the blindfold. "I'm just going to sit you down here." A chair scrapes the floor, then he's guiding me into it. My hands rest on a table in front of me.

"Uh, Jared, if I break my curfew again, I'll never be let out of the house. The rest of the party crowd will be here soon, right?"

The covering over my eyes falls away, and I blink against the light. The familiar living room of the lake cabin is the first thing to come into focus.

A shiny black handgun is the second.

"You won't be joining the party tonight." Jared Campbell stands in front of me, his trembling hands clutching the pistol.

"Are you insane?" I leap up from my chair, only to be shoved back down. I'm instantly reminded of the sheer strength in this athlete. "Jared, what are you doing? Put that thing down."

"I'm gonna have to ask you to stay right where you are."

My heart shudders to a stop. "Why are you doing this?" So confused. Mind reeling. Have to get out of here.

"You couldn't leave it alone, could you?"

I shake my head, bewildered and dazed. "I have no idea what you're talking about."

"The Brotherhood. I tried to warn you, but you wouldn't take the hint—getting Kelsey Anderson all stirred up again."

Something falls into place in my mind. "The fire. That was you, wasn't it? Did you break into my house?"

He takes a step back, the gun still aimed right at my heart. "I thought maybe it would scare you into going back to New York. I wish it had. I wanted it to. I didn't want it to come to this."

I can't breathe in here. Can't think. "You could've *killed* me. And my stepbrother. How could you do that?"

He slams one hand on the table, and I want to bounce out of my skin. "I didn't want to! Don't you understand? Doesn't anybody understand me?"

"I can't understand anything when you've got a gun aimed at me!" I scream back. No, I have to stay calm. He's only growing more agitated. I have to calm us both down. "Tell me what this is about, Jared. I deserve to know." Seeing how I'm going to die for it and all.

"I know you went to Tulsa to meet with Reggie Lee. I know you talked to his girlfriend."

"How could you know that?"

He shrugs. "Brittany Taylor. She may be annoying, but she's useful. She's been following you around for weeks."

Okay, that girl is just evil. "You and your boys planted drugs in Reggie's locker, didn't you?" Empty eyes stare back at me in response. "Why?"

He scrubs a hand over his face. "Because he was going to talk. We'd promised—we'd *all* promised."

"Promised what?"

"That no one would ever know about the Brotherhood. But . . ." His Adam's apple bobs. "Things went wrong last year. It got to Reggie."

"I know about the night Zach Epps had the wreck." Nothing like going out with a lie on your lips.

Sweat bubbles at Jared's temple. "It was a horrible night." He

JENNY B. JONES

shakes his head. He's there. "We had the initiation for Reggie and Zach all set up. Then the storm came. But there was no turning back—that's our way."

And it's worked so well for you too.

"So Reggie and Zach raced each other." I fill in the blanks. "And Zach lost control."

"We had to keep it quiet. They could never know that we had been there, had been a part of that. We all agreed, just like when we lost Carson Penturf. But Reggie buckled. He came to me at the beginning of school, told me he had to go to the police and come clean. But you can't go against the Brotherhood."

"So you planted the drugs in his locker, knowing it would get him suspended and end any chances of a college scholarship."

"It was a warning. And it worked. He didn't want to risk jail any more than the rest of us."

"And Carson?" I can't peel my eyes away from the gun. "He didn't really commit suicide, did he?"

"We decided his challenge was to climb down a cliff in the dark—no tools, no flashlight. Nothing but his bare hands." His eyes swim with pain. "He was halfway there. Then his foot slipped and he fell."

"What if you had gone and gotten help? What if he could've been saved? Who gave you the right to play God to these people? They were your friends."

"Shut up! You think I don't know that?" His wild eyes scare me.

"Jared, it's not too late to turn back. You've been pressured by Coach Dallas. It's gotten to you. I think we should go to the police—together—and talk to them. Tell them what your stepbrother has driven you to do."

"Dallas?"

"The parties? The initiations? I know this is his lake house."

Jared snorts. "He doesn't even know we use this. He's too busy with his girlfriend in Tulsa and blaming me for every mistake the team makes."

"He forced you to start the Brotherhood again so—so the team would win again like they did when he was in school and he could keep his job."

"I am *so* sick of hearing about his winning streak! Who cares?" he yells. "I've done everything—everything! I've trained, I've watched game films, I've done anything I could think of to make myself better. It's never going to be enough."

My brain clears like I've been doused in ice water. I've been so blind. *It's been Jared all along.* "Your brother knows nothing about your new little boys' club."

"And he's not *going* to know. The Brotherhood will go on as we are—a new breed of players. We will grow closer and stronger."

"And deader!" Okay, that's not a word, but grammar is the least of my concerns. "This is crazy. It has to stop now. All of it. You have to come clean." *And put the gun down while you're at it.*

"I liked you, Bella. I really did."

Did? Past tense?

Walking backwards, he goes to the coffee table, opens a small drawer, and pulls out a pen and paper. He places them in front of me.

"You're going to write."

"For some reason I really don't feel all that inspired at the moment."

He ignores me. "You're going to compose a suicide letter to your mom."

"What?" I squeal. "I would *never* take my own life! Nobody would believe that in a million years. Look, I won't say a word about the Brotherhood." At least not while an unsteady weapon is in my face. "Just drop the gun. This isn't worth it. What's happened so far have been accidents. What you're doing now? Um, yeah, that's called murder. And I don't think your stepdaddy's going to be too happy that his star player has to miss a game because he's in the big house for shooting someone."

"Don't sit there and judge me. You don't know what it's like living with my stepdad and his wonder child."

"And how does asking your friends to bungee jump in front of trains and shooting me fix any of that? Honestly, your little group is the dumbest thing I've ever heard of. Couldn't you get your boys to bond over something a little safer—like a campout or . . . some Guitar Hero?"

Jared wrenches my arm, his face contorted in rage. "Shut up! Nothing is going to get in my way!"

"Okay." I hold up my hands and slowly ease out of his grip and press myself into the back of the chair, wishing I could disappear into it. *God, I need some serious help here. What do I do? If there's a verse on dealing with psychopaths, I seem to have forgotten it. Totally need some guidance right now.*

"I've never been good enough for my stepdad. Can't ever measure up to Dallas. Well, I'm sick of being the loser. Our team's going to state this year. I *will* get a scholarship to play football, and then I'll leave this town and never look back."

I try for a softer approach. "I know it's been rough. I can't imagine what you've gone—"

My phone blasts in my pocket—the song I have programmed for Luke.

"Don't touch it!"

Think! "I . . . It's Luke Sullivan. I've been, um, seeing him."

Jared picks up the phone. "The theme from *Jaws*?"

"Yeah, we're going through a rough patch." I swallow. "This is the time he calls every night, and if I don't get it, he'll send out a search party. He'll know something's wrong." The phone continues to sing, and I feel my chance slipping through my fingers. "My step-dad's a wrestler. Do you really want him tracking me down right now?"

"Turn it on speaker. And get rid of him." He jerks the gun toward my cell. "Tell him you're okay. If you say one word, Bella, I will use this thing."

Please, God. I snap open the phone. "Luke?" I push a button and his voice fills the cabin.

"Where are you? I have some really important news. It wasn't—"

"—Charmin toilet paper in the school bathrooms like we'd thought? I *knew* it." I keep my eyes trained on Jared.

Get rid of him, he mouths. He moves the pistol closer.

"Um, Luke, *sweetie,* we'll talk about the story for the paper later, okay?"

"Bella, are you—"

"In fact, right now I have to let you go because I'm working on the other article. But I miss you." *Please find this believable, crazy boy with waving firearm.* "Talk to you soon." I start to disconnect, but Luke's voice stops me.

"Bel, just one more thing. The piece you're writing tonight.

Would that happen to be the bird-calling story or maybe the one about the dangers of making out in SUVs?"

"Hang up," Jared hisses. "Now."

"Bird calling!" My voice is chipper and light. "That's the one."

My lifeline to Luke is lost as Jared rips the phone from my hands and throws it across the room. "That's enough." He gestures to the paper. "Start writing."

"And then you're going to kill me?" Anger begins to replace fear. Who does this guy think he is?

"No, I'm not going to kill you." He reaches into the pockets of his cargo shorts and extracts a plastic bag. "But these pills will."

chapter thirty-nine

I would like to say that when I faced death I had all sorts of deep, inspirational thoughts. That poetry sprang from my lips, and God imparted timeless wisdom into my soul. That I greeted my imminent demise with grace and sweetness.

"Jared, you're a *moron*! Do you realize Fred Flintstone is in this bag? Are you planning on killing me with way too much vitamin C?"

He grabs the ziplock and looks inside. His face flushes red. "I didn't mean to grab those. There are just a few in there. I raided a bunch of medicine cabinets this week." His voice shakes like he's running out of steam.

"At least tell me what I'm taking. Besides a prehistoric multivitamin."

His eye twitches, as if I've offended him. Like I'm really worried about his feelings at this point. "Most are from my parents. The white ones are my mom's migraine pills. Those will make you really sleepy. And that's a good thing." Is he reassuring me or himself? "These purple ones are Dante's acne prescription."

My pulse slows. The roar in my head ebbs.

And some measure of peace fills me—because I don't think this is going to kill me.

Basically I'm going to take a really long nap and wake up with clear skin.

Jared continues to take the pills out and set them on the table. "My stepdad's antidepressants. Those are pretty good for stress."

I should probably eat those first.

"And his blood pressure meds." He sneers and I wonder how I ever thought he was cute. "Maybe if he'd back off on me, his numbers wouldn't be so high."

"I can't imagine him finding any fault with *you*." Hysterical laughter bubbles up like lava.

"Stop it!" He waves the gun like a slippery fish.

"Are these—" I pick up a pill and inspect it close. Then double over in giggles. "Birth control? You took somebody's birth control pills?" And this guy's in AP? "Is there a high risk of pregnancy on the way to the Pearly Gates?"

"I just grabbed stuff, okay?" he shouts. "Clearly I'm not cut out for this."

"No, hey." I touch his arm. "I think you're doing a *swell* job."

"Stop laughing." His hand cracks across my cheek.

My smile disappears and I taste blood.

"Oh, I'm sorry. Bella, I didn't mean to—" He rests the gun on the table, his hands grabbing my face, holding my cheek. "Please forgive me, I—"

I dive for the gun. My hands inches away. I can almost feel the cold metal on my fingertips.

"No!" He pushes me onto the floor, overpowering me with his

strength. When I pull myself back up, the gun is firmly in his grip. "Get back in the chair. You have a letter to write."

"There's still time to back out of this. You don't want to kill me."

"I'm not killing you. You're killing yourself."

"And if I don't take the pills?"

His jaw locks. "I'm responsible for the Brotherhood. Nobody is going to get in my way. Bella, you can either do this the easy way or the painful way. If you don't write the letter and swallow the pills, I will put this gun to your head and pull the trigger."

"And you'll go to prison for the rest of your life."

"No, I won't. I know exactly what I'm doing."

Yet he doesn't look certain at all. He looks scared—mixed with a little psycho. And a dash of nuts.

I must stall him. Surely Luke got my hint that we were at the cabin. And *surely* he went for help. Like Jake. Or the police. Or the National Guard.

"You realize Luke knows, don't you?"

"I suspected." He waves away the idea, like it's not worth discussion. "I'll deal with him later tonight."

"With what? Vitamin E and cough drops?"

Jared points the gun inches from my nose. "Enough talking! Pick up the pen."

It's not so much that I'm scared he'll actually pull the trigger. It's more about being scared of his shaking hands *accidentally* pulling the trigger. I don't want to die with an ugly eye. Even mortician's makeup can't hide this bruising. Nobody will walk past my casket and say, "Oh, doesn't she look natural?" They'll say, "It looks like markers pooped on her face."

"You need to start downing the pills. It will take awhile for them to kick in. Start with the white ones first."

For a full twenty seconds I don't move. I study the room. The distance to the door. The location of the nearest heavy object. The number of steps to the kitchen for a knife.

"Eat them!" Jared pounces on the table, grabs a handful of pills, and forces them into my mouth. I bite his hand, and he yelps. Then smacks my other cheek. "Get them out from under your tongue. Swallow them!"

He cocks the gun.

I force them down and my earlier confidence begins to fade. *God, please help me.*

Jared passes me his water bottle. "The letter should be simple. Make it to your mother. Tell her that you've missed New York so much that you can't go on. You're miserable."

What a coincidence—so are you.

"You miss your dad. Your friends. Your boyfriend." He stops. "You're cheating on your boyfriend with Luke?"

"Yes." My head bobs spastically. "I . . . um, just love the menfolk. Can't get enough of them." I can't stop nodding. "Love me some boys." And if I *don't* walk out of here alive tonight, they'll know something's up by my mention of Hunter in the letter. Like I'd miss that two-timing sleaze.

He gestures to the paper with his weapon, and I pick up the pen.

Dear Mother,
 This freak of nature is holding a loaded—

Jared rips the paper from the table and shreds it to pieces. He slams down a new piece. "I'm warning you, Bella." He thrusts another handful of pills into my palm. I somehow choke them down.

"How are you getting home?" I ask. "It's not like you can take my car."

His smile is something from a Stephen King novel. "Brittany Taylor."

"Oh." I scrape a film off my tongue with my teeth. "Isn't she sweet."

In between forced servings of meds, I scribble out my first paragraph, telling my mom how much I miss New York and that Truman brought me nothing but pain. Next I include instructions for taking care of my cat and other hints that this letter was forced.

I look up from my work and the room tilts to the left. That's not good. "Have you ever considered medication?"

I close my note, my writing growing sloppier by the letter.

I love you.

And then I add a line in case these really are my last words to my mother.

You were the best mom ever. Be happy with Jake. And tell Dad I love him—and he needs a new decorator.

I lift my pen. "What if these things don't kill me?"

Jared taps the barrel of the shiny gun.

I grab a few more white capsules. "I'm sure these will do me in nicely."

"Sign the note."

"I don't feel so well."

He pops some red tablets past my teeth, leaving my mouth so full I have to breathe through my nose.

God, I'm sorry for everything I've ever done. Forgive me for the way I treated Budge. For not giving Jake a chance. For hating every one of the bimbos my dad brings home.

I'm vaguely aware of tears slipping down my cheeks.

Forgive me for not getting involved in church here. For not being a good friend to Lindy. And for watching Sex and the City reruns.

"I . . ." Why won't my tongue work? "Can't . . . finish."

Jared places the pen in my fingers and picks up my hand. Together we make the first letter of my name.

The room swirls and twirls. Nap. I need to lay my head down. Oh, what pretty lights I see! I want to go to the pretty lights! Here I come! Who's that giggling? Is that me? Oh, I love to giggle!

"Hold the pen still!" Jared roars in my ear. But I don't care! "Finish the letter or I'll—"

A loud crash explodes to my right. The door.

And Luke's there. He's calling out something.

"Bella!"

How nice of him to come and visit. Helleww, Luke!

Look how fast he runs. Like a linebacker. Or is it a quarterback? A quarterliner?

Wait. The gun. Jared's raising the pistol.

Oh. That's not right.

Must. Stop him.

But so tired.

My legs—they're in cement. So heavy.

Focus, Bella. Focus. Move. Eye on the target. God, give me strength.

With all that I have left, I throw my body toward Jared. "Noooo!"

My limp form flops.

Flails.

Falls—right into Jared.

The gun goes off. So loud. Hurts my ears.

Luke dives onto Jared, his fist plowing through my captor's face. Jared rolls over. He's out.

"Bella!" Luke scoops me in his arms. I hear more giggling. I think it's me. The sound—so far away.

His hands are all over me. *So not appropriate, young man.*

He lifts them to his face. Blood. *Ick, whose blood?*

"Luke . . ." The pretty lights are fading. It's getting dark. "No party tonight."

He pushes the hair from my face. "You saved my life. I came here to rescue you, and you saved my life. We got onto Jared's MySpace page from Zach's computer. Jared filmed every initiation. It was all there. I'm sorry I couldn't get to you in time."

I reach out a hand and pass my fingers over his lips. "You know, you're really not so bad. Hey . . . wanna make out?"

Luke's mouth smiles. His eyes don't. He holds me closer. Tighter. "Maybe later."

A siren. Why do I hear sirens? Maybe there's a parade. I do so love a good parade.

"Hang on, Bella. Please. Stay with me."

"Luke." Can't get my voice above a whisper. "The story—I want back on the story."

"Bella Kirkwood . . . I think you just *became* the story."

The blackness pools all around me. Snuffs out the twinkling lights.

It pulls me down.

And I let it take me away.

chapter forty

The casket is covered in a spray of wildflowers.

The soloist sings "I'll Fly Away." No instruments, just a voice.

There is sadness. Yet also a reluctant peace.

Sun filters through the trees, the light coming through the branches like a band of halos.

Death would have its day.

So life can begin again.

"Hand me a tissue," Budge says, his tie a stiff knot at his throat. "I have something in my eye."

With my good arm, I reach into my purse and pull out a Kleenex. He takes it and gifts me with a rare, small smile.

"Friends and family"—the pastor takes his place in front under the canopy—"we are gathered here today to celebrate the life of a son, a friend, and a football hero. Zachary Epps was this—and so much more."

My left shoulder throbs where Jared Campbell's gun left a bullet. It was just a week ago, but when I close my eyes, I still see it there, fresh and new in my mind. Though parts of it are foggy, like the ambulance ride. Getting my stomach pumped. The surgery to extract the bullet. But I remember the fear. And the chaos.

The preacher finishes and asks if anyone would like to say a few words.

Some of his teammates stand to their feet. Noticeably absent are Dante, Reggie Lee, that Adam guy, and, of course, my favorite kidnapper, Jared, who's looking at the world through some metal bars right now.

Next to speak is Kelsey. She still looks no wider than a pencil, but her voice is mighty and carries to the few hundred gathered. She speaks of love and loss and all that Zach was to her.

"Anyone else?" The preacher scans the crowd as Kelsey sits down. "Let us pray, then."

"I'd like to speak." Beside me Budge stands. I hear him swallow, and I say a quick prayer for him.

"Last year I lost my best friend. He loved his girlfriend, and he loved his family. And he loved that car." The crowd laughs, sharing a memory. "It could have been any of us. He made a mistake and got caught up. But the real Zach Epps would've wanted us to forgive. And live. Because if Zach knew how to do anything, it was live life to the fullest. And to be who we are—not who others want us to be." Budge blinks at moisture in his eyes. "I'll always carry that part of my friend with me. Always."

I can't help but smile as a small group from the Truman band breaks into "Free Bird." Only in Truman. But it fits.

I merge into the line and shake hands with Zach's family. When I get to Kelsey, she pulls me into a hug. "Thank you," she says. "Thank you." Tears flow unchecked, and she waves a hand in front of her face, unable to speak.

I hug her again. I don't need her words. Just the hope that she's going to rejoin the living. And I think she will.

Exiting the canopy, I spot Lindy with some friends, and I walk to them.

"How's the shoulder?" Lindy asks.

It hurts like someone's holding a blowtorch to it. "Not bad."

"Are you taking your pain pills?"

"Nah, something about forcibly puking them up last week makes me not want to down any more." Just the thought makes me want to barf. "I see you're wearing one of the dresses we bought in New York."

Lindy twists a piece of her flatironed hair. "As soon as I get home, it's Nikes and sweats."

"So how's Matt doing?"

"He's grounded for life for one thing."

"Still not ready to declare your undying love and adoration?"

She smiles, her lips a nice shade of Chanel pink. "He needs a good friend. And that's what I'll be." She winks. "For now."

"Bella Kirkwood?"

I turn around at the tap on my shoulder.

"I'm Pam Penturf. Carson's mom." She wrings a tissue in her hands. "I just wanted to thank you for what you did—exposing the truth about the football players." Her voice breaks, and I awkwardly pat her arm. "I couldn't believe my son would kill himself. It's haunted me, you know. I've carried that burden around, thinking what could I have done? How could I not have seen it?" She daubs at her eyes. "I feel like he can rest in peace now—like we all can. Anyway, I just wanted to express my gratitude." I'm wrapped in another hug. "You have no idea what you've done for me." She holds the tissue to her face and hurries away.

I spot Luke standing with another group. His eyes catch mine. He nods toward Mrs. Penturf and smiles.

I ride home with Budge. Even he didn't think driving a hearse to a funeral would be appropriate, so I have the pleasure of seeing him behind the wheel of my cute little Bug.

"Hey, where are you going?" Budge turns into a subdivision instead of heading toward our old dirt road.

"Gotta make a quick detour." He stops the car at a two-story house. "Won't take long." And he bails out of the Bug.

I lightly rub my shoulder, lean my seat back, and close my eyes. Minutes pass.

I jolt awake when my door flings open. Budge stands there. A cat in his arms.

My cat.

"Moxie!" I grab her and hold her close.

"Yeah, she's decided to come live with you again. I . . . um, seem to have been healed of my allergies."

I run my fingers through the cat's silky fur, a suspicious eye on my stepbrother. "Sounds miraculous."

He cracks a smile. "Amen, sister."

chapter forty-one

~~~~~~

*I*t's hard to digest a hot dog when you're looking at thirty- and forty-year-old men in spandex. Seriously.

"There's Dad!" Robbie claps his hands then whistles through his teeth at a volume that could shatter eardrums.

"Are you ready for a smackdown? Are you ready for a fight?" The crowd goes wild at the announcer's dramatic spiel. "Tonight in the Tulsa Athletic Arena, we present our regional champion—Captain Iron Jack!"

Our family stands and yells. I lift up a sign with one arm.

"Hold on to your popcorn as he takes on the force from Biloxi—Mississippi Mud!" A man in a hideous poop brown Onesie circles Jake on the stage.

"Did I miss anything?" Luke Sullivan fills the empty seat beside me, and I have to look twice.

"What are *you* doing here?"

My mom reaches over me, waves at her new hero, then returns to yelling for Captain Iron Jack.

"Your mother invited me. Wants me to do another feature in our paper."

"Fabulous," I droll. Images of him crashing through the cabin door and yelling my name flutter through my mind. A faint memory of him holding my hand in the ambulance. Waking up in the hospital and seeing his worried face.

"You know"—he leans in closer—"we haven't really had a chance to talk since everything happened."

Mmm, he smells good tonight. Or maybe I'm high on wrestler sweat fumes. Yes, that's definitely it.

"I just wanted to thank you for, um, you know, saving my life."

I laugh and roll my eyes. "It was the drugs. Had I been thinking clearly . . ."

He opens his ever-present messenger bag and pulls out a paper. "I just submitted this to a national contest—sponsored by Princeton University."

I look at the words. My article on the football scandal. "Are you serious?"

Luke nods his dark head. "It was a great piece, Bella. And when I read it, I learned something about you."

This ought to be good. I cross my arms and wait for the zippy insult. "And that is?"

"You . . . are a writer."

"I'm a—" I blink hard as the words circulate in my brain. Below us Jake twirls Mississippi Mud over his head.

"Writer." Luke's eyes shine brilliant blue in the dimmed lights. "I'm sorry I doubted you. I honestly didn't know you had it in you."

That makes two of us.

"This was your moment, Bella. You went through the fire and came out on the other side. I'm proud to have you on my newspaper staff."

His hand touches mine as I hand the paper back. "Do you say that to all the girls who save your life?"

Luke's laugh is rich and sends happy chill bumps along my skin. "Just you, Kirkwood. Only you."

"And thanks for rescuing me from Jared." My face flushes with heat. "It's not every day a guy breaks down a door for me."

My editor in chief winks. "Don't get used to it."

We watch the rest of the match, cheering and booing at all the right moments.

And life is all about right moments, isn't it?

Okay, so Truman isn't Manhattan. And I'll never get used to stepping around cow pies in the yard. Or being ten minutes late to school because the neighbor had to take his tractor for a ride.

And back in August I had no idea why God would punish me with this place, with this life. But like Luke said, I guess it was my moment. I was meant to be here all along. And who knows where this path will lead? Maybe by this time next month I'll have forgotten all about Macy's and Times Square and love nothing more than a trip to Target and peaceful walks through our pasture with Betsy the licking cow.

Yeah.

That is *so* not happening.

acknowledgments

*E*very book is a group effort. I couldn't do it without the help of so many in my life. I would like to thank:

My heavenly Father. I stay tired. I stay stressed. I stay hunched over a keyboard. But I also remain amazed and humbled and awed. Thank You for giving me the opportunity to share the coolness of Christ.

My family for putting up with my end-of-deadline moodiness and outrageous demands for food delivery and for reminding me to brush my hair and shower during the final weeks.

My friends for listening to me gripe about my family harassing me about showering and brushing my teeth.

My students who consistently come up to me and say, "Please put me in your book." It's so sweet. My next series will focus on a girl named KelseyRaynaKarlyKensleeJohnJamieCourtneyAllieSydney SueJayson. Should be a big hit.

All those who follow my blog at jennybjones.com. I appreciate you stopping by to read all about my snow addiction, my cat woes, my inability to turn away from fajitas, and other fascinating items from my thrilling life.

My lifelong hero, Carol Burnett. Though you will never read this, you are funny personified and made a huge impact on my life. Though I will always think the role of Annie should've gone to a young unknown named Jennifer Jones, I will forever hold you in the highest regard.

Everyone at Thomas Nelson for giving me a chance—a big chance. I'm so proud to be part of the team.

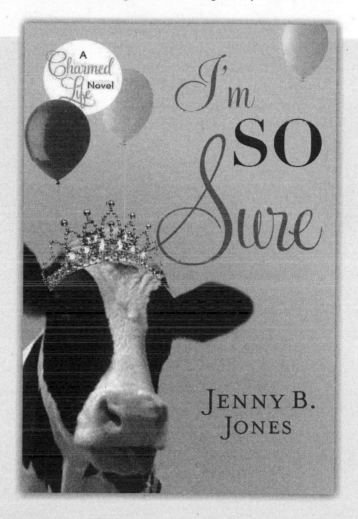